The Arrangement

LAURA TAYLOR

ALSO BY LAURA TAYLOR

THE HOUSE OF SIRIUS
(A wolf-shifter urban fantasy series)

Book 1: Wolf's Blood
Book 2: Wolf's Cage
Book 3: Wolf's Choice
Book 4: Wolf's Guile
Book 5: Wolf's Lie
Book 6: Wolf's Gift
Book 7: Wolf's Bane

THE GATE OF CHALANDROS
(A paranormal romance series)

Book 1: Whisky and Lace
Book 2: Wings of the Night
Book 3: Inferno (coming soon)
Book 4: Obsidian Scales (coming soon)
Book 5: On the Other Side (coming soon)

THE ELEMENTS
(An omegaverse romance series)

Book 1: Hurricane
Book 2: Deluge
Book 3: Lava

MISSING PIECES
(An omegaverse soulmates romance series)

Book 1: Collision
Book 2: Confusion
Book 3: Conundrum

LOST AND FOUND
(An omegaverse romance series)

Book 1: Redemption of a Slave
Book 2: The Runaway
Book 3: Rescue for a Rebel

STAND-ALONE NOVELS

Until Dawn
(A post-apocalyptic adventure)

The Arrangement
(An omegaverse romance)

CHAPTER ONE

CYCLE ONE
OLIVER

"Oliver Levy?"

Snapped out of his daze at the imperious words, Oliver leapt to his feet, then immediately felt foolish. The new recruit sitting next to him in the doctor's waiting room gave him a look of irritation, then went back to flicking through his magazine, leaving Oliver to make his sheepish way over to the nurse who had called his name.

"Doctor Connor will see you now," she told him, leading the way down a pristine white hallway and into one of the many non-descript consulting rooms.

Inside, Dr Connor was waiting, a middle-aged woman with a motherly air. "Welcome back, Oliver," she greeted him, rising to shake his hand, and he took a seat in the sterile grey chair beside her desk. "As you know, we've had the results of your tests. Are you ready to go over them now?"

The question was laced with concern, but Oliver didn't bother bracing himself for the news. Given the symptoms he'd been suffering over the past year, and the research he'd done in his own time, his diagnosis was a foregone conclusion.

"What have we got?" he asked, feeling a cold chill as a metaphorical door closed on the most recent stage of his life, leaving him to face a new and terrifying future.

"Just so you're aware," Dr Connor began, "I've had your case reviewed by one of our senior specialists. And his interpretation of your results was a solid match to my own." She spread out a small bundle of reports on the desk in front of him, though he didn't bother looking at the columns of figures; hormone levels, blood pressure, red cell count, iron levels – it seemed that every aspect of his physiology had been analysed, and every number was pointing to the same answer.

Connor took a deep breath. "I'm sorry to inform you that you've been diagnosed with Caloren's Syndrome. As an omega, you've no doubt heard of this condition before?"

Even if he hadn't, the last twelve months had been an instructive introduction to it. "It's when an omega's body is unable to regulate its hormonal cycle," Oliver recited mechanically. "It results in prolonged heats, elevated body temperature, low blood pressure and a variety of chemical imbalances throughout the body."

Dr Connor nodded sympathetically, and Oliver found himself wishing she'd just ditch the wide-eyed compassion and get on with telling him how the hell he was supposed to adapt his life to this disaster. For all his research into the causes and symptoms of Caloren's Syndrome, there had been a startling lack of information on how the disease was treated.

"That's the nuts and bolts of it," she agreed. "The elevated body temperature is the real crux of the problem. That's the cause of the vast majority of complications that arise in affected omegas." 'Complications' was a gross understatement. Without appropriate management, the omega's body went into overdrive during their three-monthly heat cycle, raising their body temperature well above the 38.5 degrees centigrade that was characteristic of the episodes. Left unchecked, omegas had suffered temperatures in excess of 43 degrees, causing long-term brain damage, or more commonly, the death of the sufferer.

"Caloren's Syndrome has a predominantly genetic etiology," Connor went on. "It has no known cure, and only one treatment has ever proven to be effective." Her tone of voice was not at all encouraging, and Oliver fought down the wave of panic that threatened to rise. "Before we continue, please understand that I mean no offence by what I'm about to say. But you may find the treatment to be rather shocking."

Her reticence was no surprise, even given her profession. Ever since betas had suddenly developed the capacity to reproduce some 1500 years ago, the population of alphas and omegas had started to decline dramatically. Genetic scientists had spent the past fifty years trying to understand what had caused the sudden shift in human reproduction, but even now, there were no clear answers, only hypotheses and educated guesses.

But omegas now accounted for a paltry 0.5% of the population, with alphas numbering a fraction lower, at 0.47%. Discussing one's secondary gender had become taboo, with the entire world apparently content to pretend that everyone was a beta, the phase of human history in which omegas – both male and female – had borne children now passing into a well-planned obscurity.

"You needn't apologise," Oliver said politely. "You're a medical professional. I'm hardly going to hold your recommended treatment against you. So tell me: what do I have to do?"

"The only way for a Caloren's omega to successfully regulate their cycle requires intensive exposure during the heat to alpha pheromones and biochemistry." Connor's lips pressed together in a tight line, but before Oliver could really process the implications of her statement, she blurted out a phrase that made his blood turn to ice in his veins. "You're going to have to find an alpha who's willing to mate with you."

"This is absolutely ridiculous," Oliver muttered to himself. It was three days since his ill-fated appointment with Dr Connor, and he'd spent every spare minute since then poring over any and every medical report he could find on omega physiology. There had to be another option. What Connor had suggested was out of the question. Repeated sex – and most likely, rough, degrading sex, given the way most alphas behaved – with a random stranger? The very idea was abhorrent.

Ignoring the dull drone of noise in the office around him, he turned back to the report on his computer. The diligent employee in him knew he should be working. The omega was too busy panicking about a promising future suddenly cut short.

It has been found that, with appropriate management, a Caloren's omega can expect to experience heats of normal duration – between thirty to forty-eight hours, as is the case with non-Caloren's omegas.

Well that, at least, sounded promising. Dr Connor had been far less optimistic in her estimation of what Oliver could expect, even if he adopted her outrageous recommendations. As it stood, Oliver's latest heat had lasted nearly two weeks, the spiking body temperature accompanied by searing cramps, vomiting, dizziness and migraines. But as desperate as he was to find a way to alleviate the symptoms, Connor's suggestion that he go and *mate* with…

Not make love, not even have sex. No, when an omega and an alpha got together, it was referred to as *mating*, a base, animalistic rut that many people believed lowered the rarer genders to little better than animals.

There had to be another way.

In order to achieve this result, however, it has been found that an omega needs to be mated at least twelve times throughout the heat -

Oliver clicked the X at the top corner of the screen, closing his eyes in disgust. Yet one more report, supposedly by a very progressive and experienced scientist, who had once again proven himself to be nothing more than a parrot for the conventional 'wisdom' of the day. Was that really all anyone was going to come up with? *Go and spread your legs for the first randy alpha you find wandering the streets and let him rut on you like a dog…*

Oliver's phone beeped just then, and he fished it out of his pocket, glancing at the reminder message. "Damn it." He'd completely forgotten his follow-up appointment with Dr Connor. Locking his computer, he grabbed his backpack and let himself out of the engineers' office, heading across the courtyard, past the cafeteria, and down the long corridor that led to the medical wing of the compound.

In that regard, at least, he was fortunate. The International Space Association, or ISA, was a sprawling organisation that included astronomers, physicists, engineers and astronauts, all working together to expand the earth's knowledge of space. Oliver was an engineer, part of a brilliant team tasked with designing the equipment that kept the international space station fully operational. One of the perks of working for the organisation was that they had their very own medical wing, where doctors provided a full range of services to the employees, as well as conducting research on the effects of space travel on the human body.

Arriving at the entrance to the medical wing, Oliver opened the door, but immediately had to step back as a group of t-shirt-clad, muscle-bound test pilots burst through the opening. Oliver stood patiently to the side, holding the door for them, unsurprised when they paid him absolutely no mind. In fact, the last man in the line was the only one to acknowledge him in any way. "Thanks," the man said, with a grin and a wink, before immediately forgetting that Oliver existed, rushing off to catch up with his friends.

Damn jocks. A part of him could see the appeal of the group of high-flyers. They were fit, athletic, outgoing and they had jobs that were the envy of adrenaline junkies everywhere. They got to participate in zero-gravity test flights, they were the test subjects for the rocket simulators, they road-tested the space suits and mechanical arms that the real astronauts would be using. On weekends, according to the rumours, they were into all manner of adventure sports, kite-surfing, rock-climbing, base-jumping and goodness knows what else. They were also, in Oliver's opinion, uncouth brutes who had little interest in anything but themselves – as the group who had just barged past him had demonstrated.

Back in the waiting room, Oliver checked in with the reception desk, then took a seat. Over the past six months, he'd spent countless hours in this room, trying to find a comfortable position on the hard, plastic chairs, waiting for his name to be called, waiting for the chance to continue on with his life as he had done up until now. Until a year ago, his omega gender had been all but irrelevant. Once every three months, he'd gone through a heat, forty hours of hormonal surges and erratic sexual desires, and on the odd occasions that the entire thing had occurred on a weekend, the rest of the world had been none-the-wiser. When it had taken him out of work, he'd merely had to stroll down the hall to the medical wing, get a certificate from the doctor and present it to his boss, and no more questions had been asked.

But all that had changed, two months after his twenty-sixth birthday, when a simple, forty-hour heat had turned into eighty hours, then a hundred, then a hundred and twenty. Then the tests had begun, a seemingly endless quest for answers as to what the hell had suddenly gone so wrong with his body.

"Oliver Levy?"

Oliver stood up, following the nurse down the hall, as he'd done dozens of times before.

Dr Connor was waiting, patient and supportive, and he took a seat, feeling his gut roll at the thought of the conversation to come.

"How are you feeling?" Connor asked him. "I got the impression our last appointment was something of a shock for you."

Oliver wanted to scream, yell, break things, rage at the world for the hand he'd been dealt. Instead, he folded his hands in his lap and took a slow, steadying breath. "It was rather a shock," he agreed. "It's not so much the mating itself..." God, how he hated that word. "...as it is the long-term repercussions of it. Short of finding a new alpha every three months, the implication is that he and I would end up as a mated pair. I'll admit that I've never witnessed such a pair firsthand, but there are plenty of anecdotes about how they operate. Mated alphas are notoriously possessive, and nobody has ever bothered updating the archaic laws that let them get away with it!" He was getting upset now, and made an effort to calm himself. None of this was the doctor's fault; there was no point taking it out on her. "I would be forced to quit my job. The alpha could claim possession of my house." It was a gorgeous, two bedroom cottage he'd bought two years ago, neat and tidy, his own little oasis away from the world. "He would be able to access my bank account, sell my car, basically take control of my entire life!"

Connor frowned, fiddling with a pen in her lap. "I know it's difficult to imagine your life changing so much, but it's by no means a foregone conclusion that you'd lose everything. There are alphas who are perfectly happy for their mates to continue working. This is the twenty-first century. Both alphas and omegas are far more progressive these days than they used to be."

Oliver sighed in frustration. "Name one example of a happily mated alpha/omega pairing? Because at least once a week, there's a report all over the news that yet another omega has committed suicide because they couldn't stand living as a prisoner in their own homes."

Connor floundered for a moment, clearly scrambling for an answer. "There have been cases of omegas taking their alphas to court," she said eventually. "They're filing for divorce, they're suing for financial loss. I know it's not a cheerful picture, but at least they're making a point, and fighting for conditions to improve -"

"There have been exactly three cases in the last five years that omegas have won," Oliver interrupted. He'd done his research just as well as she had. "And all of them involved grievous bodily harm inflicted upon the omega by the alpha. So yes, if my partner tries to kill me, the courts will stand in my favour. But aside from that, they don't want to know."

There were a number of pamphlets on the desk, titled various nauseating catch-phrases like 'The Submissive Omega' or 'Pair-bonding; a user's guide'. Looking at them was like staring down the barrel of a gun, a cold, dismal representation of his future. "Is this really the only option? There's no other research underway? No drugs to suppress the hormonal cycle? Please, there's got to be *something*."

Connor pressed her lips together in a thin, tight line. "Medically speaking, we're unfortunately out of options. I'm sorry, Oliver, but that's the cold, hard truth. But might I suggest... you could try talking to Robert Anderson. As the administrator of the ISA, he'd already have access to your personnel file, and given your pattern of illness over the past year, I'd be surprised if he hasn't connected the dots by now. He's the sort of man who knows people, who know people. If anyone can help you, he could. But if not," she added, "then please don't do anything rash. We have access to a wonderful team of therapists and legal advisers... I'm sure we'd be able to work *something* out."

Unfortunately, Oliver shared none of her optimism.

CHAPTER TWO

OLIVER

One of Oliver's more refined qualities was that he wasn't a procrastinator. Quick to make decisions, efficient in taking action, there was rarely anything overlooked or left undone in his life. So he'd wasted absolutely no time in making an appointment to see Robert Anderson.

"Mr Levy," the man greeted him, standing up to shake his hand, and Oliver was reminded just how tall Anderson was. His voice was deep and booming, his hair greying, though it still grew thickly over the top of his head, and the creases around his eyes gave the man what people referred to as 'character'. "First, let me congratulate you on the mechanical arm your team designed. It's a marvel! A true marvel. Once we get it installed on the space station, it'll halve the need for space-walks, a huge improvement to astronaut safety. They'll be able to make adjustments to the outside of the station from the comfort of a computer terminal. It's brilliant."

Oliver couldn't help but smile, despite the dark cloud hanging over him. "I really only worked on the gearing system," he said modestly. "But it was an honour to be a part of the project. We have an excellent team."

"That we do," Anderson agreed, beaming at him. "Now, how can I help you?"

Oliver had spent the better part of an hour rehearsing what he might say. Should he start with the usual prevarication, *I'm afraid I've received some bad news, etc, etc?* Should he jump right in with *I need to ask for your help?* Should he approach the whole thing in a sideways manner, talking about omega rights and trying to deduce what Anderson's stance on the whole issue was?

In the end, he'd come up with no clear answers, and so he floundered for a moment in the face of the obvious question. "I was wondering if you're familiar with Caloren's Syndrome?" he asked finally. Anderson was a

7

direct, decisive sort of man, and he'd probably appreciate a fairly direct approach.

But instead of giving him a simple 'yes' or 'no', Anderson's face instead melted into an expression of deep concern. "Oh, no, I'm so sorry," he said. "They've given you a diagnosis?"

It shouldn't have been a surprise that Anderson was already abreast of Oliver's recent troubles. Though he wouldn't have been privy to any of the specifics of his medical records, the man was sharp as a whip, and it wouldn't have taken much for him to put two and two together. Extended absences every three months combined with regular medical appointments laid out a fairly convincing pattern.

Oliver nodded, feeling suddenly emotional. Plenty of people on the team here had commented over the years that Anderson was like a father to them, stern when he had to be, but gentle and compassionate whenever life managed to get the better of them. "Doctor Connor said I should talk to you," he explained, deciding to just cut to the chase. "She said you might know of a suitable solution."

Anderson smoothed down his moustache, a thoughtful look settling on his face. "Solutions to this sort of problem are in short supply. That's not to say I can't help," he rushed on, when Oliver's face fell. "But the bigger question is what are you really trying to achieve here? Given that there's not much I can do about your medical condition, what's the best case scenario you can see coming out of this?"

Oliver's gut lurched. That didn't sound promising. "I was hoping you might know of someone in an appropriate medical field who's come up with a treatment plan. That's what Dr Connor seemed to imply."

Anderson shook his head. "Unfortunately, to my knowledge, no one has yet been able to invent that particular miracle. I suspect she was anticipating a more *practical* sort of assistance from me."

"I don't follow," Oliver admitted. There was a knot of tension in his left shoulder, and he felt the muscle slowly tightening as the conversation went on.

"Just for the moment," Anderson said, "humour me a little. Biologically speaking…" He hesitated, then lowered his voice. "Excuse me for being indelicate. But given the current state of medical knowledge, pairing up with an alpha is really your only option."

Oliver let out a harsh sigh. Just one more person getting his hopes up, only to dash them to the ground.

"But my original question is still valid," Anderson said. "Given the limitations of your situation, what would be your best-case scenario, moving on from here?"

Oliver frowned in confusion. "I don't really understand the question. I have to find an alpha to 'support' me. What other choice is there?"

Slowly, Anderson removed his glasses. He rubbed the bridge of his nose as he set them carefully on the table. "Let me explain something to you, Oliver. May I call you Oliver?"

"Of course."

Anderson fixed him with a steely look, and Oliver braced himself for some sort of lecture. Quite honestly, he'd had enough of those from Dr Connor, but he'd come here asking Anderson for help, so it was the least he could do to actually listen. "In designing a space station – or any of the components for it," Anderson began, "there are two main ways we can go about deciding what we're going to build. Now, the first option is the most obvious – we ask ourselves 'What are we *able* to do?' What technology do we have, what materials are available, how much money can we spend, and so forth.

"But there's another way to approach things – and in my mind, a far better way – which is to ask 'What do we *want*?' What is the ideal system we want to build to achieve the specified result? Only once we've got an answer to that question do we start thinking about *how* to build it. We work backwards, from the solution, to the method by which we get there. If we don't have the technology, we invent it. If we don't have the materials, we design them. Innovation at its finest, and that's one of the things I like so much about space-age development. So let me ask you again, young man – what do you actually want?"

The question was absurd. There was no way he could have what he wanted. "I want to find an alpha who will let me continue my life just as it is. I want to keep working. I want to keep my house. I don't want any interference in my financial affairs. I want someone who will just show up once every three months, provide what I need, then disappear until I need him again." It was a ridiculous request. Aside from the impossibility of convincing an alpha to not claim the omega he was mating with, there was also the more realistic challenge that the arrangement held almost no benefit to the alpha. Okay, so they got free sex once every three months, but what if they got a better offer for any given cycle, a free holiday, an unmissable concert, and decided they had better things to do? What if they met someone else, decided they wanted a stable relationship and promptly cut off their arrangement with Oliver, leaving him stranded?

Or for that matter, what if Oliver found a romantic partner at some point in the future? How was he supposed to explain to them that he needed to sleep with someone else on a regular basis? It also did nothing to solve the problem that Oliver had no desire to have sex with a random stranger in the first place.

Anderson folded his hands in front of him, contemplating the request. "That's quite an ask," he said, stating the obvious. "But not an entirely unrealistic one. You'd need an extremely laid back alpha, with very modern morals and ideals. Someone with no other commitments. Okay, how about this?" he said, suddenly changing tack. "How would you feel – assuming I can locate an alpha that you approve of – if I offered him a small financial sum as compensation for the inconvenience to him? I'm not saying it's not an inconvenience to you as well, mind you. Of course it is. But if I can look at this from a purely selfish perspective for a moment... You, Oliver, are one of the best engineers this place has seen in a decade or more. We can't afford to lose you. I would like nothing more than for you to find a suitable alpha, even just for your own happiness and wellbeing, but at the same time, it benefits the ISA if we find someone who will allow you to keep working here. And in that case, it might be within my power to find some pragmatic ways to sweeten the deal."

Oliver forced himself to consider the proposal. At first glance, it grated badly. Paying an alpha meant that Anderson – and by extension, Oliver – was effectively reduced to hiring a prostitute to serve his needs. But the more he thought about it, the more he could see the practical benefits of such an arrangement. It added a certain stability to the relationship, it assuaged Oliver's guilt at simply using another human being for his own purposes, and the payment meant that the alpha in question would be completely aware of all the conditions of the deal right from the start, cutting down on the likelihood of hurt feelings or messy arguments further down the track.

"That would be acceptable," he said finally. Then a frown creased his forehead. "But do you actually know someone who would consider that kind of offer?"

Anderson tilted his head, not a yes, not a no. "Perhaps. I have one or two potential candidates in mind. Let me ask a few questions, and I'll get back to you."

Oliver opened his mouth to agree, but then another problem crossed his mind, and he sat up straight in alarm. "You're not going to... Are you going to tell them who I am? Nobody even really knows I'm an omega at the moment," – though some of the engineers on his team had likely guessed – "and if word got out -"

"Oliver, relax!" Anderson said soothingly. "The man I have in mind is as reliable as they come. I wouldn't even be considering this if I believed there was any significant risk to your reputation. Like I said, you're a damn good engineer, and selling you out does neither of us any good."

For now, it was the best answer Oliver was likely to get, and far more than he'd been hoping for just half an hour ago. "Okay," he agreed weakly, praying that Anderson would come through. Between the endless rounds of tests and the days he'd spent raging against his own diagnosis, he had less than two weeks until his next heat. And if they hadn't come up with a solution by then, he was in a world of trouble.

CHAPTER THREE

OLIVER

In the end, it took Anderson a full week to get back to him, and by the end of it, Oliver was a quivering mess of anxiety. He took a seat in Anderson's office, bracing himself for the worst. If no one suitable had been found, the only other option was to hire a prostitute – a real one this time, rather than a clandestine fill-in – and hope he could be paid enough money to keep quiet about Oliver's status.

But it seemed that for once, the fates were smiling on him. "I have good news," Anderson said, the moment he was seated. "I've found an alpha who is entirely willing to cooperate with your conditions. He's single, he's laid back, and he's agreed not to curtail any of your current freedoms. And just in case you're inclined to think that's just lip-service to get himself the job, what he actually said was, and I quote, 'I've got way too much shit in my life already to worry about babysitting a grown man twenty-four-seven'." It was typical of Anderson to be blunt, and Oliver took no offence to the statement. "In this case, I think a little self-interest on his part works nicely in your favour. And the added bonus is that, based on what I know about each of you, I have a *reasonable* expectation that you'll get along fairly well."

"Sounds like an absolute angel," Oliver muttered. "So what's the catch?"

Anderson shot him a wry smile. "Too good to be true, eh? Well, he does have a few 'quirks', if I may put it that way, that you might find a tad annoying. He's an extrovert," – translation: he talks too much – "he can be a bit untidy," – code for 'he's going to trash your house' – "and he never quite mastered the art of thinking before he speaks." Whereas Oliver had always been taught impeccable manners and had practiced diplomacy until it was an art form. "But on the positive side, he's trustworthy, he has a very liberal view of the role of omegas in society and he's... well, shall we just

11

say he's easy on the eyes. If that sort of thing matters to you," he added. "He also works for the ISA, which adds a certain convenience to the arrangement."

He worked for the ISA? That pulled Oliver up short. "You mean I'll be *working* with him?" That sounded dreadful, coming in to work, having to make polite small-talk with a man who'd seen him naked, having to perform a perpetual dance of pretending they didn't know each other that well, when in fact they would know each other *intimately*...

"He's in a different division," Anderson said quickly. "The worst that might happen is you'd pass each other in the hallways once or twice a week. I'd never put you in a position where you were actually on the same team as your man."

Oh. Well, that didn't sound so bad. Okay, time to bite the bullet. "So, who is he, exactly?"

"Before I tell you, I'll need you to sign a confidentiality agreement," Anderson said, sliding a sheet of paper across the desk. "It's the same one he had to sign before I told him your name." Bless the man, he'd thought of everything. "It basically forbids you from publically exposing him as an alpha or discussing any of the details of your arrangement with anyone other than medical personnel or myself."

Oliver skimmed through the document, relieved to see that it was straightforward, yet comprehensive, covering all the necessary bases. He picked up the pen and signed his name at the bottom.

"Okay," Anderson said when he was done. "Your new alpha 'assistant' is Jet Wilder."

Oliver blinked. "Sorry, I'm not familiar with that name."

"That's more or less what he said when I told him your name," Anderson said with a smile. But the next thing he said made Oliver's heart drop into his stomach. "He's one of the test pilots. He's waiting in the next office. Would you like me to call him in?"

What? The man he was supposed to sleep with, the one who would see him at his most vulnerable and possess the ability to destroy his reputation and demolish everything he had worked for, was one of those arrogant, swaggering muscle-heads? Why didn't he just go and jump off the nearest bridge? It would be a lot simpler and a lot less painful than having to deal with one of those irresponsible adrenaline junkies.

"Oliver?"

Oliver made an effort to pull himself together. "Yes, uh... Yes, of course. Bring him in." With just over a week to go until his heat, he didn't have many other options at this point.

Anderson left the room and returned a moment later, the pilot in tow, and to Oliver's acute irritation, he felt his heart speed up and his face flush.

Easy on the eyes. It was certainly true, black hair falling roguishly across his face, playful lips, a body that had most certainly spent long hours in a gym.

A moment later he realised that yes, he had actually seen him before, wandering the hallways of the compound. In fact, he remembered, this had been the man who'd thanked him for opening the door the other day. The thanks and the smile had been appreciated. The wink, on the other hand...

"Hey, I'm Jet," Jet introduced himself, offering his hand. Oliver shook it automatically.

"Oliver," he replied, though it was obvious Jet knew who he was. But good manners should never be overlooked, particularly when Jet himself was going to the effort to be polite.

"So, um... interesting times," Jet said, when the silence became awkward. Was that a smirk on his lips, or was Oliver imagining things? "I guess we should talk about some of the details of this... um... what do we call this, exactly?"

"Perhaps I should leave you two to chat?" Anderson offered, then quickly excused himself without waiting for a reply, leaving Oliver standing awkwardly in the middle of the room. Jet immediately went and plonked himself down in Anderson's chair, spinning around carelessly. "I always wanted to sit in this chair," he admitted with a grin. "Get a little taste of the *power*, before I go back to being a lowly pleb."

Oliver managed a tight smile and took a seat opposite him; on the 'employee' side of the desk, while Jet sat in the boss's chair.

"So... what Anderson told me is that you're pretty much looking for a fuck-buddy who isn't going to screw up your life, right?"

Heaven help him, he'd been in the same room as Jet for thirty seconds and he already wanted to strangle him. Oliver had never knowingly met an alpha before, since the few people who were something other than a beta tended to be incredibly tight-lipped about it, but Jet was everything he'd expected of the gender; brash, arrogant and crass, and he cringed as Jet leaned back in his seat and put his boots on the desk.

"Is that right, or am I missing something?"

"That's right," Oliver said, pulling himself out of his reverie. "I'd like to continue working in my job. I would prefer not to have to share my house with anyone. I'm looking for something discreet," – did Jet even know what the word meant? – "which is purely designed to serve a biological function."

"Hm." Jet raised his eyebrows. "Okay, so the first thing you gotta do," he said, putting his boots back on the floor and sitting up, "is stop talking like you're asking my permission for anything. The way Anderson described it, this arrangement works for me. I have absolutely no interest in micromanaging what colour socks you're allowed to wear or how many times a day you take a piss. I got my own life to deal with, and I'm perfectly happy spending my evenings meeting the boys at the pub and my weekends out on the water. Okay?"

"I'm not asking your permission," Oliver objected immediately. "I'm simply stating what I want."

"If you're stating what you want, you say 'you are not welcome to move into my house'. *Preferring* not to *share* your house is all wishy-washy. Come on, man, step up. Tell me what you want, and how you want it, and if there's anything I really have a problem with, I'll lay it on you straight."

He had a point – clear communication was necessary, but Oliver refused to stoop to Jet's level of crassness. "I would like you to make yourself available once every three months to assist with my *medical condition*, and then I'd like to continue my life as before until I require your services again."

"Right. So no going out for drinks in the evening? No catching a movie when it's raining and I can't surf? Just straight up business."

"Exactly."

"What about if we see each other at work? Am I allowed to say hello, or should I just pretend I don't know you?"

"I think a certain level of civility would be appropriate. I doubt that would arouse any undue suspicion."

"Cool. Look, I'm not going to blow your cover, man. I'm just kind of a friendly guy, and being all standoffish isn't my thing, okay?"

"It's fine. Really, it's fine. I understand."

"All right, then we gotta figure out what we're going to call this."

Oliver managed not to roll his eyes. "Really? You want code names and secret passwords, do you?"

"I want some way to explain this to my friends when I suddenly have to tell them I can't go surfing on Saturday morning. Something that doesn't involve saying 'sorry, I gotta go spend the weekend sticking my dick up an omega'. I'm sorry, am I embarrassing you?" he asked, seeing the way Oliver's face was turning red.

Finally, Oliver decided to take a leaf out of Jet's book. "Yes, actually, you are," he snapped. "I don't know what kind of barn you were raised in, but I was taught that one does not refer to 'fuck-buddies' and sticking their genitals inside things in polite company!" If he was paying attention, he would have seen the surprise on Jet's face, rapidly followed by a sudden look of meek chagrin, but now that he'd let the cork out of the bottle, the rest of what was inside came bubbling out. "I'm not sure if you realise how serious a situation this is, but if we screw this up, I could very well end up *dead*. This is far from the way I would choose to be spending my time, and even with your copious assurances that you want *nothing at all* to do with my life, I'm still going to have to roll over and take it whenever nature decides to throw me the latest curveball. What I really want to do is…" His voice cracked, and his face burned in sudden embarrassment as he felt tears pricking at his eyes. He stood up, turning around to face the wall and buying a few precious seconds to get himself together.

Behind him, there was a faint rustling sound. "Holy shit, I... I didn't realise," Jet said, his tone far gentler than before. "I thought you were... I mean, I thought... You don't actually want to sleep with me at all, do you?"

"You think this is some kind of game?" Oliver asked, without turning around. "You think I'm just trying to pick up some handsome alpha for a good time? Of course I don't bloody want this. But I have two choices right here, and that's to either be raped by someone who's supposed to be saving my life, or die."

There was a moment of silence, thick and heavy, and then...

"Hey, that was over the top! You are out of line, man!" Jet leapt out of his chair and strode across the room, shoving Oliver's shoulder so he was forced to turn and face him. "I am not *raping* you! *You* asked *me* to come here, you asked me to save your life, and shit, if you really think it's such a fucking poor idea, then you're free to go off and do your own thing, but don't you *dare* lay this on me!"

Regret caught Oliver hard, and he was shocked at his own outburst. If nothing else, then getting on the wrong side of his only hope for a normal life was a stupid thing to do, to say nothing of the sheer *rudeness* of what he'd just said.

"I'm sorry," Oliver choked out, meaning it with all sincerity. "I'm sorry, you're right, that was out of line."

Silence filled the room, cold and heavy.

"Shit, I get it, man," Jet said finally. "I mean... you haven't done this before, have you?"

"Propositioning strangers for sex? No, I haven't."

"That's not what I... well, yeah, okay. Let's leave it at that." There was another moment of silence. "But seriously, we need a way to refer to this without letting on what's really happening."

"Do you have any siblings?" Oliver asked, racking his brain for a decent idea. "Nieces? Nephews?"

"Nope. I'm an only child."

Damn. "What about an ex-girlfriend? It doesn't even have to be a real one, just make one up. Can you tell people she's got kids? Pretend one of them has a serious medical condition, something like muscular dystrophy, maybe, and every now and then you have to go and babysit her other child because the first one's in hospital? Could that work? Are you the sort of guy who would do that kind of thing?" There was no point inventing a cover story if it wasn't at least notionally plausible.

"Could work," Jet said slowly. "Maybe not a girlfriend, though. Just a childhood friend. I grew up on the west coast, so no one would look too closely at the specifics. I can tell them this friend just moved east… Yeah, it could work." He pulled out his phone. "What's your number?" he asked, and Oliver told him. "Okay, you are now 'Naomi', according to my phone. Just send me a message saying you need me to babysit Jackson, and what time I should be there, and we're all set." He looked up at Oliver, a sudden frown on his face. "How much notice am I going to get about these 'medical emergencies'?"

"Eight to ten hours," Oliver said. "I usually get a bout of nausea and a mild headache about half a day before things kick off properly. I've got pretty good at picking up on when it's going to happen."

"When's your next cycle due?"

"In about a week."

Jet looked startled for a moment. "Heck, cutting it a bit fine, aren't you? Never mind, we're sorted now." But then his surprised look became a touch more alarmed. "Hey, um… sorry if this is a personal question, but… is there any chance I could accidentally end up getting you pregnant? I mean, do you even want kids? I kind of figured you didn't, since you're not too keen on this whole scheme in the first place -"

"No, there's no chance of pregnancy," Oliver interrupted him, before he could ramble on any longer. "I had myself surgically sterilised a few years ago. Society isn't particularly sympathetic to pregnant men these days, so it just seemed wiser to avoid the whole issue."

Jet looked relieved, and strangely, Oliver found that reassuring. Anderson had said he didn't want the responsibility of caring for an omega, and knowing he wasn't prepared to deal with children only confirmed that standpoint.

"All right, then," Jet said, wrapping up the conversation. "Here's my number…" Oliver's phone beeped, confirming he'd just received a message. "Take it easy, man. I'll see you in about a week."

CHAPTER FOUR

JET

Jet parked his car in front of his apartment block that evening, feeling like he'd been put through the ringer. He had no idea what he'd expected an omega to be like, but Oliver was definitely not it. If he really had to pin it down, he supposed he'd thought he would be a meek little bookworm with nerdish glasses and a cardigan, someone with two left feet who looked at the floor when he spoke to you. It was a stereotype, and an unfair one, and he really should have been above making judgements like that. Particularly since he'd worked hard to be anything but a 'typical' alpha.

But Oliver had been a surprise. Okay, so he wore glasses, but they were sleek and stylish, rimless frames that brought out the green in his eyes. He'd been wearing a business shirt and slacks, he stood up straight, he'd looked Jet in the eye, and he hadn't been afraid to bite back when Jet had pushed him too far.

And then there had been that body, the smooth lines of him evident even beneath his clothes. It was clear as day that Oliver knew his way around a gym. His shoulders were broad, the sleeves of his shirt hugging his biceps just the right amount, stomach flat and hard, legs long and sinful. When Anderson had first told him he had an omega in need of assistance, he'd mentioned the fact that the anonymous man was 'quite a looker' – an understatement if there ever was one. Those first few seconds had had his inner alpha crowing like his team had just won the grand final!

But the conversation had gone rapidly downhill after that, and one part of it in particular had filled Jet with a cold dread. Knowing he couldn't just leave things the way they were, he let himself into his apartment and grabbed his phone, flopping down on the couch without bothering to switch on the light.

"Hey, Sullivan," he said, when the call was answered. "I need some advice, man. And I'm really hoping you can come through for me." Doctor Sullivan Kennedy was the leading authority on alpha and omega physiology on the east coast, and through a fortuitous meeting on a beach some four years prior, he was also a good friend of Jet's.

"Follow the instructions," Sullivan told him, without missing a beat. "Don't trust used car salesmen, and don't eat the yellow snow. How am I doing so far?"

"Very funny," Jet drawled. "I'm serious. And before we go any further, I just want to make the point that this is the sort of conversation that falls under doctor-patient confidentiality and all that."

There was a moment of silence, then a shuffling sound. "Just a moment," Sullivan said. "I'm going to close my office door." There was a thud, then some more rustling. "Right then. Too much to just expect a social call, I suppose," he joked good-naturedly. "What can I do for you?"

"I wanted to ask you a question. Of a medical nature. And it's kind of a delicate topic." In addition to being a doctor, Sullivan was one of only a handful of people in the world who knew Jet was an alpha.

"Everything to do with alpha/ omega physiology these days is a delicate topic," Sullivan grumbled. "God forbid anyone actually talk about the way your bodies naturally work, lest we offend some poor, vulnerable beta." This was what Jet liked so much about Sullivan. He was dedicated to his work, professional, polite, diplomatic, but he was also a realist with a cynical streak that, in Jet's mind, was far more palatable than the 'holier-than-thou' attitudes of a lot of other doctors he'd dealt with. "There's very little you can say that would shock me, so go ahead, ask your question."

"Okay, so hypothetically speaking, let's suppose there's an omega," Jet began, being careful to keep things on a very general level. Doctor or not, he had no right to be discussing the specifics of Oliver's case with anyone. "And let's suppose that he's suffering from Caloren's Syndrome, and let's also suppose, for argument's sake, that he's been sexually assaulted so he's really not on board with having sex with an alpha." As far as he was aware, Oliver had no such history, but it worked as an imaginary scenario that would hopefully get him the right sort of answers. "In that situation, what are his options?"

Sullivan huffed out a breath. "You sure know how to ask the tough questions. Well, let's see... Oh, heck, Jet, you have to understand that alpha/ omega research is still very much in its preliminary stages. You're aware, I suppose, that medically speaking, mating is still the only reliable treatment for Caloren's?"

Jet flinched at the words, though not because it wasn't the answer he'd been hoping for. "Can't we just call it 'having sex' instead of 'mating'?" he snapped. The whole bloody world was determined to reduce them to nothing more than animals.

There was a pause on the end of the line. "Do you find that term offensive?" Sullivan asked, sounding a touch baffled.

"Yeah, actually, I do."

"I'm so sorry!" Sullivan apologised immediately. "It's never even occurred to me that alphas and omegas might object to the term. I'll make a note of that. Something to keep in mind for my future patients." There was a faint rustling sound, and Jet could imagine the doctor rummaging around for a pen and something to scribble on. "Now, back to the original question," he said, once he'd sorted himself out. "Let's look at this from a purely physiological perspective. There are a number of receptors in the omega's body that need to be stimulated to regulate the hormonal cycle. I believe I've narrowed it down to the two most important ones, but as I said, my research is still a work in progress, so don't take anything I say as gospel.

"The first key is pheromones; the omega needs to be able to smell an alpha's scent. That means prolonged exposure at close range throughout the heat. The second part is that the omega's body needs to absorb a particular protein found in alpha semen. This is really the part that makes sex such a necessity. The proteins are absorbed through the wall of the omega's reproductive tract, they enter the bloodstream and then go on to regulate the omega's hormonal production, which in turn regulates their body temperature, blood pressure, muscle tone – all the things that cause the symptoms of Caloren's Syndrome.

"Now, of course, it's never quite that simple," Sullivan went on. "There are also a number of secondary stimuli that I haven't yet been able to work out the importance of. One of them is the manual stimulation of the reproductive tract. There are various nerve endings that may require physical stimulation, but given that there aren't all that many Caloren's omegas in the world, I haven't been able to -"

"So that would be… okay, sorry to interrupt," Jet stuttered out, trying to keep up with the barrage of information. "That last part, just ignoring the rest of it for a moment, could theoretically be achieved with a dildo, right?"

"If you're only talking about the physical stimulation, then yes," Sullivan agreed.

Jet grabbed a notepad and pen off the coffee table, scribbling down a few notes. "Okay, good. That's one part of it sorted. What else have we got?"

"I'm also working on a theory that saliva may contain one or more chemicals which interact with the omega's physiology. Kissing, I mean," he clarified. "It may be necessary for the alpha and the omega to kiss each other."

"But that's unproven at the moment, right?"

"All of this is unproven. And I'm getting the horrible feeling that you're going to paraphrase this, wrap it up with a neat little bow and give some very dubious advice to some poor omega looking for a way out."

Yes, that was exactly what he was going to do. "I'm not going to put anyone at risk of harm," he said truthfully. If he wasn't able to scrape a plan together out of this, or if that plan failed, then he would be fulfilling his duty to Oliver the old fashioned way. "So let me see if I've got this. The omega needs to be exposed to an alpha's scent, he needs to 'insert proteins into his reproductive tract'," – Oliver would be so proud of him for using such clinical terms – "and he may or may not need to stick a dildo up his ass?" Unlike Oliver, Sullivan had no objection to his crudity.

Sullivan sighed. "Have you listened to the part where I said this was an unproven theory?"

"Absolutely," he promised, almost able to hear Sullivan roll his eyes. "Like I said right up front: this is a hypothetical omega. Just theories and ideas, man, that's all."

"Good grief, I don't know who gives me more grey hairs, you or my fourteen-year-old daughter. Fine, go play with your theories," Sullivan said with a sigh. "Although..." His tone turned suddenly speculative. "If you come up with any ideas that might warrant further research, you will let me know?"

Jet hesitated at that. How would Oliver feel, knowing he'd been discussing his problems without his permission? "I'll see how it goes," he said, dodging the question. "No point starting the oven before you've plucked the chicken."

CHAPTER FIVE

JET

It took Jet three days to come up with what he considered to be a workable plan, and two more to collect everything he needed. And not a moment too soon. At 2 p.m. on a lazy Saturday, his phone beeped, and he idly checked the message… then sat up ramrod straight, spilling his beer in the process. *Can you babysit Jackson this afternoon? After dinner is fine.*

Jet hastily typed a reply. *Can I come now? Something interesting to discuss.*

A simple 'Okay' was the response, so he threw a few things into a bag – some clothes, his toothbrush, the supplies he'd gathered – and headed out the door.

Twenty minutes later, he was pulling up outside a house that looked every bit like it suited its owner. The front yard was tidy, a hedge row neatly trimmed, the grass recently mown. The house was small but modern and stylish, functional with no additional frivolities. Very much like Oliver himself. Jet checked the address – yup, this was definitely the place – and got out of the car, snagging his duffle bag on the way.

Oliver opened the door before he got halfway across the porch, and for a split second, Jet was surprised to see him wearing jeans and a t-shirt. A moment later, he told himself he was being stupid. Had he really expected the man to be sitting around his own home in a business shirt and slacks?

"Hey, how's it going?" he greeted him.

Oliver made an attempt at a smile and failed miserably. "As well as can be expected. Thank you for coming." It was no surprise that Oliver wasn't looking forward to this. But hopefully Jet had some good news for him.

He stepped through the door as Oliver held it open, not surprised to find the inside of the house very like the outside – tidy, stylish, and clean. Not a dirty coffee cup or a stray magazine to be found.

"So I've been doing some research," he said, jumping straight in, at the same time as keeping his announcement vague. No point telling Oliver exactly where that research had come from. "Most of it was about why an omega needs to have sex with an alpha, from a purely physiological perspective. I've come up with a few theories, and possibly some plans to make things more comfortable for you, so I wanted to come early and have a chat." Hopefully, Oliver would be willing to not only listen, but add his own ideas to the plan. On the other hand, given how uncomfortable he'd been during their last discussion, there was a possibility he'd just shut Jet down. If he refused, though, they were in for an awkward couple of hours while they waited for Oliver's heat to hit.

Oliver stared at him blankly for a long moment. "Would you like some coffee?" he offered suddenly, and Jet blinked at the unexpected change of topic. Was Oliver saying no, or was he just deflecting, or…?

No, of course not, Jet realised suddenly. His host was simply neurotically polite, focusing on manners before his own discomfort. Damn, it was going to take some time to get the hang of this guy.

"I'd love one," he said, more to appease Oliver than because he really wanted it. "White with two sugars." Realising he was still standing there holding his duffle bag, he set it neatly beside the sofa, then followed Oliver into the kitchen.

He'd been expecting the instant stuff, quick, easy, cheap… but of course, Oliver would never stoop to such an inelegant option. He set about spooning grounds into an espresso machine, then started frothing some milk. As he stood there, watching Oliver's precise movements and nit-picky concern over the two stray grounds that spilled onto the counter, Jet couldn't help wondering what the hell had possessed Anderson to put the two of them together. They couldn't have been more different. Surely there must have been some other alpha in the International Space Association better suited to helping out a high strung omega with a metaphorical stick up his ass. Because, Jet thought darkly, he'd made it perfectly clear that he didn't want a literal stick up there.

Minutes later, he was handed an expertly made cappuccino, and the pair of them headed for the sofa.

"So what's this grand idea you've had?" Oliver asked, staring into his cup.

"I'm not entirely sure it's going to work, but I figure it's worth a shot," Jet said. He outlined the details that Sullivan had shared with him on the chemical requirements of an omega's body, and the tentative conclusion he'd reached that maybe, just maybe, they didn't need to have intercourse after all.

"The way I see it," he said, coming to the end of his explanation, "is that all you really need is a way to stimulate the right nerve endings and to administer the necessary proteins into your... reproductive tract." He fumbled over the description just slightly, trying to remember not to offend Oliver. "So I've prepared a few things," he ploughed on, reaching for his duffle bag. "First up, I've got two of my workout shirts for you." He handed Oliver two large, zip-locked bags, each containing a sweaty t-shirt. "That should take care of the pheromones."

Oliver, for his part, had still said nothing, and the carefully neutral expression on his face wasn't giving anything away. Was he about to laugh at Jet? Or tell him the idea was ridiculous? Or maybe he was so offended he'd just been rendered speechless? Then again, he'd probably never been handed a sweaty, stained singlet before and told to go sniff it.

"The physical stimulation part was fairly obvious," Jet said, trying to bolster his courage as he reached into the bag and pulled out a weighty phallus. He set it on the coffee table, noting the way Oliver's eyes widened. Instantly, he decided to leave out the other detail he'd been about to share – that he'd specifically chosen one that was as close to his own size as possible. Alphas, on average, were fairly large in the downstairs department, and he wasn't sure if that size was an important factor in stimulating the right nerves.

"The last part is fairly crude at the moment, but if things work out, we can always refine it later." He retrieved the last two items – a packet of disposable plastic cups and a plastic dropper, the sort that might be used to administer medicine to a baby.

Oliver stared at the objects blankly, and Jet felt his face flush as he realised he was going to have to explain this one. Oliver clearly wasn't picking up on his suggestion just from the items themselves. "Basically I can jerk off into a cup, then you can... manually insert the liquid yourself. It's not perfect," he rushed on, as Oliver still gave him no response, "but you don't actually have to touch me at all, you get to take care of yourself in privacy, and..." He trailed off, finally running out of steam.

Oliver reached out slowly, picking up the dropper. He turned it over in his hands, then his eyes flickered over Jet's body, a quick dip down to his groin, then off to the side, where he seemed to find the curtains inexplicably fascinating.

"You're serious about this?" he asked finally.

Jet wasn't quite sure how to respond to that. "Of course I am," he said, with a frown. Why would he be suggesting it if he wasn't? But a moment later, he re-evaluated his position here. He'd made a number of assumptions about omegas in the past, and Oliver was disproving a lot of them. So it was entirely possible that Oliver had made similar assumptions about him as an alpha. This was his opportunity to prove himself above the crude stereotypes. "Listen, buddy," he said. "I know alphas are supposed to get all hyped up over the chance to get with an omega, and I've heard some pretty awful stories about that sort of thing. And I assume you have too." A faint nod was his answer. "But it was pretty clear the other day that you're really not into this, and quite honestly, being with a guy who doesn't want me has never been my thing.

"Like I said at the start, this 'alternative method' thing is just theory at this point. I honestly don't know if it's going to work, and if it doesn't…" He looked Oliver in the eye, the weight of their situation bearing down on both of them. "If it doesn't, then we'll still have to have sex. I'm not going to know how much your heat if affecting you, so *you* have to be prepared to make that call." Oliver nodded, a small, defeated movement, though Jet was well aware of how seriously he was taking things. "But until then, I'm prepared to give this a try and see what happens."

Oliver pressed his lips together, looking distastefully at the dildo. "It's fine, in theory. Don't get me wrong, I really appreciate the idea. It's far better than anything anyone else has offered me. But…" He eyed the plastic cups apprehensively. "I was of the understanding that an alpha needed fairly close contact with an omega for you to be able to… 'perform' adequately."

Jet barked out a short laugh. "Yeah, don't worry about that," he said, feeling himself flush. Even a couple of hours out from the real start of his heat, he could already detect the scent Oliver was putting out. As time went on, it was only going to get stronger. "I think just being in the same room as you is going to be enough to get me revved up." His cock was already twitching with interest, though he kept telling the damn thing to shut up and wait its turn.

But Oliver's face suddenly fell at the statement. "In the same room? Oh. So, um… you want me to watch you…?"

It took Jet a moment to catch on, but when he did, his jaw dropped, and he suddenly found himself backpedalling as fast as he could. "What? Oh, shit, no! That's not what I meant. Sorry. I'm really sorry. I just meant… I can go in the bathroom or something, that's fine. I just meant we don't have to be getting all up close and personal for you to affect me."

"Oh." Oliver looked relieved, and the alpha in Jet worked hard not to be offended. As much as he wanted to deny the stereotypes, there was an instinctive part of him that very much wanted his omega to want him.

"Well, then…" Oliver shrugged, a far cry from the enthusiastic response Jet had been anticipating. "It's a workable plan," he conceded. "Let's try it. And if it doesn't work…" He grimaced, and Jet pretended not to notice. "…then we can still fall back on plan A."

"Sounds like a plan." His coffee cup was empty, and following Oliver's example of neatness – it was his house, after all – Jet headed for the kitchen, washing the cup and setting it on the draining board to dry.

Oliver was still sitting on the sofa when he got back, toying with the dropper. Even despite the improvements in their plans, Jet still felt sorry for him. Oliver was about as proper as they came, and privacy aside, there was absolutely nothing dignified about what he was going to have to do.

"So, how soon do we need to start?" Jet asked. As with most alphas, he had little real idea about how an omega's body worked. He'd done some reading when he was younger, but basic sex education didn't even mention the secondary genders, and the medical texts tended to wrap things up in such convoluted jargon that no one without a medical degree could understand it.

"Not for a while yet," Oliver said idly, then suddenly seemed to snap out of his daze. "I should show you around. I'm so sorry, I'm not really in a good frame of mind today. I'm normally a lot more hospitable." He leapt up, not giving Jet the chance to dismiss his agitation. "This is my bedroom," he said, leading Jet down a short hallway and opening the first door. It was a wide room with a double bed, neatly made, no clothes out of place – a stark contrast to Jet's bedroom at home, which was a whirlwind of discarded clothes, rumpled sheets and random shoes lying about. "The second bedroom is this way." He opened the door to a small but serviceable room with a neatly made single bed. "You're welcome to use it, either for sleeping, or just for some privacy. The bathroom's just across the hall. I have an ensuite in my room, so you'll have this one to yourself."

He headed back to the kitchen, where he showed Jet where the cups and spoons were. "There's tea and coffee in the pantry. I've got bread, biscuits, fruit – help yourself if you're hungry. Based on previous experience, I don't think I'm going to be in a fit state to offer you much in the way of cooking, so feel free to make something when you want it. You brought a change of clothes, I assume?"

"A couple of different things, yeah," Jet confirmed. "How long are we expecting this to last?" Their last meeting had been unfortunately vague on a couple of the details.

"According to the medical texts, if we provide adequate stimulation to my various chemical receptors, it should last about two days." Such a clinical way of phrasing it. "My most recent heat lasted two weeks. I'm sincerely hoping this one doesn't last that long, but then again, if it does, I'll probably die of hyperthermia before we actually get that far."

The macabre words were delivered in the same clipped tone that Oliver had used for pretty much everything he'd said today, and it was only then that Jet really latched onto the truth – blindly obvious, once he'd seen it, and yet Oliver was doing such a damn good job of hiding it.

Oliver was terrified. And why wouldn't he be? As far as Jet was concerned, this was, at worst, an embarrassing inconvenience. At best, it could be viewed as a weekend of decadent sexual indulgence. But for

25

Oliver, even at its very best this was a gross imposition on his privacy and personal freedom. And if things took a turn for the worse, it could well be a death sentence. What a way to put things into perspective.

"Hey, can I just say something here?" Jet blurted out, stopping dead in the doorway to the kitchen, nearly causing Oliver to walk right into him. "I know this is a lot for you to deal with, and none of it's pleasant, and all things being equal, I know you wouldn't be choosing to do this. But I'm here for you. I promise you, Oliver, I will do whatever you need me to do to make this as safe, and successful, and comfortable for you as possible. Anything you need, just ask. If I'm doing something you don't want me to, just ask me to stop, and I will." He desperately hoped he'd be able to live up to that promise once the hormones kicked in.

For the first time since he'd arrived, Oliver managed a smile. It was a small, shy one, weak and uncertain, but it was a smile. "Thank you," he said softly. "I appreciate it."

CHAPTER SIX

JET

As the afternoon stretched on and began to slide into evening, Jet lay sprawled on the sofa, flicking through a surfing magazine he'd brought with him. Oliver was currently sitting in an armchair, sock-clad feet curled up beneath him, reading a novel. Or at least, he appeared to be reading. Jet himself had spent the last fifteen minutes staring blankly at the same article, his erection throbbing uncomfortably beneath him, the scent of Oliver's heat thick in the air. He couldn't help but wonder if Oliver was experiencing the same discomfort.

But if he was, then why didn't he damn well say something? Jet had made the point again and again that the ball was in Oliver's court here. All he had to do was say the word and Jet would be scurrying off to supply him with his first 'treatment'. As it was, he could barely keep his eyes off the long column of Oliver's throat, the way he occasionally chewed on his lower lip, those elegant fingers caressing the corner of the page…

Oblivious to Jet's quiet observation, Oliver calmly turned the page, shifting his position just a fraction. Doing his best to put his discomfort out of his mind, Jet turned back to his magazine. The article was about a big-wave surfer in Hawaii, something that would normally have been more than enough to hold his attention, but right now, all he could concentrate on was how good the surfer looked standing there, his board under his arm, his wetsuit peeled down to reveal toned abs and thick biceps.

What would Oliver look like beneath his shirt? He had a lean build, that much was obvious, but did he work out? Did he have hair on his chest, or would it be naturally bare? What colour would his hair be as it trailed down to his groin? The same blonde as his head, or a shade darker? An image popped into his mind of Oliver's cock, nestled in amongst the hair, the skin pale, his girth swelling in Jet's hand -

Okay, enough was enough. Abruptly, Jet rolled onto his side, craning his neck to look at Oliver. "Hey, do you think maybe it's time for us to get started?"

Oliver looked up at him in surprise. "Oh. Um… yes, I suppose it is." The man looked cool as a cucumber, Jet thought with irritation, though he nonetheless breathed a sigh of relief at the agreement. He wasn't sure what he would have done if Oliver had said no. What was the appropriate etiquette when you wanted to excuse yourself from the room to go rub one out, when your host was sitting just metres away?

"Okay, great." He swung his legs off the sofa and stood up, aware that he was giving Oliver an eyeful in the process. There was absolutely nothing subtle about the current bulge in his pants. He picked up a plastic cup off the coffee table and pointed vaguely in the direction of the bedroom. "I'll just be… over here."

His hands were undoing his belt buckle the instant he had the door shut. His cock sprang out, thick, hard and seeping fluid, and Jet spared a scant moment to wonder whether omegas had a similar reaction to alphas as alphas had to omegas. Oliver hadn't seemed the least bit affected, and here he was, ready to shoot at the drop of a hat.

Sure enough, it took no more than three or four strokes to bring on his climax, fluid spurting into the cup as Jet let his head fall back against the door, a muted groan rumbling from his chest.

With fumbling hands, he fastened his pants again, ignoring his belt for the time being, and stumbled back into the living room.

Predictably, Oliver avoided looking at him as he took the cup and disappeared into his bedroom. The instant the door was closed, Jet made a dash for the bathroom. One meagre climax hadn't been nearly enough to take the edge off his raging arousal, and it should take Oliver at least a few minutes to administer his first round of 'treatment'. Plenty of time to take care of his own needs.

Jet's second climax came almost as easily as the first, and he cursed as he caught the offering in a wad of toilet paper and dropped it in the bowl. Holy hell, he'd sorely underestimated the potency of Oliver's scent. It was like anticipating a summer rain shower and instead stumbling into a hurricane!

Breathing hard, Jet wrapped his hand around his length, the scent of ripe omega thick in his nostrils. What would it feel like to press the throbbing head of his erection into Oliver's tight passage? To hear him moan beneath him as he thrust in and out? How much of a bloody fool had he been to come up with this convoluted work-around, when he could have been buried balls-deep in Oliver at this very moment…

His third climax, thankfully, cleared his head a little, and Jet was immediately scolding himself for his selfish thoughts. *Get your brain out of your bloody dick*, he thought roughly. Oliver was finding this hard enough as it was without Jet turning into a lecherous oaf. Sex was absolutely off the cards, he reminded himself, until or unless Oliver let him know that their current method wasn't working.

Did he have time for round four? He decided he did, anticipating that it would take Oliver a while to get his head around what he had to do, and a little while longer to actually work up the courage to do it. Was he using the dildo, he wondered, as he worked his shaft again. Would he be moaning? And would Jet be able to hear him if he went and stood in the hallway…?

No, you are not allowed to go and eavesdrop on Oliver, he scolded himself again. He'd spent half his life insisting to other people that alphas weren't the randy perverts most people seemed to think they were, and by God, he wasn't going to prove them all right now. His fourth climax came on a sob, nerves strung taught with pleasure, legs shaking, his breath coming in rough gasps. Now, though, he could at least think straight without wanting to undress Oliver with his eyes – or worse – every time he glanced his way. He flushed the toilet, straightened his clothes and washed his hands, splashing cold water on his face as he prepared to return to the living room. The scent in here wasn't quite as strong, giving him a much-needed reprieve.

He could do this, he assured himself firmly. After all, Oliver was expecting him to be revved and ready to go, so surely he wouldn't mind if he had to excuse himself now and then? That, after all, was the whole reason he was here.

By the time Oliver emerged from his bedroom, Jet was sitting peacefully on the sofa, his attention back on his magazine. Oliver looked decidedly flushed, though Jet noted that both his hair and his clothes were all in the right place, and if he hadn't known better, he would have assumed that he'd been doing nothing more interesting in his room than watching television. He offered Jet a tight smile and took a seat, picking up his book again.

But he'd barely read a single line when he turned to Jet, a worried frown on his face. "How often do you think we'll need to…?"

Jet stared back at him blankly. "I have no idea. I guess it depends how you feel." *How are your symptoms?* He wanted to ask, but didn't know if he was allowed to. *Did you feel better after you took this dose? Did you have any trouble inserting the dropper? Did you use the dildo?* That last one was an absolute no-no, and Jet stared at his magazine, trying to get his riotous thoughts in order. "You said hyperthermia was a serious risk. Are you monitoring your temperature?"

"That's a great idea," Oliver blurted out, leaping off the chair and rushing for the bathroom. He returned with a thermometer under his tongue, and they waited impatiently for the minute or two it took for the thing to beep.

"Forty," Oliver said, as he read the number. "That's too high." He glanced at Jet, a stray peek at his groin telling Jet exactly what was going on in his head. *No sex until all other avenues have been exhausted*, he reminded himself.

"Maybe you need another dose," he suggested instead. "Did you feel any better after the first one?" He tried not to think about what Oliver had been doing in the bedroom, stripping his pants down to his knees, his ass high in the air as he –

"You don't think it's too soon?"

Jet shook his head. "Honestly, I have no idea. But if we're going to give this thing a shot, we may as well do it properly. Why don't I give you another dose? Or two. And we'll see where we get to." He was doing his best to watch his language, given how upset Oliver had been the last time they'd discussed this, but to be perfectly honest, he felt awkward as hell sugar-coating everything in clinical terms.

"I'll be right back," he promised, not waiting for an answer as he escaped to the bedroom again. Two climaxes later, he was handing the cup back to Oliver and settling in for another uncomfortable wait on the couch.

This time when Oliver returned, he was looking far more relaxed. "I think that worked," he reported. "The cramps have gone and I'm not feeling dizzy. I'll wait a few minutes then see if my temperature's come down."

"Okay. Good. That's a promising start, then, right?"

The look of relief on Oliver's face almost made up for the disappointment of not being able to touch him. "I think we just might have a chance of pulling this off."

CHAPTER SEVEN

OLIVER

The next few hours trickled by in fits and starts. At first, Oliver had requested Jet's services every half hour or so, and after that first batch, his temperature had dropped to a high but tolerable 38.7 degrees. Then, as the night wore on, the gaps got longer, one hour, then two, and then finally at one in the morning, Oliver announced that he was going to try and get some sleep. After making sure Jet was comfortable in the spare bedroom, he climbed into bed, far less apprehensive than he'd been in months. He didn't honestly expect to sleep much, his body hot and uncomfortable, his mind a mess of wayward fantasies, but it seemed the stress of the past few days had finally caught up with him. Two minutes after his head hit the pillow, he was fast asleep.

Oliver woke to a searing pain, his entire body feeling like it was on fire. His guts were cramping, sweat pouring off him and when he tried to stand up, the room spun like a rollercoaster. He clutched the door frame, panting for breath as he tried to remember what the hell was going on. He was in heat, he remembered dimly, and it seemed Jet's clever idea to bypass the necessary mating had been a failure after all. He needed… He needed an alpha, his mind screamed at him, even while his more rational side rebelled against the idea. He didn't want sex, didn't want to mate with some random alpha who would just rut upon his body like he was an object instead of a person.

But the pain was unbearable, and Jet was just down the hall, five or six short steps away, ready and willing to provide relief from the burning heat and raging cramps.

The first step almost undid him, pain causing him to double over even as he leaned against the wall for support. "Jet... Jet, please..." The words came out weakly, too soft for Jet to hear, and he forced himself to take another step, then another. "I need... please, help me..."

Just two more steps... one more... then his hand was on the handle of the door. Should he knock, he wondered briefly? Deeply ingrained manners asserted themselves, reminding him that one did not just wander into another man's bedroom unannounced. But the pain won out, and Oliver flung the door open, staggering against the frame in order to remain upright.

But just when he'd thought the heat surging through his body couldn't get any worse, he caught a glimpse of the naked man lying on top of the rumpled sheets. Instantly his mouth was watering at the thought of putting his hands on that smooth, tanned flesh, of feeling those firm muscles beneath his fingers. Unfortunately, the effort to stay standing proved too much just at that moment, and his knees buckled, hitting the floor with a thud.

Fortunately, the noise was enough to wake Jet. He rolled over in bed, a weary hand lifted to rub his eyes as he stared blearily at the man who'd just stumbled into his space.

"Jet, I need... Please, I can't..."

Jet's mind seemed to be working rather more quickly than Oliver's, and it took him mere seconds to assess the situation. "Holy shit, are you okay? No, of course you're not. Fuck, what the hell happened?" Oliver felt himself being lifted, and then the warm sheets of Jet's bed were rising beneath him, soft and comforting. The scent of alpha was thick in the room, a balm to his screaming nerves. "I need... Jet, please..."

"Fucking hell, I can't... Oh God, you smell so good... Jesus, don't lose it now, Wilder..." Oliver heard the sound of plastic rustling, then a rhythmic flapping sound, though he was in too much pain to really figure out what was happening. Jet was here. Jet with his tantalising scent and scorching-hot body, and that thick shaft between his legs that both terrified and enticed Oliver.

"I'm going to... Oh, shit, where's your dropper?" Jet was gone in an instant, but before Oliver could even summon the strength to moan his name, he was back again, and Oliver felt hands fumbling at his waistband. "Come on, Ollie, turn over. I'm really, really sorry about this, but I don't think you can do it yourself right now." He felt something small and cool pressing at his entrance, and he opened to it willingly, a night of feverish dreams fuelling an arousal that was almost as distracting as the pain. "That's one dose," Jet informed him. "I'm going to..." A guttural moan followed, then a curse. "Shit, missed the cup. Hang on, buddy. This won't take long." A minute passed, then that thin pressure was at his entrance again, and this time, when the liquid squirted inside him, a wave of soothing coldness came with it. "How's that? Ollie? Come on, talk to me."

Jet disappeared again, then returned, and Oliver felt him pressing something inside his mouth. "Don't bite down, okay? That's a thermometer. I need to know what your temperature is." Seconds ticked by, then there was another moan. Clarity returned in slow degrees, and this time, when Jet went to insert the dropper, Oliver was alert enough to realise what he was doing. He felt a wave of shame at the knowledge. "Hold still," Jet said, his voice deep and soothing. "This'll make you feel better, I promise." More cool liquid, and then the thermometer beeped. Jet took it out of his mouth, Oliver still too wrung out to do more than lift his head. "Forty-one. That's way too high…"

"It's okay," Oliver murmured, attempting to roll over. Gentle hands stopped him, and he felt Jet pulling his pants back up. "Feel better now. The cramps are going…" The embarrassment, on the other hand, was staying right where it was. "I'm okay. Really." He managed to adjust his clothes, then flopped over onto his back.

Jet was peering down at him, a look of stark concern on his face. "Hey, buddy. You back with me?"

Oliver nodded, resisting the urge to hide his face. "Thank you. I'm sorry. I'm so sorry…"

"This is not your fault," Jet told him firmly, then pressed him back when he went to sit up. "Just take a breather, okay. Fuck, where are my pants?" He rummaged around on the floor and slid into a pair of tracksuit pants, then came to sit beside Oliver on the bed. "It's working, yeah? Is it working?"

It was, much to Oliver's relief. The cramps faded out, the fire in his veins cooling as he caught his breath. Some minutes later, the room finally stopped spinning, and he managed to sit up.

The first thing that struck him was how light it was. He glanced at the clock on the nightstand. 9:00. He'd slept for eight hours?

"Thank you," he said again, baffled and amazed by Jet's reaction to the emergency. But embarrassment prevented him from commenting on it just at the moment.

"What the hell happened?" Jet asked. "We were doing so well. But then you just… boom, you're burning up, and shaking, and…"

The answer was obvious, now that he was able to think clearly. "We slept for too long," Oliver replied. "Eight hours. All the reports say we're supposed to…" *Oh, come on, just say it,* he thought to himself. "…to have sex about once every three hours." Mating was still too crude a word, though when he'd stumbled into the room Oliver had been more than willing to spread his legs and let Jet mount him.

Jet glanced at the clock, as if only just realising it was morning. Then he let loose a string of curses that would make a sailor blush. "Sorry. I'm so sorry, I didn't even think of that."

"It's a learning curve," Oliver said, to distract himself from the fact that another man had just seen his naked asshole for the first time in his life. "Now we know for next time."

The reminder was like a bucket of cold water, even more effective than Jet's 'donations', if that was possible. Because this wasn't a one-off, Oliver remembered. This was his life for the foreseeable future. Once every three months, he'd be back here, depending on Jet for his health and safety, his independence a long-forgotten ideal of the past. His relief fading once more to despair, Oliver rolled out of bed, not quite managing to meet Jet's eyes.

"Let's get some breakfast," he suggested, trying to keep his tone light. "We didn't eat last night, and you must be hungry."

CHAPTER EIGHT

OLIVER

They had coffee and toast on the back patio, neither of them saying much, until about an hour later when Oliver felt the first twinge of returning cramps. He set down his coffee cup, still not quite over the embarrassment from the morning. "Um… might I request a… another round of… assistance?" he stammered out finally.

Jet leapt up like his seat was on fire. "Yes. Sure. No problem." He rushed off like he couldn't get out of there fast enough, and while he waited, Oliver couldn't help but succumb to a new wave of regret. Jet apparently relished the excuse to get away from him, and he had the black thought that perhaps there wouldn't be a next time after all. Asking a stranger to have sex with him was one thing, but what Jet had had to do that morning was above and beyond the call of duty. Perhaps he was disgusted by the whole process, and wanted nothing more to do with Oliver? He was too honourable a man to abandon him right here and now, but it would be entirely reasonable of him to tell Oliver at the end of this that he didn't want to do it again. He'd have three months to find a new partner, and no one could really say that was an unreasonable amount of time to make alternative arrangements.

Jet returned a moment later, and it was Oliver's turn to excuse himself, taking care of the necessities quickly and eschewing the dildo that still sat unused on his nightstand.

Returning to the patio with a fresh batch of coffee, he sat in silence for a moment. But the odd thought he'd had that morning kept circling in his mind, and finally, he decided he had to say something, if only for his own peace of mind.

"Thank you," he muttered, then shook his head, knowing he would have to explain himself better than that. "I mean... thank you for being here, of course, but also, I wanted to thank you for..." He trailed off.

"For what?" Jet was sitting at the far end of the table, nose buried in his coffee.

"This morning, when I came into your bedroom. You were naked, and I needed you, and I thought you might have..."

Jet frowned, then suddenly his eyes opened wide. "You thought I might just hang it all and have sex with you anyway?"

Oliver stirred his coffee morosely. "It wouldn't have been an unreasonable choice," he pointed out. "Most people would have."

"Most people are complete assholes, if that's what they would have done," Jet spat, his lip curled in disgust. "We talked about this. I said I would do whatever I had to do to look after you, and that would have been an absolute betrayal of everything you asked of me. I'm not -" He cut himself off and stood up, stalking away across the patio. "I'm not some mindless alpha who just wants to get his rocks off," he said, facing the wall at the back of the garden. "If the method we're using didn't work, then so be it. But it *is* working."

Well, that hadn't gone according to plan. Oliver had just been trying to thank him, and he'd ended up insulting him instead. What was he supposed to say now? "Why did you even suggest it?" he couldn't help asking, even though he was probably going to regret it. "The new method, I mean. Please don't take this personally, Jet, it's not a comment on you individually, but... the fact is, most people, most *alphas*, would have taken the chance at free sex and run with it. And I'm genuinely grateful for the fact that you didn't," he added, trying not to dig too deep a hole for himself. "But I don't understand why."

Jet spun around, his coffee sloshing out of his cup as he did so. "The first time we talked about this, you fucking accused me of raping you! So excuse me if I don't want to be *that asshole*. And by the way, you're making a hell of a lot of assumptions about what 'most alphas' would do. How many have you actually known? Seriously, how many people have you known for a fact were alphas, and how many of them ran around being narcissistic shits and blaming it on their gender?"

Oliver felt his face pale at the pointed question.

"Well?" Jet prompted him, when he didn't reply.

Oliver cleared his throat. "None," he said finally. "This is the first time I've actually known for certain that someone was an alpha." Omegas suffered just as many stereotypes as alphas, and they were equally as unjustified. He was a horrible hypocrite, on top of everything else he'd put Jet through, and his last hopes faded away that Jet would ever be willing to go through this with him again. "I'm sorry." He stared at his cup, not able to meet Jet's eyes. "I should know better."

"Yeah, you should," Jet agreed. "How would you feel if I told you that omegas all wanted to get it on all the time, and you stumbling into my bedroom this morning while I was naked was a clear sign that you secretly wanted me to 'do' you right and proper?" Oliver didn't reply. "Think about that for a while," Jet suggested harshly. "And while you do, I'm going to be in my room, reading."

The afternoon passed in tense silence, Oliver retiring to his room to read while Jet ended up binge-watching some TV show in the living room. Exhausted from the night before, Oliver announced he was going to bed at nine o'clock in the evening, making sure he set his alarm clock for midnight, for his next treatment. By the time the alarm woke him up, Jet was in bed, and it was the work of a few short minutes for Oliver to administer the dose and for both of them to be once again curled up beneath the blankets.

Sleep, however, didn't come so easily this time, and Oliver lay awake for a long while, unable to stop himself from dwelling on his argument with Jet. Anderson had all but guaranteed he was a decent guy, and Jet himself had proven again and again that he was cut from a different cloth than the average alpha, the sort who was featured on the evening news, invariably charged with disorderly conduct or public drunkenness, or in the more unpleasant cases, with some form of public indecency or sexual assault. So given that Jet had gone out of his way to help him, why was Oliver so reluctant to trust him? By the time his alarm went off at 6 a.m. he was no closer to an answer, and was now dreading the day to come; not just another day of slow torture as his body rebelled against him, but of treading on eggshells around Jet, unwilling to annoy him even the slightest bit more, for fear he'd simply abandon this project and leave Oliver hanging.

He switched off the alarm and automatically reached for the thermometer on his nightstand, having got used to taking his temperature every hour for the last full day. He'd felt perfectly fine at his three o'clock wake up, but his temperature had still been a touch high, indicating that his heat wasn't quite over, no matter that his other symptoms seemed to have settled down.

This morning, however, he was relieved to find his temperature back down to normal: 36.9 degrees.

How was that even possible, he wondered? Last time, his heat had gone on for nearly two weeks. It was far too much to expect that one single round of 'assistance' from an alpha was enough to reset his cycle entirely.

He got up and had a shower, set coffee brewing, then took his temperature again. 36.9 degrees. He took his blood pressure with the machine he'd bought from a pharmacy, and it, too, was normal. No dizziness, no headache, no cramps.

"Hey." A bleary-eyed Jet stood in the kitchen doorway, shirtless, with his hair sticking in all directions. "How'd you sleep?" He headed straight for the pot of coffee, then suddenly paused, looking around as if he was confused. Oliver wasn't entirely sure, but he thought he saw him subtly scent the air.

"A little restless," Oliver admitted. "I have some good news, though. It seems your plan has been a resounding success. By all appearances, my heat has ended." Assuming it finished sometime between 3 a.m. and when he got up this morning, that meant it would have been just shy of forty hours long – smack in the middle of the statistical norm.

Jet just stared at him for a moment. "Shit. Wow. That's awesome," he said finally. "I thought you smelled different this morning." It was a crass thing to say, the physiological interactions between an alpha and an omega generally considered too crude to discuss in polite company, and Oliver opened his mouth to scold Jet for the reference... before hastily closing it again. *Let it go*, he told himself firmly. He'd already done enough to upset a man who had been nothing but kind to him.

"If everything's back to normal, I was considering heading in to work this morning," Oliver told him. After two nights of lost sleep, showing up at work wasn't the most appealing idea, but a deeply ingrained sense of responsibility wouldn't tolerate him calling in sick simply because he was tired. "We have time for breakfast and a shower first," he offered, not wanting to sound like he was kicking Jet out. "Or maybe you wanted to go home for a change of clothes?"

"Yeah, okay," Jet said, through a yawn. "Just let me get some coffee into me, and I'm good to go."

Half an hour later, they were both standing on the front porch, dressed and fed, and awkwardly uncertain about how to wrap things up.

"So, um..." Jet shifted uneasily from one foot to the other, and Oliver braced himself for the announcement that he wouldn't be doing this again. "Think about whether you want to find something a bit less hodge-podge than a dropper and a plastic cup," Jet said. "But otherwise, are we all set for three months' time?"

Oliver felt his heart skip a beat. Was he serious? "I think this set-up worked extremely well," he said, feeling a wave of both relief and trepidation. Jet was coming back? "It would be an honour to have your assistance again."

CHAPTER NINE

CYCLE TWO
JET

Sorry for the short notice, but could you please babysit Jackson this afternoon? I'll need you here about midday.

Jet rolled over in bed, the message having come through at the ungodly hour of 5:30 in the morning, and he groaned into his pillow as he tossed the phone aside.

Then, cursing his lack of foresight, he realised that now he'd actually have to get out of bed to pick the thing up and reply to Oliver. He slid sideways, fumbling about on the floor in the dark as he hung halfway off the mattress. Eventually finding it, he quickly typed a reply. *No problem. See you then.*

He already had a couple of t-shirts prepared, having been anticipating Oliver's message. In the weeks since Oliver's last heat, he'd done some reading on the subject, wanting to know more about what to expect, and how best to help Oliver manage his symptoms. One of the things he'd learned in the process was that most omegas' cycles tended to be fairly consistent every three months, though they could vary by up to a week or two.

Today was a Tuesday, and so the next message Jet sent was to Anderson. *Working from home today. Special assignment.* The cryptic message was the easiest way to tell Anderson exactly why he wouldn't be at work, while removing any risk that anyone else could accidentally stumble upon information they shouldn't see.

The sudden knowledge of exactly what he'd be doing today was enough to chase away any chance of getting back to sleep, so instead, Jet got up and went to take a shower.

Two minutes in, he turned the heat way down, letting the cold wash over his body and willing his sudden, insistent erection away. There was nothing terribly exciting about jerking off into a plastic cup, he reminded himself, but his body completely ignored the attempt at logic. He still vividly remembered the scent of Oliver, the way it had filled every corner of the house as the weekend had worn on, and the brazen dreams he'd had as a result. He tried to think of something else. After all, he'd be spending most of the afternoon getting his rocks off. Surely he could wait another six hours?

Thirty seconds later, his erection was in his hand, gasping moans escaping his throat as he spilled himself against white tiles.

Okay, time for a pep-talk, he told himself, as he turned off the shower and grabbed a towel from the rail. The next two days were going to be full of temptation, and there was absolutely no excuse for crossing that line and doing *anything* that Oliver would object to.

Five hours later, Jet pulled up in front of Oliver's house, duffle bag in tow. Last time, it had been a relief that the heat was over so quickly, not only so that Jet could get the hell out of a house saturated with omega pheromones, but also because it hadn't caused a huge interruption to his routine; no awkward questions from his friends about what he was doing, no extended absence from work that would need a plausible explanation. He was hoping for a similar result this time around, but he'd brought some clothes for an extra day, just in case.

Oliver opened the door, and Jet froze in his tracks, mouth hanging open as he stood on the doorstep. The scent of omega hit him like a freight train, and for a moment, he wondered how the hell he'd forgotten just how potent that smell was. Biologically speaking, the scent was designed to attract an alpha and excite him enough to ensure a mating took place. It was little comfort to realise that nature had laid its trap very, very well.

"How's it going?" Jet asked, throat tight, finally managing to get his feet to move him through the doorway. "You look warm."

He did; there was a bright flush to Oliver's face and a faint sheen of sweat on his arms. He'd chosen shorts over jeans this time, and Jet idly wondered whether it was a concession to the temperature, or for 'ease of access'.

"I'm sorry for pulling you out of work," Oliver said as he shut the door – as if he'd had any choice in the matter.

But Jet just shrugged. "I made a deal with Anderson, right back when he first asked me to do this. I still get paid while I'm here. I'm all for altruism and all that shit, but I can't just burn through all my leave so I can sit around on your couch and watch crappy TV. Oh, and by the way," he added, "you're getting paid too. That was one of the conditions I gave Anderson. Omegas get a raw enough deal as it is, without you having to put up with more bullshit because of things you can't control."

Oliver seemed genuinely surprised by the news, and Jet wasn't entirely sure why. "You... Oh. Thank you. Anderson hadn't told me." Last time around, given that the heat had fallen on a weekend, it probably hadn't come up.

"Hey, I know Anderson's got a soft spot for you, but with everything else he has to deal with on a daily basis, he probably just forgot." Idle small talk was doing nothing to distract Jet from the throbbing bulge in his pants. No matter how hard he tried, he couldn't stop thinking about how damn good Oliver looked, his hair slightly mussed, his green eyes a tad unfocused behind spotless glasses. His pupils were dilated, and a reckless instinct had Jet wanting to step forward and press his lips to Oliver's, to slide his hands up inside that pale blue t-shirt and trace the outline of firm abs beneath smooth, heated skin...

An instant later, he remembered all the internal scolding he'd given himself the last time around. *Don't slap his ass when you walk past him. Don't stare at his crotch. Don't stand at his door trying to hear whether he's jerking off or not.* He would be on his best behaviour, Jet reminded himself. He'd done this before without making a fool of himself. There was no reason he couldn't do it again.

"Would you like some coffee?"

Damn Oliver and his impeccable fucking manners. What he'd really like was to disappear into Oliver's spare bedroom and get to work on filling those damn plastic cups. "Yeah, I'd love one," he forced himself to say, not quite managing to drag his eyes away from Oliver's ass as he walked ahead of him into the kitchen. Damn, it was going to be a *long* day.

CHAPTER TEN

CYCLE SIX
OLIVER

Sitting at his desk at work, Oliver was halfway through his second cup of coffee for the morning when the headache hit. It came on quickly, as they often did, and he put the cup down, anticipating the nausea that would arrive next. Ten minutes later, it had, and Oliver pulled out his phone, sending a quick message to Jet.

It had been a year and a half since they'd begun their unusual relationship, with an admittedly shaky start and no shortage of arguments along the way. There were still days when Oliver failed to see what Jet was getting out of the arrangement, but even so, he wasn't going to complain. True to his word, Jet had done nothing to interfere with Oliver's life, no restrictions on his finances, no curtailing of his leisure time, not even an innocent invitation to go out for a beer after work. He'd been the epitome of discretion, and Oliver had thanked Anderson more than once for putting them together. For all their differences and disagreements, he couldn't have asked for a more loyal or more thoughtful assistant.

He sent a quick email to his boss, telling him that he'd be leaving early, then set about finishing up what he was working on and tidying up his desk before he headed home. Though the heat wouldn't hit full-force for another eight hours or so, trying to concentrate at work was still an uphill battle, and despite the scarcity of alphas in the world, he was still wary of running into one unexpectedly while he was smelling like an upmarket cologne vendor and not thinking terribly clearly.

His own scent was actually a bit of a mystery, he mused as he drove home. As an omega, he was entirely unable to smell it. A few of his colleagues had commented once or twice over the years, complimenting him on the 'subtle' and 'classy' scent, which had been both informative and a relief – at least his beta acquaintances wouldn't be put off by an overpowering smell should he be late in detecting his own changing hormones.

But Jet, on the other hand – the only person Oliver knew for certain was an alpha – had said it was like being sprayed right in the face by a skunk. A really, really sexy skunk, he'd clarified, when Oliver had been horrified by the description. It wasn't that the scent was bad – it was mind-bogglingly enticing. But for an alpha, it was also overpowering, and once he got a whiff of it, it lingered in his nostrils for hours.

An alpha's pheromones, by comparison, seemed far more subtle. The t-shirts that Jet routinely provided for his three-monthly cycle smelled mostly of sweat, with a faint hint of cologne, but nothing that sent Oliver into a frenzy of desire. Rather, he found the smell rather soothing, and over the months, he'd noticed a distinct decrease in his heart rate and increase in his clarity of thought when he'd breathed the scent in.

Arriving at home, Oliver took a cool shower, staving off the symptoms of his heat for another hour or so, then checked his phone.

Odd. There was no reply. Normally Jet was quick to respond, though he'd never moved much beyond a stock-standard two-word answer.

Still, there was nothing to be overly alarmed about. Perhaps he was in the middle of a training exercise? Or running a flight simulation? He could hardly just let his electronic shuttle crash because he'd received a text message.

He would have a nap, Oliver decided, the headache already taking its toll, and by the time he woke up, Jet would have replied, and then he could relax and get on with preparing a simple dinner for them both to eat that evening.

By the time five o'clock rolled around, Oliver was in full panic mode. He'd messaged Jet five times, so far with no response. He'd called the office, only to be told Jet was offsite on a training exercise. He'd tried to call Anderson, wondering if he could pull a few strings to get a message through, but Anderson's PA had told him he was off for a few days on a fishing trip.

But it was still okay, Oliver told himself, pacing his living room as he tried to stay calm. Jet would just finish his training run, get Oliver's messages, and come over after work. He didn't really need to be here until six o'clock, and Oliver could stretch that to eight if necessary. A cold shower and a couple of painkillers would get him through the first few hours of his heat.

His phone rang suddenly, and Oliver nearly dropped the thing in his haste to answer it.

"Hi, Oliver, it's Jeanette from the ISA. I heard you were trying to get hold of Jet Wilder earlier?" Jeanette was one of the admin team. On a normal day, she was the perpetually cheerful type, so it was a shock now to hear her sounding markedly subdued.

"Yes, I was," Oliver said, his heart pounding. "Have you heard from him?"

"I have, actually, but I'm afraid there's been some bad news. Jet and two of the other crew in his team have been involved in a training accident. They've been taken to St John's Central Hospital."

Oliver plopped down onto his sofa, legs feeling weak, his head spinning. Oh, this was bad. This was so very, very bad. "How serious are his injuries?" he asked, feeling like an asshole because the only real thought in his head was 'Is he well enough to get out of bed and come take care of me?'

"I haven't been told any details," Jeanette said, "other than that it was a non-life-threatening injury."

"Okay, well… thank you for letting me know." Oliver hung up, his chest aching, his head drooping in his hands. Now what? Without an alpha, he should probably get himself off to a hospital. He had about an hour before his first symptoms began to hit, and from that point on, things would start going rapidly downhill.

Stay calm, he counselled himself, as he realised his hands were shaking. *Be sensible. Go pack a bag and drive yourself to the emergency room.* It was either that or sit here and let his body fry his own brain when his temperature went into overdrive.

His phone rang again, and this time, Oliver did drop it, so startled by the piercing noise. He fumbled on the floor, grabbed the thing and glanced at the screen…

In his desperation, it took him two tries to answer the call. "Jet! Where the fuck are you? Are you okay? They said you were in hospital!?"

"Wow, you must really be bent out of shape if you're swearing at me," Jet said, which only prompted Oliver to swear again. But before he could really get on with chewing the guy out, Jet interrupted him.

"Hey, look, I'm going to be getting out of here in less than half an hour. I got your message. We were testing one of the all-terrain vehicles for the Mars expedition, and the thing rolled. They've just got to finish bandaging my leg, and I'll be good to go."

"Do you need me to come pick you up?" Oliver offered.

There was a pause, then a rustling sound. "No, man," Jet said, his voice sounding odd. "It's coming up on six o'clock. I don't think you should be driving right at the moment. Low blood pressure and all that?"

It was a valid concern, but how else was he going to -?

"I'll get a cab. I would get one of the boys to drop me off, but then there'd be questions about why I was going to your place instead of home. Ow!" he yelped suddenly, then muttered, "Damn ankle!"

"Are you going to be well enough to... 'assist' me?" Oliver asked, praying the answer was yes.

"Yeah, yeah, I'll be fine. Hey, look, I gotta go. The nurse is back and he's glaring at me for using a phone in the hospital. Catch ya later."

He hung up, leaving Oliver staring at his phone in disbelief. That last assurance that he was fine had been about as believable as a three-year-old saying that he definitely, absolutely had not been the one to draw lipstick pictures all over the walls. It was going to be an *interesting* night.

CHAPTER ELEVEN

JET

Jet handed a couple of notes to the cab driver, then swivelled neatly in his seat, hanging his injured leg out the door. The driver got his crutches out of the back seat for him, then Jet was hobbling his way up the drive to Oliver's front porch.

As usual, he had the door open before Jet got there, only this time, instead of standing ramrod straight and plastering a polite smile to his face, he was tapping his foot, hand gripping the edge of the door like the poor thing needed to be strangled.

"Where the hell have you been?" Oliver hissed at him, no doubt to prevent the retreating cab driver from overhearing. "It's nearly eight o'clock! You said half an hour!"

Jet eased himself up the step and in the door. "You might have noticed I'm on crutches," he said as Oliver closed the door behind him. "How damn fast do you think I can -?" The retort died on his lips. An errant breeze fluttered through the door just as Oliver closed it, catching up his scent and delivering it to Jet's nose like a blast of expensive perfume. The scent was so overwhelming that he actually reached out to touch Oliver, dropping one of his crutches in the process. His hand stopped just inches from Oliver's body as the crutch clattered to the floor, his eyes fixed to Oliver's lips, his mouth suddenly watering, a surge of heat seeping through his body.

He swayed on his feet, both from the loss of his crutch and the sudden wave of dizziness that accompanied the blast of omega pheromones, and Oliver instinctively reached out to steady him.

The touch of fevered omega skin against his own – even just a hand on his arm – was like a punch in the guts, and Jet let out a moan. He couldn't help himself. His dick was suddenly trying to claw its way out of his pants and his mind was unable to focus on anything other than the quickest way to get Oliver out of his clothes. Damn it, he'd been hoping the pain in his ankle would have tempered the lust a bit. But instead, it was doing absolutely nothing to help, and Jet suspected that the delay in getting here had just made Oliver's body ramp up the pheromones even more than usual, his biochemistry unconvinced that an alpha was going to come save him this time around.

"What is it? Your leg?" Oliver asked, urging him to sit down on the sofa.

"No, it's…" He swallowed hard.

"If it's hurting I can get you some painkillers."

"No, my leg's fine." The hell it was.

Oliver let go of his arm and stood up straight… which put his groin much closer to Jet's line of sight. "I'm sorry, I shouldn't have snapped at you, but I'm… What's wrong?"

Jet had his head down, elbows on his knees, trying to take slow, deep breaths to get himself under control.

"Jet?"

"Fuck, it's *you*, okay?" Jet snapped, losing patience with the endless questions. "You smell like a high-class brothel! And… is that cologne? You're not wearing cologne while you're in heat, are you?" The scent was heavenly! Without thinking, he reached up and tugged Oliver down, getting a good whiff of his neck to see what that odd, woodsy smell was, almost like sandalwood, or cedar, maybe.

A split second later, he realised his mistake. Already overwhelmed by pheromones, that single sniff was enough to derail his brain completely. Unbidden, his hand grabbed Oliver's and refused to let go. His other hand began undoing his own belt buckle, and a dim, distant part of Jet's mind tried to tell him there was something bad about this scenario.

Oliver was trying to pull away, but Jet wouldn't have it, tightening his grip on his wrist, managing to haul himself to his feet as he moved to go after his omega -

A sudden, blasting pain in his groin finally pulled him up, and Jet collapsed back onto the sofa. "Fucking son of a bitch! You kicked me in the fucking balls, man!"

"What the hell do you think you're doing, sniffing my neck?" Oliver snarled at him, retreating to the far side of the living room. "You're behaving like a bloody Neanderthal!"

"You have no idea what this is like," Jet snapped back at him. "You get to just stand there, cool as a cucumber, while I have industrial-grade chemicals screwing with my brain. Next time you call me over, take a fucking shower before I get here. You don't want me to touch you, but you're perfectly happy to stand around with a six-foot-high neon sign in blast-proof pheromones advertising your body!" He wasn't even making sense anymore, mixing metaphors and doing something that he'd sworn a hundred times he would never do, which was to blame Oliver for this mess.

But true to form, Oliver refused to back down. "If you'd been here an hour ago, we wouldn't be having this problem!" He was sounding short of breath now, and as Jet peered up at him, the pain in his groin clearing his head a little, he realised something he'd missed before. Oliver's shirt was drenched with sweat, his hair plastered to his head, and his hands were shaking slightly. "I've had *four* showers since I came home. My temperature is currently forty-one-and-a-half degrees and if it rises another half a degree, I'm looking at brain-damage as a serious possibility. And just for fun, in another half an hour, my headache is going to turn into a migraine. So don't go thinking you're the only one feeling the effects of this, but somehow *I* still managed to not throw myself at you like a teeny-bopper at a Justin Bieber concert!"

"No, but you did bite my head off, just because I was a few minutes late. Never mind that I actually bothered to get up out of my hospital bed and hobble all the way over here just to save your ass! And yes, my ankle's fine, by the way. The real problem is the gravel rash I have all down my left side, which took two nurses three hours to properly clean. You're welcome!"

There was a heavy pause, both of them running out of steam suddenly. Oliver wiped his brow, his fingers coming away wet. A single drop of sweat escaped, tumbling down to splash onto the polished wooden floorboards.

Immediately, Jet decided to shelve his complaints. "We need to get you a couple of treatments," he said. Oliver was right; he was about to be in serious trouble here.

"Yes, we do," Oliver agreed. "Would you like to…" He gestured towards the bedroom.

"Nah, just… just go in your bedroom and shut the door," Jet ordered. Aside from the fact that staying here would be far quicker given how slow he was on his crutches, he honestly didn't think he was going to make it to the bedroom without blowing a load all over his pants.

Thankfully, Oliver caught on quickly, making a hasty retreat to his bedroom. Less than two minutes later, Jet had three doses in a cup – empty ones had been helpfully left on the coffee table for his use – and he fastened his pants, making sure he was decent before he called Oliver back.

"Oliver! Come and get it!" The bedroom door opened and Oliver emerged, swaying slightly as he made his way across the room.

"Thank you," he muttered, as he attempted to peel the front of his damp shirt away from his chest. He disappeared again without another word, and Jet flopped back against the sofa.

Fifteen minutes later, he still hadn't come back.

"Oliver?" Jet called, peering around the corner to get a look at his bedroom door. "You alive or what, buddy?"

"I'm fine," came the sharp reply… and something about Oliver's tone caught Jet's attention. He cocked his head, replaying the words in his head… but even then, he couldn't quite put his finger on it.

"How's your temperature?" he called. Oliver would get pissed off if he thought Jet was coddling him, but given the state he'd been in when Jet arrived, he figured a little follow up was justified.

"It's fine!"

Nope, something was definitely wrong. And an odd, gut feeling was telling him it was more than just the fact that Jet had been late. Oliver was nothing if not rigorously polite and he'd never before refused to answer a direction question about his health.

Jet sat there, chewing on his lip, wondering what he could say next. Neither response had convinced him that Oliver was okay, and yet he couldn't just barge into the bedroom and demand to know what was going on. For all he knew, Oliver could be in there, sprawled out naked on the bed, that thick dildo shoved up his ass, and he'd likely die of embarrassment if Jet ever happened to catch him like that.

He was going to get his head bitten off, Jet knew, but the niggling voice of his conscience just wouldn't let up. "Come on, man, talk to me. Are you in pain, or what? What's your temperature? Don't tell me it's fine, I want a number here."

There was a moment of silence, and then…

"I'm going to take a shower," came the muffled reply. The water started running a moment later, and Jet sighed. Okay, so there was nothing he could do for the moment. But in half an hour, Oliver was going to need another dose, and if he hadn't come to collect it by then, Jet was knocking on that door, embarrassment be damned.

Fifteen minutes later, the bedroom door opened and Oliver emerged. His hair was wet, he'd put on a new t-shirt, and though his face was still flushed, it was no longer the unhealthy red it had been before. "Thirty-nine-point-five," he said, not meeting Jet's eyes. He handed him a cup. "May I?"

"Sure." Jet reached for his belt buckle, then paused as Oliver continued to stand there. "Are you going to watch?"

That snapped Oliver out of his daze. "Oh, God, no!" He spun around and marched back into his bedroom, slamming the door shut. That, too, was not normal behaviour for him. Even when startled or embarrassed, Oliver had always maintained a strict sense of self control.

Knowing that Oliver's body was probably still catching up on the delayed start, Jet put three more doses in the cup, then set it carefully on the coffee table. Gingerly, he stood up, supporting himself on one crutch while he retrieved the other one from where it still lay on the floor. Then, balancing the cup in his fingers, he hobbled over to Oliver's door. If he didn't make a point now, Oliver could all too easily spend the next two days simply avoiding him.

"Oliver?" he called, knocking softly on the door. "Ready to go."

Oliver opened the door. "Thank you." Ever the polite one. He moved to shut the door again, and the fact that he didn't bother telling Jet off for being on his feet clinched the deal. Something was definitely not right here.

Quick as a flash, Jet slapped his hand against the door, stopping Oliver from closing it. "Okay, man, let's deal with this. I was late, and I'm sorry. I know you get a rough time if things don't go according to plan and I shouldn't have snapped at you. So I'm sorry."

Oliver's knuckles were white as he gripped the edge of the door. "It's fine. You were injured. I just... I was worried. So I apologise as well." The words came out woodenly, as convincing as a teenager insisting they really had cleaned their room properly.

"Talk to me, man," Jet said softly, trying to catch Oliver's eye, while Oliver steadfastly avoided his gaze. "You're not okay, that much is obvious. Is it just physical, or is there something else?"

For a moment there was no response, and Jet held his breath. *Come on, man, just tell me*, he pleaded silently. Then, like the air being let out of a balloon, Oliver's shoulders sagged. He let out a shuddering sigh and leaned his head against the door.

"Just let me do this first," he said, lifting the cup a fraction, "then I... well, I suppose I'll have to tell you eventually." With that, he closed the door, leaving Jet standing in the hallway, feeling completely baffled.

CHAPTER TWELVE

JET

Jet made his way back to the sofa and sat down, then quickly stood up again. Before actually explaining whatever it was that was bothering him, Oliver would no doubt ask if he wanted a coffee, and things would move quicker if Jet got the machine going ahead of time. He'd watched Oliver make coffee a dozen or more times, so it wasn't hard to figure it out. Coffee tin in the pantry. Top up the water in the reservoir. Milk in the jug. He didn't go as far as actually frothing it, as he'd learned over the months that Oliver was notoriously picky about having enough froth on top, and in the end, it was easier to let him do it himself.

Five minutes later, Oliver was back, and he managed a weak smile when he saw what Jet had been up to. "You should have let me do that," he said, with no real conviction. "You should be resting your leg."

The reprimand was reassuring. The flat tone it was delivered in was not.

"How about we go sit outside?" Jet suggested. It was a warm day, and the living room was feeling suffocating, with all the pheromones Oliver had been spreading around the place. He switched on the patio light and seated himself, thanking Oliver for the coffee when he brought it out.

But he'd also brought a thick envelope with him, and Jet peered at it curiously.

"It's a letter from the government," Oliver said, without being prompted. "I have…" He stopped, his voice cracking slightly, then he cleared his throat and continued. "I have apparently exceeded the allotted time available for nominating an alpha to oversee my affairs."

"You have to what, now?" Jet asked, baffled by the statement.

"It's a little-known legal requirement," Oliver explained, toying with the envelope while doing his best to look unperturbed. "When a doctor diagnoses an omega as having Caloren's Syndrome, they're required to inform the relevant government department. The omega then has twelve months in which to nominate an alpha to take control of their life."

"Take control of your... That's ridiculous!" Jet had known that alphas often held the reins in any alpha/ omega pairing, but he'd never realised it was mandated by legislation.

"I've been putting it off as long as I can," Oliver went on. "I suppose I was curious about what would happen if I simply failed to nominate anyone." He looked down at the envelope sadly. "I've just found out the answer. If I don't return the form within the next twenty-one days, authority over all financial and medical aspects of my life will be handed over to my nearest living relative. Both my parents have passed on, and I don't have any siblings, so that means my aunt will be responsible for me. Even though I've never actually met the woman." Oliver's tone was getting sharper, his anger growing as he spoke. "She and my mother stopped speaking to each other when they were in their early twenties. There's been no contact between her family and mine for more than thirty years. But according to some archaic dog's-breakfast of a law, she gets to control my life."

It was a shitty law, Jet had no argument there, but he couldn't quite see why Oliver was making such a big deal out of it.

"You know that's not necessary, right?" he asked, leaning forward, tapping his spoon against the edge of his cup. He stopped when he saw it was annoying Oliver. "Just nominate *me*. I mean, that was the whole point, right from the start, wasn't it? Can I see this?" he asked suddenly, reaching for the envelope. It was probably better if he understood exactly what he was dealing with.

Oliver pushed it negligently across the table, apparently waiting to argue the point until Jet had at least read it. Fortunately, most of the thick wad of papers was just forms to be filled in. The stuff that Jet actually needed to understand took up just two pages.

"Yeah, so nominate me," he repeated, once he'd finished. "Short term, your pay will go into my bank account, but I'll just transfer it straight back to you as soon as it comes in. Longer term, I'll talk to Anderson about getting it redirected back into your own account. There's a form in here transferring ownership of your house to me. I'll just authorise it to stay in your name, same with your car. Seriously, man, this is all solvable. Why did you even wait this long? You could have told me about this ages ago."

Oliver stared at him, mouth hanging open, a look of absolute disbelief on his face. "What the fuck is wrong with you?" he gasped out finally. "They're taking my entire life away!"

"And I'm giving it back to you!" Jet said, a touch louder than necessary. "This is just a temporary glitch. What the hell is the problem?"

"The problem," Oliver spat, leaping out of his seat, "is that after running my own damn life for the last ten years, after being allowed to be an *adult*, I'm suddenly relegated to the eternal status of a child! It's not just the money, it's every single major decision I want to make! If I need any serious medical treatment, you have to authorise it. If I want to sell my house and buy a different one, you guessed it, you have to authorise it. I need your permission to travel overseas or to open a new bank account or to change jobs. I need your help once every three months just to stay alive! And I called you this morning, and then I couldn't get hold of you, and…" His voice cracked, tears suddenly shining in his eyes. He took a shuddering breath, and the tears spilled over. "And what if you weren't here?" he asked helplessly. "What if you couldn't come, or what if you were actually in a serious accident? What if you'd died? How the fuck am I supposed to carry on with my life when it could all be snatched away at any moment?"

Now it was Jet's turn to gape at him. "Shit. I'm sorry."

"But none of this is your fault!" Oliver rambled on, angrily brushing tears away. "The entire legal system is completely biased against omegas and *no one* is willing to do a damn thing about it! You're just trying to be some noble non-asshole, but your hands are tied, and my hands are tied, and there aren't even enough omegas left in the world to start a decent revolution!"

"A revolution?! Okay, Ollie, just take a deep breath and calm down! Yes, this is a shitty place to be, but we can *deal with it*."

Oliver stalked away across the garden, stopping in front of a vine that was climbing the lattice on the western side of the courtyard. Delicate white flowers were beginning to bloom, and Oliver stood and stared at them, long minutes slowly ticking by. Finally, he turned around and came back to the table, sinking into his seat morosely. "What am I supposed to do?"

Unfortunately, Jet had no easy answers. "Look, I gotta say, I don't really understand how you feel right now," he said, trying to be as honest as possible. "I'm sitting here trying to imagine how I would feel if someone wanted to take away my career and my freedom, and yeah, I get that it sucks, but I don't really *feel* it the way you do. So I'm sorry if this plan falls short, but it's the best I can do. In the short term," he told Oliver firmly, "you're going to nominate me as your alpha, and I'm going to do everything I can to let you keep control of your own life. In the longer term, I'll see if I can get in touch with a couple of legal geeks and find out if there are any precedents for alphas granting legal emancipation to omegas. I can't make any promises, but it's worth asking the question, right?"

That, finally, earned a small smile. "I'm beginning to see why Anderson recommended you."

The next two days drifted by in fits of restless sleep and frantic desire, and by the end of it, a slow, tentative plan was forming in Jet's mind. As Oliver's heat was drawing to a close, he thought about the best way to raise the topic. He had neither a gift for tact nor an inclination to sugar-coat things, unlike his refined friend, so in the end, he decided to just come straight out and say it.

Preparing to head home, he hobbled down the steps from Oliver's porch, then around to the driveway at the side. He'd offered to call a cab, but Oliver had insisted on driving him instead. He managed to open the car door himself, and slid down more or less gracefully into the seat, but Oliver had to help him stow his crutches, then load his duffle bag into the back seat.

"You know, I have this crazy idea," he told Oliver, as he started the engine and pulled out into the road. "There's this whole worldwide industry for farmers and livestock owners who want to breed better animals. If you've got a prize-winning cow, you don't just go down the road and borrow a bull from Farmer Joe. These guys can buy semen from other sires, literally from the other side of the world, and a vet comes and inseminates their cow, and hey presto, they get a super-baby. Or calf. Whatever."

Oliver raised an eyebrow at him. "I'm torn between asking where you learned about breeding cattle, or what on earth this has to do with me?"

"I've got an uncle with a farm back east. I don't talk to him anymore cos… well, it's a long story. But I picked up a few things when I was a kid. And what's it got to do with you? Well, I know there are some serious differences between omegas and cows… but what if we tried freezing some of my jizz?" Was that the wrong word? He'd caught the momentary wince from Oliver as he said it. "You keep it in your freezer, and if I can't make it here one day, or if I'm late for some reason, then you can use the frozen stuff. We'd need to test it, to make sure it actually works, and if it does, then find out how long it could be stored for. I mean, an ice cube tray in your freezer isn't exactly like keeping it in liquid nitrogen. But if it works, it's a half-decent back up plan. Right?"

"It is," Oliver agreed. "Actually, I'm kind of annoyed we didn't think of that sooner."

"Trial and error, buddy," Jet said cheerfully, glad he'd been able to come up with *something* that might be useful. "This is all just trial and error. I'll collect some samples and bring them by next weekend." Then he snorted out a laugh. "Just label them something discrete, okay? We don't need one of your friends coming over and sticking a mislabelled ice cube in his drink!"

CHAPTER THIRTEEN

OLIVER

"Goodness, she's adorable!" Oliver held out his arms, gently taking the four-week-old baby from Celeste, one of his closest friends. "Look at all that hair!" The little girl was blonde, just like her mother, sound asleep even as Oliver nestled her in the crook of his arm. "What did you decide to name her?"

"Hazel," Celeste told him as she pulled a seat out for him. "After my grandmother." The café they were in was on the waterfront, a picture-perfect day delivering up a light breeze along with a gentle swell. The rhythmic shush-shush of the ocean was soothing, after a week of hectic deadlines and a minor system failure that had set Oliver's team back three days.

"It's beautiful," Oliver said, smoothing Hazel's hair back from her face. "And how's Tyler doing?"

"He just started kindergarten." Celeste picked up a menu, perusing the selections with half her attention. "Every day he comes home just bursting with excitement. His best friend was Larry last week, and Jeremy the week before that, but this week it's Sophie, and next week it'll probably be Larry again. Last week he wanted to be a fireman when he grows up, then this week one of the kids brought their pet hamster in for show-and-tell, so now he wants to be a vet. I keep telling him he's got plenty of time to decide, but he's so gung-ho about everything." Celeste lowered her voice. "I have to keep reminding myself it's just because he's a five-year-old, and not because he's... you know... an *alpha*."

A waitress arrived a moment later, and that put an end to the conversation until they'd both ordered, Oliver choosing a Caesar salad and cappuccino, while Celeste picked a lasagne and herbal tea.

"Did you tell the school what gender he is?" Oliver asked softly, once the waitress had left. "I know it's not mandatory anymore, but some parents still do."

Celeste shook her head. "Bradley wanted to, but I flatly refused. I want Tyler to grow up believing he's just the same as everybody else. Bradley's a beta, so he tries his best, but I honestly don't think he understands what it's like to be an alpha or an omega, that your whole life can be twisted sideways before you even start!

"But little Tyler's learning to sit at the table and eat dinner without wanting to run around all the time. He's learning to use his 'indoor voice' instead of yelling everything. He's very good at sports, but he's also got this really compassionate streak. We found an injured bird in the park the other week, and he absolutely would not give up until I'd agreed to wrap the poor thing in my sweater and drive it to a vet clinic. I'm trying to nurture all the different parts of him, so he can be who he wants to be, and not just get stuck in the box the media keeps trying to shove him into."

"It's never an easy choice," Oliver said, remembering his own awkward childhood all too clearly. "There's a fine line between giving your child support, and forcing them down a track they don't want to go down. What about this little one?" he asked, looking down at the tiny baby in his arms. "If you don't mind me asking?" He'd known Celeste for over ten years, and it was only that prolonged friendship that allowed him to dare ask the intrusive question.

"Hazel's a beta. Bradley was so relieved. With me being an omega, there's a higher chance that she'd have been one too, but we had her tested as soon as she was born, and she's just a regular old beta." The forced smile on her face faded quickly. "God, that sounds so sexist, doesn't it? *I'm so glad she's a beta, and not something inferior like you and I are.*" She shook her head. "Sorry. It's been a long week."

"I know what you mean," Oliver agreed. The waitress came back, carrying their meal.

"Oh, here, let me take her," Celeste said, holding out her arms for Hazel. "I'm used to eating with one hand." They shuffled about a bit, rearranging the plates on the table until Celeste could reach everything.

"So…" she said, once they were alone again. "What's been going on with you, Oliver?" She pinned him with a smile, but there was concern lurking beneath the surface. "You've haven't been around in months. I call, you're not available, I've tried to set up get-togethers with you but you're always busy. If I didn't know better, I'd think you were avoiding me."

Oliver shook his head. He picked up one of the little packets of sugar in the dish on the table and ripped it open, taking a deliberately long time to pour it into his coffee. "I haven't been avoiding *you*, so much as I've been avoiding *everyone*. Life's been a bit chaotic lately. I'm sorry, I meant to come and see Hazel much earlier. I've just… I've had a lot going on and I haven't been in a great frame of mind because of it."

"You want to talk about it?" Celeste offered, taking a bite of her lasagne, then she immediately interrupted herself. "Oh, wow, that's good. My mom kept telling me we should come here. This is divine! Seriously, though, is there anything you want to talk about?"

"Actually, it's about time I let you know," Oliver said, taking a deep breath. "I've been diagnosed with Caloren's Syndrome." He'd been about to ask if she knew what it was, but the look on her face answered the unspoken question.

"Oh, no, I'm so sorry! One of my aunts had it. She passed away while I was still a child, but my mom used to talk about her all the time. Oh, God, that's awful." Celeste reached out and placed her hand over his. "Are you okay? Do you have… It's going to sound so rude to ask this but… Do you have an alpha?" she asked in a whisper.

"I do," Oliver admitted. This was not the sort of conversation he'd ever expected to be having, but at the same time, actually telling someone what was going on – particularly someone who was likely to understand the struggles that came with it – was a relief. "You remember Robert Anderson? He set me up with someone. It's actually been… not that bad."

Celeste's eyebrows rose. "Having your life controlled by an alpha *isn't that bad*? Are you serious? Wait, are you still working? You're still working, right? You said on the phone you were doing a project on that new solar panel thingy."

"I'm still working, yes. He still lets me go to work -"

"*Lets you?*" Celeste looked outraged. "He *allows* you to do something that every other person on the planet gets to do without thinking about it? That pretentious, stuck up -"

"Okay, let me rephrase that," Oliver interrupted her. Her indignation on his behalf was appreciated, but in this case, it was also unnecessary. "He made it clear right from the start that he never had any intention of stopping me from working. I told Anderson that I wanted to maintain a level of independence, and he found an alpha who was prepared to agree to it." Celeste's look of disbelief was understandable. "You said yourself, you want Tyler to grow up believing he's like everyone else, and that he doesn't have to behave a particular way just because of his gender. As much as the odds are stacked against it, I think I've found an alpha who's somehow managed to defy the stereotype."

"How long have you been together?" Celeste asked, a challenge in her voice.

"A year and a half."

Her jaw dropped and she sat up suddenly, then cursed softly when Hazel let out a cry. A moment later, though, the girl was drifting back to sleep, a chubby fist shoved into her mouth. "A year and a half!?" she hissed, staring wide-eyed at Oliver. "And he's still being all considerate and non-dictator-ish? Bloody hell, you've hit the jackpot right there!" She muttered a few choice words to herself. "Okay, so I have to ask... What's the sex like? I don't mean to pry; I know you like your privacy. I'm just asking one omega to another," she went on, making sure to keep her voice low. "I've never been with an alpha – and never wanted to, mind you – but some of the stories you hear..."

Oliver felt his face turn bright red. As Celeste had said, from one omega to another, it wasn't *too* outrageous a question – not like it would have been had a beta asked him the same thing. But given the distinct lack of sex in his current relationship, he was floundering to know how to respond. Fortunately, Celeste would simply take his flushed face as evidence of his normal reticence to discuss anything private or intimate. "He's actually been... very considerate," Oliver said, thinking back on the odd, excessively polite side-stepping dance that he and Jet usually performed. He'd been a little uncouth last time, sniffing at his neck like that, but he hadn't done anything that could really be called rough or aggressive. "He's never forced anything, or been demanding or intimidating." If anything, he'd been the complete opposite, letting Oliver make the decisions, placidly going along with whatever he asked. "He's even been... well, shall I call it *oddly charming*, at times. We argue like cats and dogs -"

"Has he ever hit you?"

"What?" Oliver was shocked by the question. "No! Of course not!"

Celeste was staring at him like he was an alien species. "What?" he asked, baffled by her response.

"Are you hearing what you just said, Oliver? '*No, of course not*', for an alpha hitting an omega, like that's the *obvious* answer, not some weird aberration." Her frown deepened a touch, a hint of wonder appearing in her eyes. "You trust him, don't you?"

No, of course not. It was the obvious answer, stuck in Oliver's throat just before he said it. An omega could never afford to trust an alpha. Ever.

But back when he'd been unable to reach Jet during the start of his last heat, his immediate concerns had been surrounding Jet being injured or unable to access his phone, rather than any deliberate attempt at making Oliver suffer. If he'd been *able* to reply, Oliver knew he would have done. And besides that, Jet had been the one to come up with their 'alternative method' of getting Oliver the treatment he needed. Jet had thought of the potential solution to him being late, freezing samples for future use. "I... I don't know. I guess... yes. Maybe I do."

CHAPTER FOURTEEN

CYCLE SEVEN
JET

Dripping with seawater, Jet made his way up the sand to the beach showers, his surfboard tucked under his arm. The sun was setting, but the air was still warm, summer serving up a scorcher for the third day in a row. Once he'd showered, he loaded the board into his car, but before he climbed in to drive home, he made a point of checking his phone for messages. It was three months since he'd last seen Oliver, and by his calculations, he should be receiving a request to babysit any time now.

Bingo. There was a message that hadn't been there when he'd hit the beach two hours ago. *Can you babysit Jackson? First thing tomorrow, if you can make it.*

He sent a quick reply. Given Oliver's usual ten-hour warning, that meant he had to be there by six o'clock the following morning. Early starts, however, were nothing new to Jet. It wasn't unusual for him to be at the beach ready to catch a wave just as the sun was rising. Tomorrow was Sunday, which meant he'd be off work for Monday, so he sent a message to Anderson, knowing that if he left it until he was at Oliver's house, he'd just as likely forget. Once the blast of pheromones hit him, concentrating became a monumental effort, so it was best not to leave these things to chance.

Eight hours later, the blasting din of Jet's phone ringing jerked him out of sleep. He bolted upright, completely disoriented, and it took him a moment to work out where he was.

Oh, right. In bed. In his own apartment. Damn, he must have been sleeping like a log. Fumbling around on the nightstand, he grabbed the phone, then frowned when he saw who the caller was.

"Hey, Oliver, what's up?" he asked, sleep slurring his words.

A harsh intake of breath came back at him. "Can you come now?" Oliver managed to gasp out.

Jet was out of bed before he'd even finished the question. "You okay, man? What's happening?"

"Started early," Oliver said, then the words were punctuated with a groan. "Just woke up." Jet glanced at the clock. 4 a.m. From the sounds of it, Oliver was already deep in the throes of his heat.

"I'll be there in fifteen minutes," Jet promised. "Hang in there -"

"No. Can't. Hurts…"

"Okay, okay, listen," Jet said, putting a firm authority into his voice. He was already pulling on pants and searching for his shoes. "You've got some ice cubes in the freezer, right?" After the near-disaster of Oliver's last heat, Jet had collected twelve 'treatments' for him. He'd felt like a weird perve, pouring the liquid into an ice-cube tray, and even weirder when he'd delivered the frozen package to Oliver one weekend. "Go get some, defrost it in warm water, and use that until I get there."

He heard a moan on the other end of the line. "Oliver? You with me?"

"I'm going," he said, sounding strained. "Ice cubes… freezer… got it."

"Okay, now remember, *warm* water, not hot. You don't want to damage it."

He heard water running. "What if it doesn't work?"

It was a good question. "I'm going to be there in fifteen minutes, okay?" He tucked the phone under his chin and pulled on a t-shirt, then grabbed his bag from beside the front door. Thankfully, he'd had the foresight to pack it the day before. "Take three doses straight up. More if you need it. Don't worry about running out, I'm on my way."

For the first time since they'd started this arrangement, Oliver wasn't waiting at the door when Jet arrived. He knocked loudly, cringing as he realised he might be waking the neighbours. But this was surely more important than waking up a couple of people on a Sunday morning. A minute later, he knocked again. "Oliver? Come on, buddy, open the door."

"Coming…" The reply was weak and thready, and Jet braced himself for the blast of pheromones that was about to greet him.

Sure enough, as soon as the door opened, Oliver's scent hit him like a ton of bricks, and he reeled backwards. "Jesus, when the hell did this start?" A moment later, any thought of asking more questions vanished from his mind. In stark contrast to the previous occasions he'd been here, Oliver had apparently decided that the temperature was too much. He'd removed his shirt, standing in the doorway in nothing more than a pair of boxer shorts, and Jet's mouth went dry as he finally got a look at the man's body. He most certainly worked out, he decided in an instant. Oliver's torso was as lean as his own, his muscles less bulky, but no less defined. A six pack rippled beneath smooth skin. His legs were long, dusted with blond hair, and his boxers hung low on his hips, revealing that tantalising trail of hair that disappeared into his waistband…

Oliver was also sporting a raging erection, and a petty part of Jet's mind crowed in smug satisfaction. He'd often wondered if omegas suffered the same sexual urges as alphas, and from the way his boxers were tenting, the answer was a clear yes.

But for all the pleasure of finally getting to see the prize unwrapped, the image standing before him presented a new and dangerous problem. Even fully clothed, there had been times when the scent of Oliver had pushed him to the edge of his self control.

Focus, he scolded himself sharply, even as his heart rate sped up. Oliver was in pain. His face was flushed, his entire body coated in sweat, and from the way he was standing slightly hunched over, the cramps were clearly doing a number on him.

"Let's get you taken care of," he ordered, pushing his way into the house and closing the door. Oliver seemed rather dazed, and he didn't think waiting for him to take the lead was a viable strategy this time around.

But, true to form, Oliver still managed to surprise him. "I'm okay," he said, taking a deep breath. "I've just taken my fifth dose. It's working now. The cramps are getting better."

"No way, buddy, you look like shit. You need some of the good stuff." Where had he put the cups? Jet had left them in the spare bedroom at the end of their last appointment. He headed that way now.

"No, wait. We wanted to find out of the ice cubes work. And I think they're working."

"What's your temperature?" Damn it, they were right on course for yet another argument. No matter how these episodes played out, at some point they always managed to find something to disagree on.

"Forty-one. But I woke up late."

"That's too high! You keep telling me you're not supposed to get above thirty-nine, and every time we do this, you end up running into the forties. You need to look after yourself, Ollie! Screw the experiment. We can always find out next time -"

"I want to know if this works!" It wasn't quite a yell, but it came pretty close, and hearing Oliver raise his voice was enough of a shock to stop Jet in his tracks. "I want… I *need* some kind of freedom here, some kind of control over this mess. I want to know if there's a way for me to do this without you."

The words cut through Jet like a knife. "You want…" He'd known that all along, of course. It had never been a secret, so why did hearing it out loud make his chest constrict like he'd just been stomped on by a horse? A childish part of him wanted to turn around and go back home, and leave Oliver to his stubborn idiocy, screw the consequences. He took two steps towards the door, but the alpha in him forced him to stop. Injured pride aside, his biology simply would not allow him to walk away from an omega in heat, almost naked in front of him and just begging to be filled…

"Oliver…"

"You said you would help me."

An alpha protected his mate. Pale green eyes stared back at him from behind glass that was frosted with a touch of fog from Oliver's perspiration. Oliver was not *his mate*, Jet tried to remind himself. He had no claim here, something that his inner alpha raged against, tempered only by the promise that he was going to *protect* Oliver, even from Jet himself.

"You're an omega," Jet said helplessly. "You're supposed to fucking *want* me…"

"I do, Oliver admitted harshly. "I want…"

Jet took a step forward, so close now that he could feel the heat radiating off Oliver's naked chest. Wordlessly, he lifted his own t-shirt, sliding it over his head and letting it drop to the floor. "Then have me."

Cool breath shivered across his skin as Oliver stared at his chest. "Don't tempt me." It was a small plea, weak and airy, and somehow Oliver managed to back up a step or two. "Please, Jet…" Oliver's hand drifted down, over the waistband of his boxers, and Jet's eyes were immediately fixed on the clear outline of his erection. His own cock was throbbing, pressed uncomfortably against his jeans. Oliver's scent shifted a moment later, the frantic, sour notes replaced with a warm, smoky scent that was twice as enticing as before. Jet's heart rate picked up even more, his breath coming hard and fast.

"Shit, Oliver, I can't…" His eyes followed a bead of sweat as it trickled down Oliver's abs.

"I'm sorry," Oliver apologised. "I was too hot. I'll just go and…"

Go and put some clothes on, presumably. Was it the scent in the air, or the fact that he was still half-dazed from waking up at four o'clock in the morning that was making it so damn hard to think straight? None of this was even remotely appropriate! Nonetheless, his hand shot out to capture Oliver's wrist, while Jet's rational brain frantically commanded it to let go. His body completely ignored him.

"I want you to let me go," Oliver said coldly.

That was the promise he'd made. He'd told Oliver that if he ever wanted him to stop doing something, he only had to ask. Jet abruptly let go of his hand.

Protect your omega. There was only one way to do that. Jet spun around, marched himself into the bathroom and slammed the door. Without letting himself think about it, he turned on the shower, full blast on cold, and stepped in, still wearing his pants and shoes. The water hit him like a bucket of ice, but he didn't move, just stood there and let the cold water seep into his clothes.

But he barely felt the chill, so great was the fire beneath his skin.

CHAPTER FIFTEEN

JET

Twelve hours later, Jet and Oliver were both sitting on the back patio, enjoying the breeze after yet another warm day. Summer was slowly fading to a close, but the temperature hadn't yet begun to drop in any serious way.

Throughout the day, Oliver had continued using the frozen supplies until they'd run out, and now they were back to the real thing – a detail Jet was immensely grateful for, if only because it gave him an excuse to relieve the tension in his groin now and then. The experiment had been a success, of sorts, with Oliver reporting that although the frozen samples did the job, they weren't as potent as fresh supplies, and he'd needed four or five doses to every three of previous heats.

But that wasn't the only good news. Somehow, after they'd both calmed down and apologised to each other, the odd incident that morning had broken the ice between them. Even after a year and a half, Oliver had always maintained his rigorous politeness. There were still some things Jet simply couldn't say to him, and they'd never really talked about their unusual arrangement in any but the most superficial terms.

But in an unexpected move, Oliver had pulled a bottle of whisky out of the cupboard about half an hour ago, offering to make them both a stiff drink. It had been a surprise, given that the strongest thing Jet had ever seen him drink so far had been beer.

"You know, you don't have to wait for me to ask," Oliver was saying, the latest comment in a conversation that had been refreshingly open and frank. "If you just want to shut yourself in the bathroom now and then, you can."

Jet breathed a sigh of relief at the news. "Thanks. Thank you. Damn, you don't know how many times I've wanted to do that."

"Then why didn't you?"

"I don't know. I guess I figured… You've been so damn skittish about this whole thing. I thought you might be offended, or scandalised. You're just so…" He stopped, knowing that what he said next was likely to offend him for real.

"So proper?" Oliver filled in. "So uptight? Trust me, you're not the first person to tell me that." He took a sip of whisky, sighing as it burned down his throat. "Can I tell you a secret?"

A secret? From Oliver? How could he resist? "Of course. My lips are sealed."

"Sometimes when I… ask you for a sample," Oliver said, apparently still uncomfortable with saying it out loud, for all his recent honesty, "I don't actually need it yet. It's just an excuse for me to lock myself in my room and… take care of business."

Jet snorted, then had to set his glass on the table to keep from spilling it as the chuckle became a real laugh. "God damnit, Ollie, I have never quite managed to figure you out. Every time I think I know what you're going to do next, you just pull something out of left field."

"I've got to keep you on your toes," Oliver said, a small, secretive smile playing at his lips.

"Can I ask a question?" Jet asked, feeling bold.

"Hit me," Oliver shot back with a grin.

"What do you think of the dildo? Is it big enough? It is…" He waggled his eyebrows. "…giving you a good workout?"

There were a range of responses he was expecting. Oliver might blush and tell him to mind his own business. He might scold him for asking such a crude question. Or, if he was feeling particularly reckless, he might even say he enjoyed it. But what he actually said nearly made Jet fall off his seat.

"I've never used it."

"What? Why the hell not? I mean, that was part of the whole equation, wasn't it? Stimulating the right nerves and all that."

"I think some of your research might have been a touch inaccurate," Oliver said. "The absorption of the proteins is absolutely necessary, and the pheromones on your shirts help keep my mind clear. But the rest of it…" He shrugged. "It just hasn't been necessary."

This, after Oliver had just admitted that he was getting himself off in his room on a regular basis? "Haven't you ever just wanted to use it for the sake of it, though? I don't know what the heat hormones really do to an omega, from the sex drive side of things, but I haven't… I don't…" How should he phrase this? "I don't think I could have been that restrained."

Now they'd hit the expected embarrassed phase, Oliver blushing as he stared down at his feet. They were bare, and something about that sent Jet's blood pressure through the roof. It was just so *casual*, so far from the prim and proper image Oliver usually projected. "It just never seemed…" Jet waited for him to continue, forcing himself not to guess the end of the sentence. "…dignified."

There was so much about that that didn't make sense. He was in his own room, wasn't he? Maybe at first he'd been worried that Jet would interrupt him and find him going at it, but after nearly seven cycles, surely he'd learned by now that Jet was a stickler for respecting his privacy? "Can I ask you a personal question?" he asked. They'd come this far. He may as well jump in all the way.

"More personal than asking whether I enjoy the giant dildo you bought me?"

"Well… yeah. Maybe."

Oliver cocked an elegant eyebrow at him. "What is it?"

"Why do you do that?" Jet asked, fumbling to find the right words. "I mean, why are you so hung up on always being polite? Good manners is one thing, and God knows, we probably need more of that in the world, but you kind of take it to extremes."

Oliver took a sip of his drink, then swirled the cubes of ice contemplatively. "My parents," he said, after a pause. "It's the way they raised me. But it's not because they were particularly upper-class or anything. They weren't, actually. Dad was an electrician. Mum was a teacher. Just your run-of-the-mill middle class couple. But the anti-discrimination act only came into effect about fifteen years ago, so when I was born and my parents found out I was an omega, they were worried. I mean, they loved me. There was never any question about that. But omegas back then were universally considered to be both stupid and boorish, and they were concerned that I'd be seriously disadvantaged for my whole life for something that wasn't my fault.

"So throughout my entire childhood, there was a huge emphasis on both education and manners. Extra tuition at school, etiquette and elocution lessons. Their reasoning was that if I didn't behave anything like an omega, then maybe no one would bother asking the question, and I'd have the same opportunities that any beta had. By the time the laws changed, the lessons had stuck."

"It's not a bad philosophy," Jet admitted. "According to the rumours, you're a damn good engineer. That education certainly paid off."

"I'm very grateful to them. They've both passed away now." The detail came out of nowhere, and it hit Jet like a punch in the guts.

"Oh, shit, I'm sorry!"

Oliver shook his head. "They lived to see me graduate university. They were killed in a car accident a couple of years later, but…" He swallowed hard, then continued. "They knew they'd done the right thing. They'd given me every opportunity I needed to make it through life. I don't think they would have died with any regrets."

They sat in silence for a long moment, as the sun slowly slid towards the horizon. "What about you?" Oliver asked at length. "I don't mean this with any judgement whatsoever, but as far as alphas go – according to the news reports, at least – you're a bit unusual." He didn't need to extrapolate on the statement. As much as Jet liked to deny it, most alphas would have looked at the opportunity to mate with an omega the same way they'd have looked at an invitation to walk into an open bank vault and take whatever they fancied.

"True enough," he admitted. "I kind of had the opposite experience to you, but somehow ended up in the same place. My mother was an omega," he said, a secret that very few people in the world knew. "And my father was an alpha. Statistically speaking, omegas are more likely to have alpha or omega children. But she had Caloren's Syndrome, and my father was pretty typical of alphas back then." Namely, brutish, dictatorial and prone to fits of temper. "He was always putting her down, telling her what she could or couldn't do. If she challenged him, he'd hit her. As a kid, you don't really think about it too much, but then…" He stopped, unable to meet Oliver's eyes. He drained his glass, feeling the strong liquor pool in his belly. "When I was seven years old, she killed herself. I didn't really put it all together until I was fourteen, maybe fifteen years old. But I saw what an asshole my father was, and one day it finally clicked that the way he treated her was probably why she ended up killing herself. And… I don't know. I guess I just decided; I was never going to be like that. I was never going to be the reason why someone didn't want to be alive anymore. There's a whole pile of things I do, and things that I am, that people blame on being an alpha. I'm loud, I'm energetic, I'm an adrenaline junkie, I prefer physical activity to academic study. But for fuck's sake, there are plenty of betas who are just the same, and no one's giving them a hard time.

"For years, it was never really an issue. The anti-discrimination act made it illegal for employers to refuse to hire someone on the basis of their secondary gender, and I got this job, and everything was going fine. And then suddenly Anderson calls me into his office, and I have this amazing, crazy, messed up opportunity to prove I'm not what everyone said I was." He lapsed into silence, but he knew that wasn't the whole story, and he owed it to Oliver to tell the truth.

"Even with all the idealism in the world, it's been way harder than I ever expected. I'm sitting here with a hard-on, and half my mind is trying to concentrate on this conversation while the other half is trying to figure out how to talk you into letting me follow you into your bedroom for once and show you what an alpha's really capable of." He shook his head. "I keep telling myself that I would never, ever hurt you, but… God, sometimes…"

"Like this morning?"

"Like this morning." How the hell was Oliver just sitting there, accepting his admission with that calm, cool demeanour? He should be raging at Jet for being a randy perve.

"As I recall, a large part of your difficulty this morning was due to the fact that I firstly failed to put any clothes on, and secondly told you that I wanted you. I can hardly expect you to be the epitome of good manners if I insist on waving temptation right under your nose. It's a good lesson for me. I'll endeavour to be more careful in future."

Jet just stared at him. Where was the condemnation? The blame? The belittling reminder that he should learn to *overcome his baser instincts as an alpha*? He couldn't quite figure out what he was supposed to say next, so he took the easy way out, and swiftly changed the subject.

"Oh, by the way, the paperwork came through about me being your designated alpha. I should have told you a few days ago. It took forever, given how much they were on your back about signing the damn thing. I've already written a letter to the ISA, telling them I give you permission to keep working there." Phrased like that, it sounded horrible, and Jet understood why Oliver had been so upset about it before. In theory, writing the required letter had seemed like a mere formality. But when he'd actually sat down to do it, he'd felt utterly awful, like one of those overbearing parents who couldn't let their child chose their own path in life. "I've set up an automatic payment into your bank account every fortnight, and I've sent back the house ownership form. Haven't had a reply to that one yet."

"Thank you," Oliver said, sounding like he meant it. "And thank you for being so honest about all this. I genuinely hadn't realised how hard it was for you. But don't ever think I'm not grateful. Your help means the world to me."

A new idea popped into Jet's head, one that he would normally have dismissed, but on the back of so many odd things going on today, he decided to just go with it. "Hey, what are you doing next weekend?" he asked, before he could second guess himself. "Me and some of the guys from work are going skydiving on Saturday. How'd you like to come along?"

Oliver looked at him quizzically. "Skydiving? For fun? Don't you do that often enough for work anyway?"

"Yeah, but this is more of a social thing. Haru's bringing his wife, and Aksel's daughter is turning eighteen, so it's her birthday present, and Arnold…" He grinned, unable to help himself. "Arnold just started dating this guy who's apparently terrified of heights, and he's managed to talk him into trying it. We've got a couple of bets going on as to whether or not he's going to chicken out. And I figured it's not the kind of thing you get to do every day, so…?"

For all his attempt to sell the idea, Jet was already regretting the impulsive invitation. Oliver had made it clear from the start that he wasn't interesting in doing social things with Jet, and skydiving was pretty much the last thing in the world he would ever -

"Yeah, okay."

Jet's mouth fell open. "Are you serious?"

"Are you?" Oliver shot back at him.

"Yes! Absolutely. I just didn't think you'd say yes."

"I don't know anything about skydiving," Oliver said. "I'm assuming there's some sort of training beforehand?"

"Don't worry, you'll be going tandem. There's a half-hour intro with some instructions and stuff, but really, all you have to do is strap in and enjoy the view."

Three days later, once the pheromones had worn off and he was finally able to think straight again, Jet got comfortable on his couch and dialled a number on his phone. He'd been putting this call off, anxious about saying too much, and nervous about going behind Oliver's back. But he'd also made certain promises to him, and if he was going to fulfil them, he was going to need help.

"Jet. Haven't heard from you in a while."

"Hey, Sullivan. How's your research on omega physiology going?"

"On hiatus at the moment. I've had some bad news. My mother was diagnosed with cancer. She's been having chemotherapy, and I'm on extended vacation to look after her. She's improving, but it's been a slow road."

"Shit, I'm sorry," Jet said. "That's rough." Now what? He could hardly just demand that Sullivan abandon his mother to help Oliver. "Is now a bad time? Should I call back in a couple of weeks?"

"No, don't be silly. I'm assuming you need some advice? How've you been going with your 'theories' on omega heats?"

To heck with it. He may as well at least tell Sullivan what was going on. "Interesting progress on that score, actually," he said. "The first thing I need, though, is do you know any lawyers who specialise in omega legal cases?"

"I know a couple. Tell me you haven't gotten yourself into trouble?"

"Not me, no," Jet reassured him. 'But I have a friend who needs some legal advice."

"On what in particular?"

"Caloren's omegas being emancipated from their designated alphas."

There was a pause, and it went on so long that Jet wondered if the call had been cut off. "Sullivan? You there?"

"Yeah, I'm here. Damn, man, you sure know how to pick them. You know that omegas lose ninety-nine per cent of their cases, right?"

"That's why I need the best. Someone who knows the laws inside out and can argue a case like a walking encyclopaedia."

"Interesting." Sullivan made a thoughtful noise. "Okay. I'll send you the name of a guy. He's an alpha, but don't let that put you off. And don't worry, he's publically out as an alpha, so I'm not telling you anything I shouldn't. It gives him an edge in court when he's arguing against alpha defendants. Was there anything else?"

"Well, yeah, actually there is. But this one might be a bit trickier. I was kind of hoping you might be willing to dust off your lab coat and jump back into a bit of research. I know it's not a good time, but it's important. Not just for me, but potentially for every Caloren's omega."

"I'm intrigued. Tell me more."

"Last time we spoke, I asked you for ideas on how a Caloren's omega could get through a heat without having sex with an alpha. We've come up with a few ideas -"

"We?" Sullivan interrupted. "Dare I ask who 'we' is?"

"I can't say," Jet said, knowing he was already walking awfully close to a very fine line. "But I was thinking maybe you could design a couple of medical trials? Write a paper. Start challenging the conventional wisdom on the subject."

Sullivan laughed. "You don't do anything small, do you? Let me just grab a notepad," he said, and Jet waited while he rustled around. "Okay. All set. Now, tell me everything."

CHAPTER SIXTEEN

OLIVER

"How does it fit?" Jet asked Oliver as he shimmied into a bright orange jumpsuit. "You're a bit taller than me, so I've given you a size up."

"Seems pretty good," Oliver said, stretching his arms out to the side then crouching down in a squat. "Comfortable but not too baggy."

"Okay, let's get you into a harness, then I'll run you through the training."

Oliver followed him over to the harnesses, glancing around anxiously. "So who exactly am I going to be jumping with?" Jet had said he'd be going tandem, but other than that, he'd been rather scant on the details.

Jet stopped in his tracks, shooting Oliver a surprised frown. "Me," he said simply. "Who else?"

Oliver's eyebrows rose sharply. "You?"

Jet looked a little baffled. "Is that a problem?"

Was it? "No, of course not," Oliver said quickly. "I just wasn't expecting…"

"Don't worry, we're all properly qualified." Jet shot him a grin that managed to convey a degree of sympathy at the same time. "Look, I know we have a reputation for taking risks, but I would never, ever take any chances with someone else's life. Come on, stop looking at me like that," he complained, when Oliver didn't reply. "I've earned a *little* bit of trust by now, haven't I?"

Oliver ignored the way his heart was pounding and managed a smile. "Yes, you have."

"You needn't sound so bloody happy about it," Jet griped, as he started walking again.

"May I point out that I'm about to jump out of a perfectly good plane at fifteen thousand feet," Oliver reminded him. "I think I'm entitled to a few nerves."

He stepped into the harness Jet offered him and shrugged the straps up onto his shoulders. But as Jet did up the buckles, he kept glancing over to the left, and Oliver was nervous enough to call him out on it. "Perhaps you might pay a little more attention to my harness, and less to Arnold's infamous boyfriend?"

Jet smirked at him, taking one last glance then returning his attention to Oliver. "He's looking a little green over there. I'm just keeping track of my investment."

"What has to happen for you to win? Or shouldn't I ask?"

"I've got fifty bucks on him making it into the plane, but not actually jumping. I just don't want him to bail too early."

Oliver nodded, then raised a shrewd eyebrow. "And how much are you set to make if *I* chicken out?"

Jet looked scandalised. But only for a moment. "I'm counting on you following through, buddy. I've got a hundred bucks riding on that, so don't you let me down."

Oliver chuckled. "I'll try my best," he promised.

The training was fairly straightforward, some basic instructions on how to hold his body and where to put his arms. "For newbies, the parachute ride is the fun part," Jet told him. "Great view from up there. For us veterans, it's all about getting down as fast as you can so we can go up again. Okay, you're all set. And don't worry; I'll do all the hard bits – pulling the chute, steering, hitting the landing site. I gotta go check in with Aksel, but I'll be back in a few."

Left to his own devices, Oliver wandered over to the side of the building, watching the colourful parachutes circling as the previous batch of skydivers made their way to the ground. Once she was suited up, Haru's wife, Liandra came to join him. "Your first time?" she asked with a grin.

Oliver nodded. "It seemed a good idea when Jet suggested it. I'm not so sure now, though. What about you?"

"This is my third jump," Liandra told him. "It took Haru three years to get me to go the first time. I kind of regret taking so long about it, though. It's an absolute rush! You'll love it. And Jet's a great teacher. He was the one who took Arnold on his first jump." She gave him a sideways look. "You and Jet, by the way. You two seem pretty close. Are you and he, you know…?" She raised an inquisitive eyebrow, leaving the rest of the question open.

Oliver shook his head, slightly embarrassed by the insinuation. "No. Just friends."

"Hey, you're not trying to talk my boy out of it, are you?" Jet asked suddenly, reappearing at Oliver's side, Haru tagging along behind him.

"Wouldn't dream of it," Liandra said. "I was just telling him how much he'd enjoy it."

"That's my girl. Come on, we're just about ready to go."

"So, I gotta ask," Haru said, as they headed for the plane. "How the hell did you get so buddy-buddy with someone from engineering? No offence," he added quickly, glancing at Oliver. "You guys do great work. We just tend to move in different circles."

Oliver felt his gut lurch at the question. He'd been so caught up in the idea of jumping out of a plane that he hadn't even considered all the peripheral questions: how did he and Jet meet? How long had they known each other? Why was Jet including him in his exclusive 'boy's club'?

But before he could get too flustered, Jet jumped in for him. "We just had this crazy week a while back," he said, picking just the right tone for the explanation, the vague disinterest of a not-particularly-interesting story, but not so negligent as to make anyone think he was avoiding the question. "We kept running into each other in the hallways, like five or six times in a week, and literally bumped into each other, one time. Spilled coffee all over the floor. But we just started chatting after that, I guess." He shrugged, and Oliver was grateful for once that Jet was so good at running off at the mouth. "This seemed like the sort of thing Oliver would enjoy."

Aksel met them at the door of the plane. "All aboard!" he crowed, helping his daughter inside. "Everybody ready? No one having second thoughts?"

Knowing what he did about the bets, Oliver decided to ignore the wry look of doubt Aksel shot him. Presumably, he was set to lose some money if Oliver had the courage to get into the plane, and he was doing his best to unnerve him.

"It's now or never," he said, managing to sound far more confident than he felt. Jet climbed in, a wide grin on his face, and Oliver didn't give himself time to hesitate, just clambered in after him. Inside, the plane was surprisingly small, no seats, just a long, thin tube. Jet made his way to the rear of the plane, then turned around, settling in with his legs spread. He patted the floor between his thighs. "Right here, buddy," he told Oliver. "Squish up close."

Oliver sat down, leaving a respectable distance between them, but apparently it wasn't close enough. "I'm not kidding," Jet told him. "Move back. We've got to get twenty people in here. This isn't the time to get all shy on me."

"Twenty people?" The plane didn't look big enough to hold half that many.

"Every time we go up, it costs time and fuel," Jet explained. "Gotta make the most of it."

Not sure whether he was joking or not, Oliver wriggled back another inch or two... and then realised that Jet was serious. Haru was right in front of him, and he shifted backwards until he was almost on top of Oliver. Trying to make space, he wriggled back a bit more, disconcerted to feel Jet's strong thighs on either side of him.

Haru's wife was next, then a couple that Oliver didn't recognise... but then there was apparently a delay at the entrance. Arnold was kneeling just inside the plane, his boyfriend lingering outside the door.

"It's totally safe," Oliver heard him say. "We've got the best safety record on the east coast. It's *extremely* unlikely that a chute would ever fail, but even if it does, we've got a back-up. And we've *never* had a secondary chute fail."

"Trouble in paradise," Jet muttered from behind him. "Come on, buddy, get in the plane..."

A moment later, Arnold climbed out again, and another handful of participants climbed in. There was another pause, and Oliver heard Jet mutter a curse.

"He's not going to do it," Haru said softly. "He's not going to..."

Arnold stuck his head inside the plane. "Sorry folks, looks like you'll be doing this one without us." There was a collective groan from Jet and his friends, a couple of the others calling encouragements from further down the plane. "No, really," Arnold confirmed. "We'll see you when you land." He disappeared again, and Jet cursed again.

"It's all up to you now, Oliver," Haru told him cheerfully. "Jet's pride is on the line. You sure you've got the guts for this?"

He wasn't sure at all, but Oliver nodded anyway. "No problem," he said, his voice sounding tight. "Though Jet is *definitely* going to owe me a beer after this one."

The door closed, and minutes later, they were in the air. Before he knew it, the door at the front of the plane opened again, and Oliver experienced a moment of panic as the reality of what he was about to do hit home. There was no ground outside that door, no safety net, just a huge expanse of open air, followed by a very, very hard landing...

"You okay?" Jet asked, his mouth right next to Oliver's ear. "All kidding aside, you are allowed to bail if you really think you can't do this."

"I'm fine," Oliver croaked out, as three more people disappeared out of the door. Christ, the nerve of these people!

"Okay, well... How about you let go of my leg and head for the door then?"

It was only then that Oliver realised he had Jet's ankle in a death-grip, his knuckles turning white as he held on. He forced himself to let go, then shuffled awkwardly towards the door.

He felt Jet fiddling with his harness. "Okay, all buckled in. Last chance, buddy. You good to go?"

"Let's do this," Oliver said, his heart pounding in his chest. His lungs felt tight, like he couldn't get enough air. At Jet's instruction, he eased out onto the rail... and then they were falling, the air rushing up to meet them, while Oliver was sure he'd just left his stomach behind in the plane.

After what seemed like hours, but was probably only actually a few seconds, he felt Jet tap his shoulder, and as he'd been instructed, he spread his arms out, lending stability to their downward plunge – if freefalling could ever be thought of as even remotely *stable*. But once that first part was over, their bodies reaching terminal velocity, he was startled to find that it felt more like floating than falling. A grin spread over his face, and he forced himself to look down, the earth a wide open ball beneath them. It was terrifying and exhilarating, and Oliver had the odd thought that it was a lot like falling in love – a terrifying plunge, but once you were falling, there was nothing you could do but enjoy the whole ride down...

The minute's ride passed quicker than he would have believed. He felt another tap on his shoulder and tucked his arms away, then there was a sudden lurch, and he knew Jet had just pulled the chute. They slowed, and then it felt a lot like he was flying.

"You okay?" Jet asked him. It took him a moment to find his voice. "Oliver?"

"Yeah. I'm okay. Wow. Oh my God, that was crazy..."

He heard a chuckle. "The worst part's over. Now you just get to enjoy the view."

It was as beautiful as Jet had said it would be, wide open paddocks criss-crossed with roads that seemed miniscule from way up here. There were clouds dotted above them, and spiralling below, he could see the other parachutes floating downwards.

Some five minutes later, they were coming in to land, and Oliver lifted his legs, skimming over the grass as Jet brought them safely to the ground. He unbuckled them from each other, and Oliver stood up on shaking legs, unable to wipe the grin from his face.

He turned around to face Jet and saw a mirroring grin shining back at him. "That was amazing," he said, his heart still thumping as he caught his breath.

"Want to go again?"

Oliver laughed. "Maybe one day. But not right now. I think I just need to have a nice, quiet sit down for a bit." Now that it was over, he wasn't afraid of admitting he'd been terrified.

Jet slung an arm around his shoulder and gave him a squeeze. "Nicely done, Ollie. You just saved me a hundred bucks." Then the grin faded, and a look of genuine admiration settled on Jet's features. "No, seriously, buddy. Well done. I am so damn proud of you."

Half an hour later, the whole group was settled in the centre's café, coffees and a few snacks spread out on the table in front of them. Aksel's daughter was tapping frantically on her phone, no doubt chronicling the whole thing on Twitter, while Liandra and Askel were teasing Arnold about his choice in men. His boyfriend looked embarrassed, but had stood by his decision to back out, and Oliver gave him a supportive nod. This sort of thing wasn't for everyone, and there was no shame in knowing one's own limits. Jet had just excused himself to go to the bathroom, and as soon as he was gone, Haru sidled up to Oliver while the others were occupied.

"So, level with me," he said quietly, taking a sip of his coffee. "You and Jet. What's the real story there?"

Oliver shrugged deliberately. "There's no story. He just mentioned you were all going skydiving and asked if I wanted to come. That's it."

"So you're not into guys, or what?"

Oliver's eyebrows rose at the impertinent question. "No! I mean yes, I am, but there's nothing going on between me and Jet. Really." It was the truth, as far as it mattered. For all their 'extra-curricular activities', they weren't in any kind of romantic relationship.

Haru made a humming sound, and the look on his face seemed a little disappointed. "Fair enough. Just asking," he said. "But... maybe keep an open mind on that one. I've known Jet a long time, and trust me, I can read the signs. He's into you."

Oliver didn't quite know how to respond. He opened his mouth, intending to ask Haru why he thought that... but a moment later, the bathroom door opened and Jet emerged. His eyes caught Oliver's immediately, another grin settling on his face, and Oliver was forced to leave the question unanswered.

CHAPTER SEVENTEEN

CYCLE NINE
JET

It was 10:30 in the morning when Jet's phone rang, and he answered it quickly, expecting it to be Oliver. He was due for his next heat any day now, and Jet already had an overnight bag stowed in his car and a couple of worn t-shirts sealed in zip-lock bags.

But instead of Oliver, Jet saw the call was from Sullivan Kennedy. They'd been in regular contact since Jet had told him his ideas about providing 'protein samples' to Caloren's omegas six months ago, and the doctor had proved to be a total godsend. Despite his mother's ill health, he'd managed to devote a couple of hours a day to his research, displaying an impressive enthusiasm for the new ideas.

"Sullivan, my man! How's your mom doing?"

"Officially in remission," Sullivan reported happily. "Her hair's growing back and she's joined an aqua-aerobics class to try and get some of her fitness back. So all's well on the home front. Sadly, though, I can't say the same about the research."

"Can't get enough donors?" Jet guessed. There weren't many alphas who were willing to come out about it. Even though the medical trials would be confidential, it wouldn't be a surprise if the few alphas around felt antsy about it. "I said I'd help you out with that if you needed me to." The short-term plan was to collect fresh samples from alphas – provided they agreed to undergo medical testing and had been declared fit and healthy – and then the longer-term plan was to try to manufacture a synthetic analogue.

"That's not the problem," Sullivan told him. "It's not a shortage of alphas. It's a shortage of omegas. My last research subject passed away from medical complications nearly three months ago, and I haven't been able to find any more willing participants since then."

That made no sense. "There must be dozens of omegas out there looking for a better solution," Jet objected. "Maybe not in this city, but you could put out a request for volunteers right across the country. All you'd need is three or four participants to get started, right?"

"True," Sullivan agreed. "But it's not that simple. In order to participate in a clinical trial, omegas need permission from their alpha partner." It was a fact so obvious that Jet could have slapped himself for failing to think of it. "And what alpha is going to let their omega join a trial that could end up allowing them to leave the alpha?"

"Fuck me," Jet swore. "God, human beings can be assholes sometimes."

"I won't argue with you there," Sullivan said. "So the only real option is to find an omega right after their diagnosis, before they designate an alpha as their partner. I've put out the word to a couple of contacts in the field, but now it's just a waiting game, until we come up with some suitable candidates. I don't suppose...?" Sullivan trailed off.

"You don't suppose what?"

"Do you think that perhaps this omega you're working with would agree to join the trial? I know you've been awfully circumspect about him – or her," he added. "You've never even told me if it's a man or a woman. But do you think they'd consider it?"

"That's a tricky one," Jet replied. "It's a 'he', by the way. But he's intensely private about his gender – as most omegas are – and the truth is, he doesn't even know I've been talking to you. When we started this arrangement, we both agreed to keep the whole thing entirely confidential. I might even be breaking the law just by talking to you now." The original agreement had allowed for him to talk to 'medical personnel', but he wasn't sure this was really what the clause had intended. "I don't know how he'd react if I told you were running medical trials on an idea we've been testing on him." Jet had had this debate with himself in the past. On one hand, Oliver was desperate for a way to regain control of his own life, and Jet was fairly sure he'd be keen to help other omegas do the same. But on the other hand, the trust between the two of them was still fragile, even after all this time. Oliver was still very much in a position where he had everything to lose, if anything went wrong, and Jet was terrified of doing anything that might break that trust.

But before he could decide whether or not he should talk to Oliver, another idea circled back, interrupting his train of thought. "Hey, you said your last omega patient died of 'medical complications'. What the heck is that about?"

"You must know the side effects of an omega's heat," Sullivan said, sounding confused. "High temperatures, migraines, cramps, low blood pressure. That's why it's so important Caloren's omegas have a supportive alpha. If any of those symptoms aren't managed properly, the result can be life-threatening."

"So how did this guy die? Why wasn't he being 'managed' properly?"

"He fainted from low blood pressure and fell down the stairs," Sullivan told him flatly.

"But why wasn't his alpha taking care of -"

"Jet," Sullivan interrupted sharply. "Are you aware of the post-diagnosis life expectancy for Caloren's omegas?"

The question caught him off-guard. "No. What? Why would...? I'd have thought that, assuming they can find a willing alpha, they'd live as long as any other omega."

The silence that followed was ominous, and Jet's stomach dropped. "Sullivan? Talk to me, man."

"I'll send you through some data. But I should warn you, it's not pretty."

"How long are they expected to live?" Jet demanded. "What's the issue? Does having sex with an alpha stop working after a while, or what?" Was he inadvertently putting Oliver at risk by not having intercourse? Was their manual work-around actually doing him more harm? He dreaded the idea of explaining that to Oliver.

"Read the reports," Sullivan said. "It's too complicated to explain it all now. And if you have any more ideas on how to improve the statistics, I'm all ears."

It was just after 6 p.m. when Jet pulled up in front of Oliver's house. The routine text message had come through just after he'd hung up from talking to Sullivan, and he'd sent a quick reply, then dived into the reports Sullivan had emailed him.

By three o'clock, he'd been wishing he hadn't. As it was, his stomach was a swirling mess of anxiety. A neatly printed stack of papers sat on the passenger seat of his car, but he hesitated before picking them up. Did Oliver need to see this? Would sharing them do more harm than good? But then again, their relationship so far had been built on honesty and the deliberate decision on Jet's side to treat Oliver with all the respect that an independent adult deserved. It wasn't his place to try and protect Oliver from reality, no matter how tempting it might be.

With a grimace, he picked up the papers, slung his duffle bag over his shoulder and marched up to the front door. He likely wouldn't get around to mentioning the reports until tomorrow morning at the earliest. As soon as the pheromones hit, he'd be too focused on trying to keep his hands off Oliver, and Oliver would be preoccupied with managing his physical symptoms. It was only about halfway through the heat that their frantic biological reactions calmed down enough for them to think about something else for a while.

Jet knocked on the door, tapping his foot and bracing himself for Oliver's scent to hit him. As he waited, he idly noted that he was so concerned about Sullivan's news that he didn't even have a real erection yet, his cock only standing at half-mast in his jeans.

Snapping out of his daze, Jet realised he'd been standing there for a while. Oddly, there were no lights on inside the house. He knocked again, then wandered around the side...

Damn. He'd been so lost in thought that he hadn't even noticed Oliver's car wasn't there. An instinctive surge of concern hit him, but a moment later, he told himself to stop being silly. He was just overreacting from the already stressful news of the day. Oliver was probably just running late. Maybe a meeting had gone over time, or he'd got stuck in traffic. Telling himself to just calm down, he went and took a seat on the front step. Oliver would be home any moment.

Ten minutes later, he was pacing the porch, debating whether or not to phone Oliver. He hated the idea of being an overbearing ass; Oliver was an adult who was perfectly capable of looking after himself. But at the same time, they were on a tight schedule, and it was now heading for 6:30. They'd nailed down Oliver's cycles pretty well after all this time. Six o'clock had been the time he'd been due to arrive, and in general, they had no more than an hour to play with before Oliver's symptoms started causing him serious problems.

He was just about to give in and call Oliver when his phone suddenly rang. He answered it, making an effort to sound calm, rather than the raging ball of anxiety he really was. "Hey, man, what's up?"

"Jet?" Oliver sounded rather breathless, which did nothing to calm Jet's frantic nerves. "I think I might be in trouble."

"What's going on?" Jet was instantly all business, those seven little words inspiring an odd instinct in him that he wasn't entirely sure what to do with. He'd had moments during test flights or out on the water while he was surfing that had forced him to make quick decisions or take urgent, drastic action. He'd had his share of work-place injuries, and once, he'd saved a fellow surfer from drowning when he'd been dumped by a rogue wave. But the surge of adrenaline he felt just then was orders of magnitude more intense.

"I was in the city," Oliver said his voice rough, his breathing uneven. "We had an offsite meeting and it ran overtime. Then I got stuck in traffic. I've had to pull over in a shopping centre. I don't think I can drive. My head's spinning, my hands are shaking. I'm not going to make it home..." He sounded terrified, barely holding himself together.

"Okay, where exactly are you?" Jet demanded, already running for his car.

"The Waterford Centre, on Granville Road."

"I know the place. You stay there," he ordered. "I'm going to come get you. Just sit tight. And whatever you do, *do not* get out of the car." If there were any alphas within a hundred metres of Oliver, they'd detect his scent in an instant. Jet dreaded to think what would happen next.

"I'm at the eastern end of the parking lot," Oliver said. "Near the library entrance."

"I'm on my way," Jet promised him. "I'll be there in fifteen minutes, tops."

CHAPTER EIGHTEEN

JET

It was a small miracle that Jet wasn't pulled over by the cops on his frantic drive to the shopping centre. He pulled into the parking lot, cruising slowly up the row as he looked for Oliver's car.

There it was, the last one on the left, and he pulled up right beside it. Oliver was clearly in a bad way, his head leaning back on the seat, his eyes closed. Jet got out of the car and knocked on the window, and Oliver jumped so badly he nearly hit his head on the roof. He opened the door, but didn't get out of the car.

"How's it going, buddy?" Jet said, trying to breathe through his mouth as the wave of pheromones hit him. He had to keep it together long enough to get them both home...

"Hurts," Oliver said weakly. "Dizzy. Oh God, you smell good..."

Jet opened the passenger door of his own car. Holding his breath, he leaned over Oliver, pulling his legs around, then he helped him to his feet. *Protect your omega*, he commanded himself. That driving urge to keep Oliver safe was the only thing powerful enough to overcome the urge to mate him right here and now.

"Come on, Ollie. Turn around. Sit down, mind your head. That's it..."

Suddenly, a new and startling scent caught Jet's attention, breaking through the haze of pheromones. It was a scent he'd never smelled before in his life, but he knew immediately what it was: the challenge of another alpha. A primitive corner of his mind kicked into gear, and suddenly the world sharpened into vivid clarity.

Letting go of Oliver, Jet straightened, turning around slowly to see two men standing near the rear of Oliver's car. Damn it, he should have been paying more attention to his surroundings! How was he going to protect his omega if he didn't pay attention?

"Well, well, what have we here?" the nearest man said. He was the alpha, Jet knew, the scent rising off him sharp and pungent. The other man was a beta, simply tagging along for the ride, as he would have been completely unable to detect anything unusual in Oliver's scent.

"Nothing that's any concern of yours," Jet said. "Where are your keys, buddy?" he asked Oliver softly. They would have to leave his car here and pick it up in a few days, but he at least needed to lock it before they abandoned it.

"Here," Oliver said weakly, handing him the set from a tightly clenched fist.

"Come on, don't be selfish," the alpha said. "He smells like a bitch in heat. I'm sure there's enough for us to share."

Not taking his eyes off the pair, Jet closed the door to Oliver's car. "I'm giving you a warning, cos I'm feeling *real polite* at the moment," he told them, feeling an urge to bare his teeth and snarl. "If I was you, I'd just turn around and walk away." He locked the door, then pocketed the keys. A fight was inevitable, but if he could stall them long enough by keeping them talking, maybe he could at least get Oliver safely tucked away inside his car.

"Now, that's not very nice." The alpha stepped closer. "Someone should teach you some manners."

"Put your legs in," Jet told Oliver sharply, then suddenly he was ducking out of the way of a meaty fist. The punch threw the alpha off balance – for all his willing aggression, he clearly hadn't had any formal training in fighting technique – and Jet used the opportunity to slam him into the side of Oliver's car, then shove him backwards into the other man. While they were scrambling for balance, he scooped Oliver's legs up and tossed them into the car, then locked the door and slammed it closed.

The two men were back on their feet by now, fists up, ready for a fight... but Jet suddenly dashed away, around to the driver's side of the car. Before they'd quite realised what he was doing, he leapt into the driver's seat and slammed the door, locking the entire car with the press of a button. He fumbled to get his keys out of his pocket, praying they didn't just smash a window in their fury. Doing so would almost certainly break one of their fists, but alphas high on pheromones had been known to do more reckless things than that.

"Hey! Open the door!" The alpha was banging on the window, while his pal stood back, looking uncertain now that Jet was trying to leave.

Jet ignored the man trying to beat up his car and started the engine, glancing at Oliver as he put it in gear. He'd taken his glasses off and was sitting slumped in his seat, hand pressed over his eyes. His seatbelt wasn't done up, but for the moment they had bigger problems. The beta was standing directly behind the car, so instead, Jet put it in first. He put his foot down and the car shot forward, thumping over the curb in front of him, then landing in the next row with a thud. Undeterred, he spun the wheel to the right, taking off down the row and leaving the two losers chasing after him, fists flailing in the air.

He headed quickly for the exit, then down the next street, then decided he really needed to get Oliver strapped in. "Hey buddy, do you think you could do your belt up for me?" he asked, as he pulled in to the curb. He put the parking brake on, peering at his companion as he waited for a response.

None was forthcoming.

"Oliver? You okay?"

"Headache," came the thin reply. "Lights are too bright."

"Okay, look, I'm just going to do your belt up." The last thing he needed was Oliver being thrown about the car if they had an accident. With the way today had been going, Jet wouldn't have been surprised if the disasters just kept coming. He leaned over, grabbing the buckle... and then he was pulling back with a curse. Or, at least, he was *trying* to pull back. His nose was hovering just an inch above Oliver's neck, and to his own mortification, he let out a low moan, his eyes drifting closed as he felt his brain turn to mush, all of his available blood pooling in his groin.

He had to get them *home*, he reminded himself frantically. They were parked on a dark street, in the middle of nowhere, and Oliver was far from safe here. His omega had to be *safe*.

Get your head on straight and drive, a voice snarled at him.

But it seemed the sudden proximity to a trusted alpha was doing a number on Oliver, as well. His eyes opened, dark and hooded in the dim light of the car. Jet felt a warm pressure on his thigh, and he looked down. Oliver's hand was slowly sliding northwards, and there was nothing in the world that could make Jet stop him. "You smell good," Oliver murmured. Jet's fist tightened, and he felt cold metal bite into his skin. Right. The seatbelt.

"You need to do up your seatbelt," he told Oliver woodenly, pulling the buckle over and clipping it in place. "And we need to get home."

"Want you," Oliver slurred, and that, finally, was what got Jet's attention. He put a hand on Oliver's forehead, only confirming what he already knew. The heat rolling off the guy was almost enough to burn him.

"We need to get home," he said again, slumping back into his seat and putting the car in gear.

Oliver's hand remained on his thigh the whole way there.

"How's your headache?" Jet asked Oliver, as he hauled the man out of the car. He was being as helpful as a toddler who didn't want to go home from the park, his legs limp, his torso flopping all over the place. Jet managed to lock his car, then guided Oliver up the front steps. If any of the neighbours happened to see them, hopefully they'd just think he was drunk.

His duffle bag was still on the doorstep where he'd left it, so he simply stepped over it for the time being, settling Oliver on the sofa, then he ducked back outside to grab it. "Oh, fuck," he muttered to himself, the bundle of reports Sullivan had sent him still sitting neatly on top, and the reminder of the day's revelations was almost enough to pour cold water on his throbbing arousal.

Almost.

The truth was, there was still a hard, raging place in his mind that he couldn't quite get hold of. An instinctive fury rose up now and then, followed by a malicious glee that he'd gotten rid of the other alpha so easily. *Oliver is mine*, a voice chanted roughly. *My omega*. Jet shook his head, unnerved by the possessive aggression and entirely uncertain where it was coming from. All the way home, the scent of the unfamiliar alpha had stayed with him, lingering in his nose like raw sewage. Oliver was *his*. No one else could have him!

"We need to get your temperature down," he told Oliver, knowing he'd likely have to help him administer the first doses. He hadn't had to do it since that first time when they'd underestimated how often Oliver would need to be treated, but for all their growing familiarity with each other, Jet didn't think Oliver would really appreciate the necessity now.

To his surprise, though, the instant the door was closed, Oliver seemed to recover. Not entirely, of course – his body was still throwing off staggering amounts of heat – but he seemed more alert than he had been since Jet had met him in the parking lot. "Thank you," he said, his voice coming out almost like a purr. "My very own knight in shining armour."

"How's your headache?" Jet asked again. He slid down onto the sofa beside Oliver. A distant part of himself watched in consternation as he helped him take his jacket off.

"What headache?" Oliver leaned into him, a flirty little smile playing at his lips.

"Cramps? Dizziness? Come on, Ollie, help me out here."

"Okay," he agreed, then without warning, he started unbuttoning his shirt.

There was a reason why he shouldn't be doing that, Jet's rational mind tried to remind him. They needed to get Oliver a treatment, to start getting his temperature down. "No, no, stop for a second," he said, taking Oliver's hands to still them. The sliver of smooth, tanned skin beneath the fabric was doing nothing to help him focus.

Trying to concentrate, he stood up, tugging Oliver up with him. He started steering him towards his bedroom. The sensation in his groin was odd, and distracting because of that very oddness. Always before, when

85

Oliver had been in heat, the arousal had licked at him like living flames under his skin. Now, though, it was more like a slow burn, decadent, like melted chocolate over his tongue.

The scent of unfamiliar alpha lingered. Driven by a strange instinct, Jet stopped suddenly, as they rounded the corner into the hallway, and pressed Oliver back against the wall. He could feel the heat radiating through two sets of clothing, though they weren't quite touching, the air between them hot and ripe with anticipation. He tilted Oliver's head up with a gentle finger, lowering his face to breathe in the scent of him, sandalwood and smoke, and a deeper scent that was all male. One stray hand rose, lingering over the remaining buttons on Oliver's shirt. Perhaps if he just undid one more... or maybe two...

Like a bucket of cold water, he suddenly realised what he was doing. And what he was about to do.

"Oliver," he growled, mind struggling to find the words he needed to warn him of the danger. "We can't..."

"Jet..." He felt a hand on his chest, searingly hot through his shirt, and his groin surged in response. "I want..."

Desperately, Jet tried to pull away. "No. Really, you need..."

"I need *you*!"

With a jerk, Jet ripped himself away. What the hell did he think he was doing? "Get the hell out of this room," he snapped, wiping his face, as if that could rid him of that tantalising scent. "Go in your bedroom. Lock the door! Now, Oliver!"

Realisation seemed to hit Oliver in a rush. Eyes wide, hands shaking, he turned around and bolted through the doorway. The lock clicked shut a moment later, and half a second after that, Jet found himself plastered to the door, desperate to remove the barrier that stood between him and his omega.

But Oliver still needed him, needed the relief that only his body could provide. Too overwhelmed to even think about modesty or privacy, Jet unzipped his pants right there, outside Oliver's door, palming his erection desperately. Thank God they hadn't turned any lights on, he thought dimly, otherwise the neighbours would be getting an eyeful. The blinds weren't yet shut, and Jet didn't have the energy to deal with that right now. Instead, he stumbled into the kitchen, picking up a drinking glass, as he couldn't quite wrap his head around finding a plastic cup just at the moment. He headed back to the bedroom door, drawn like a moth to a flame, and spent himself into the glass with no more stimulation than the image of Oliver's face in his mind.

Breathing hard, he rested his head against the door, trying not to think about the fact that he was masturbating right outside another man's bedroom. There was no question that Oliver would be able to hear him, and Jet would have to apologise later. Round two followed on a sigh, and round three brought a gasping moan that made Jet wonder what Oliver sounded like when he came. He'd admitted in the past that he got himself off, behind that locked door, but he must have been pretty damn quiet about it, because Jet had never heard so much as a peep through the wooden barrier.

Jet thought about doing up his pants, but couldn't quite be bothered to deal with the discomfort of stuffing his throbbing erection back inside his clothes. Instead, he simply set the glass on the floor.

"Ollie... Don't open the door just yet. There's a glass out here for you. Just give me a minute to go away..."

A muffled reply came through the door, then Jet was forcing his legs to carry him away down the hall. The door to the second bedroom swung shut behind him, and he lingered just long enough to hear Oliver's door open.

His omega was safe. He'd done his job.

His knees buckled finally, and he sagged down onto the floor beside the bed. The bed sheets smelled of Oliver, for some reason, though he couldn't think why he'd be sleeping in this bed, when he had a perfectly good one of his own.

Nonetheless, the smell of omega – not omega in heat, but just the normal, everyday scent of him – soothed Jet's frazzled nerves. He opened the draw of the nightstand and pulled out a cup. A moment later, hot jets of white fluid were spurting into the bottom of it. He leaned his forehead on the blanket, inhaling the scent of Oliver, and stroked himself again, his erection not softening in the slightest before he was once more right on the brink, nerves jangling as he ran a thumb over the head. Helplessly, he imagined that it was Oliver's hand instead of his own, imagined what it would be like to have the man spread out naked in front of him, moaning in pleasure, a willing omega finally accepting his alpha.

CHAPTER NINETEEN

JET

"Is it all right if I come out?" Oliver called from behind his bedroom door. He asked again, slightly louder, before Jet summoned the strength to get up off the spare bed and answer the question.

"Yeah, it's cool, man. How are you feeling?" Seven hours had passed since they'd arrived home, and thankfully, Oliver had had the good sense to stay locked in his bedroom for that entire time. Jet wasn't entirely sure what he'd have done if he'd been faced with a dazed and seductive omega again.

The door opened a crack, then wider, as Oliver saw Jet leaning against his own bedroom door, fully clothed and apparently back in his right mind. After climaxing a prodigious fourteen times, Jet was finally feeling more like himself. Temptation was still a fiery beast lurking beneath his skin, but it was back down to manageable levels, no worse than it usually was during Oliver's heats. He'd showered as well, ridding himself of both the lingering scent of the other alpha, and the lust-soaked smell of his own omega.

But the instant the door opened properly, temptation flew right back in the window, setting up camp in Jet's groin like squatters in a vacant building. Oliver was standing there wearing a fuzzy bathrobe, a tantalising triangle of skin exposed at his neck where the two halves didn't quite meet.

"Feeling better," Oliver said. "My temperature's come down, though the headache went away pretty much the moment we got home." He looked down and blushed. "That was quite odd, actually. As soon as we were in the car, the cramps stopped. I was still hot and dizzy, but nothing like as bad as before. Why would that be? Do you want some coffee?"

With his head still swirling with desire, the sudden change of topic threw Jet off balance again. "Coffee? What? Yes. No. It's two o'clock in the morning, Ollie. Why do you want coffee?"

Oliver looked momentarily confused. "Oh. Well, hot chocolate then?" Despite the late hour, they'd both been too revved up to sleep. Even now, Jet was feeling a strong, protective urge, and he'd had a hard time calming his anxiety when he couldn't be in the same room as Oliver.

"Hot chocolate would be good. Let's do that."

Five minutes later, they were both seated comfortably, Jet on the sofa, Oliver curled up in the armchair, which seemed to be one of his favourite spots. He looked like a big, fluffy cat, feet tucked under him, the white bathrobe billowing around him.

"I have a theory," Jet began, wondering if what he was going to say would sound crazy. "I think maybe the reason I was behaving the way I was, and the reason your symptoms went away, is linked to that other alpha. I don't know if you could detect his scent, but I certainly could. It had a weird effect on me. It made me feel invincible, like I could take on a whole army single-handed. Maybe it did something to you, too?"

"Actually, that's something I've been wondering about," Oliver said. "They were gunning for a fight, and you would have been more than capable of taking them on. So why didn't you fight them?"

"Did you want me to fight them?" A primitive part of Jet's mind was suddenly prepared to do just that, to drive right back to the shopping centre, track the men down and give them a good beating, if that's what his omega wanted.

Oliver snorted. "No, of course not. But I thought..."

"You thought that's what alphas do?"

Oliver shrugged. "Yeah."

They'd come far enough now that Jet was beyond the need to feel offended by the misunderstandings his gender created. Well, okay, the misunderstandings that *Oliver* had. If anyone else had maligned his gender, he'd have had some sharp words to say about it.

"To be honest, I don't entirely know why I didn't," Jet said. "If they'd come at me, I'd have happily handed them their asses. But the whole point was to get you to safety. And once you were in the car, the safest thing was to just get the hell out of there. You were in my car. You were willingly coming with me. I guess I just didn't feel like I had anything to prove to them."

Oliver nodded, and he fell silent for a moment. But then... "What about when we got home? What was that?"

Oh, shit. Jet had known he'd have to explain that one sooner or later, and he'd been dreading the conversation. On top of everything else that had happened earlier in the day, it was a wonder his brain hadn't simply exploded yet.

"One of the men was an alpha," he began, not quite knowing how that was relevant.

"I know. But we were well away from them by the time we got here."

Jet thought back to that hard possessiveness, the need to claim, to own, and he felt sick at the thought of his own instincts taking over, of causing him to harm the very person he was supposed to protect. If he didn't want to admit that side of him to himself, how was he supposed to explain it to Oliver?

But before he could come up with a decent explanation, Oliver spoke again. "You weren't hurting me," he said, looking Jet straight in the eye. "You were actually incredibly gentle. And I thought... No, maybe I shouldn't say that."

"Shouldn't say what?"

"We're both still pretty high-strung right now," Oliver pointed out. "I don't want to make that worse."

Jet shrugged, knowing that it was a fair point.

"You were crowding me, up against the wall, but you weren't actually touching me, and then you got all snarly and told me to get away from you. I don't understand why."

"Because I..." Because I wanted to kiss you. "Because I thought I was going to hurt you. I thought I was going to lose control of myself, and I couldn't stand to do that to you." He said it to the floorboards, as if absolution could be found in the creases of the wood.

Oliver was looking at him strangely. "I don't think you would have," he said, though Jet could see no reason at all that would lead him to that conclusion. "You were sniffing my neck," – he touched the small scent gland there unconsciously – "and it doesn't get much more potent than that. It actually seemed to calm you down for a moment."

Oliver moved then, shifting across from the armchair to the sofa. Jet automatically slid over, giving him more room, but Oliver kept coming, closing the gap between them. "I just want to test a theory," he said, at Jet's alarmed look.

"No, not a good idea," Jet said, tilting his head away to avoid breathing in too much of Oliver's scent. "You're still all high on pheromones and shit, and this is... Oh, hell..." The scent was going straight to his groin, his erection pressing hard against his jeans. "Oliver, please..."

"I don't believe you would hurt me," he said again.

Unable to help himself, Jet pressed his palm down over the bulge in his pants, rubbing himself through the fabric. "You don't know what you're doing," he warned Oliver again. Unbidden, his other hand slid around Oliver's waist, pulling him closer. He tilted his neck up, giving Jet clear access to that decadent gland on his neck. Rumour had it that it tasted even better than it smelled. Was he wearing anything beneath the bathrobe? Jet's head was spinning, and he desperately tried to cling onto sanity. "You don't want to sleep with me," he reminded Oliver, praying that he'd regain some semblance of rationality.

"No, I don't," Oliver agreed. "But that doesn't mean we can't have a little fun."

"No, uh, yes it does. I mean no, we can't," Jet rambled, trying to extract Oliver's hand from where it was sneaking beneath the hem of his shirt.

Suddenly, Oliver's shoulders sagged, his lips forming a tantalising pout. "You don't want me," he said forlornly.

"Look, I don't know what that other alpha's pheromones did to you, but you're not thinking straight."

"That was hours ago," Oliver said. "Anything he did would have worn off by now."

"Then how come you've never done this before? Usually you're all prim and proper, and making sure we both keep our hands to ourselves. Stop that!" Oliver had taken one of Jet's hands and slid it inside his robe. "Oliver, listen to me. You're not thinking straight. Trust me on this one, buddy. I promise, you'll thank me tomorrow."

"Why are you being so stubborn?" Oliver asked. He leaned forward and brushed his lips lightly along Jet's jaw.

All of a sudden, Jet realised what was missing. Pheromones! Of course! He scrambled off the sofa, grabbing the bag he'd left by the door. He rummaged around inside, coming up with his two sweaty shirts. He ripped one out of its plastic wrapping and thrust it at Oliver. He'd completely forgotten to give them to him, in all the drama of rescuing him from the shopping centre and both of them having a minor meltdown.

"Here, breathe that in," he ordered, shoving the fabric at Oliver's face with a sigh of relief. Oliver wasn't losing his mind, he was just pheromone deprived. And since Jet was the only other source of scent available, getting up close and personal with him had been the only option. Of course, Oliver probably wasn't processing any of that on a rational level, and Jet cringed at the inevitable embarrassment Oliver would feel once the heat wore off and he realised what he'd been up to. Jet resolved to simply brush the incident off, far more comfortable with it now that there was a rational explanation.

"You look pretty tired," he told Oliver, as the omega curled up on the sofa, legs tucked up, head pillowed on Jet's t-shirt. "You want to go to bed? Try getting some sleep?"

Oliver shook his head, snuggling his face into the shirt like a kitten.

"Okay, then how about I just turn off the light. I'll set my alarm for three hours' time and give you your next dose. I'll be in the bedroom if you need me."

Oliver hummed a faint reply, eyes already closed, fingers clutching the shirt like a child with a favourite blanket.

CHAPTER TWENTY

JET

"You said there was something important you wanted to talk about?" Oliver emerged from the bedroom, hair wet and dressed in clean clothes. The lingering scent of omega pheromones was fading now that Jet had opened the windows, and after a marathon fifty hours, Oliver's latest heat was finally over. The length of it had been of some concern, with his average being closer to forty hours, but as Oliver had calmly pointed out, these things did tend to vary. Forty-eight hours wasn't unheard of for omegas, so fifty was only just outside the norm.

"There is. A couple of things, actually," Jet said, bracing himself for the conversation to come. The stack of reports from Sullivan had sat ignored for the past two days, other concerns more urgent – like Oliver's sudden cuddliness, or an inexplicable paranoia that had had Jet double checking that every window and door in the house was closed and locked.

The first issue was the easier one to deal with, though it was by no means good news. "I got in contact with a lawyer who specialises in omega cases," Jet began, as they both took a seat on the sofa. "He's worked on emancipation cases in the past. There is a bit of good news. Two of his cases were for omegas who wanted to divorce their alpha partners. They were successful, and both of them were restored to, and I quote, 'the approximate financial position they were in before entering the relationship.'"

"Not exactly fair," Oliver said, wariness in his voice. "In beta couples, unless there's a solid prenup, the assets of the relationship are generally split equally between the two parties."

"Nothing in this world is particularly fair towards omegas," Jet said. "But it's a start."

"So that means I could potentially apply for emancipation from you? You've been an absolutely marvellous partner, by the way," Oliver added, good manners back in full swing. "Please don't think I have any problem with the way you've been handling all this."

"Hey, I'm not taking any of this personally," Jet told him. "You want the freedom to be your own person. I get that. But unfortunately, it's not going to be quite that simple. Both successful cases were for non-Caloren's omegas. The lawyer I spoke to is one of the best – and don't worry, Anderson's agreed to foot the bill. Something about you really brings out his soft side. Anyway, the lawyer checked all the legal precedents he could get his hands on, and the answer is fairly simple; a Caloren's omega cannot be legally separated from an alpha unless he or she is also capable of surviving physically without said alpha. We can't buy your freedom until we find a way of bypassing your biochemistry. On the plus side, the fact that your alpha is perfectly willing to sign an emancipation order makes the process significantly smoother, if we ever reach that stage."

Oliver let out a long sigh, his mouth twisted into a frown. "It's not the worst news," he said finally. "It means there is a way, if we can only figure out how."

"Which brings us to the next bit of news," Jet said, far more apprehensive about this part. "I have a confession to make. And I'm not really sure how you're going to feel about it."

"Why would I not like it?" Oliver asked, the wary caution back.

"Because in the strictest sense of the agreement, it may have violated our confidentiality clause. I never mentioned your name," he rushed on, as Oliver raised an imperious eyebrow. "But I have mentioned some of the methods we've been using to control your heats."

"And who exactly did you mention this to?"

"A doctor friend of mine. He's been studying omega physiology with a focus on physical and chemical changes during heats. I told him about it as a potential way of allowing other Caloren's omegas to avoid having to pair up with an alpha."

"How very altruistic." Jet couldn't tell if Oliver was being sarcastic or not. "And why are you bringing this to my attention now?"

Jet ran a hand through his hair. Sometimes, Oliver could be so damn hard to read. That perfectly civilised veneer could be hiding either wild enthusiasm about the idea of helping other omegas, or unmitigated outrage at having a trusted friend go behind his back.

"He's looking for volunteers for a clinical trial he's running. He wants to take our anecdotal success and turn it into hard research. But finding omega volunteers is difficult."

"It can't be that hard," Oliver said with a frown. "Surely there would be a way to contact potential candidates through their regular GPs? Privacy laws allow for that sort of thing, so long as the research institute isn't given any personal data until the candidate has agreed to participate in the trial."

"I said pretty much the same thing," Jet said. "Well, not the bit about privacy laws, but I figured there must be plenty of omegas out there looking for a better option."

"So what's the issue?"

Okay, crunch time. Somewhere, Jet thought darkly, an overweight soprano in an opera house had just begun the first warbling notes of her final song. "He sent me through some research papers about the side effects of heats in Caloren's omegas. One of his colleagues did a retrospective analysis of a lot of the studies and came up with…" How was he supposed to phrase this? "I'm really not sure if telling you this is a good idea. There's a fairly good chance it's going to do more harm than good. I don't want to hide things from you – I swore I would always respect your right to make your own decisions. But there are some things you might just be better off not knowing."

"Presumably some of the 'side effects', as you call them, of extreme heats are rather unpleasant?" Oliver guessed. "You must realise I've done a fair bit of reading on this topic myself."

Jet shrugged. "Maybe. Maybe not."

Oliver chewed his lip, tapping a long, elegant finger against his chin, and Jet was glad that he was at least considering the idea seriously. All he really wanted to do was throw the report in the bin, or better yet burn the damn thing and pretend it had never existed. But neither would be fair to Oliver. He had the right to decide for himself.

"Let me see it," he said finally. Heart in his throat, Jet handed over the papers. *'Life expectancy of Caloren's omegas after diagnosis'*, the title read, in a boxy font. The information was dry and hard to read – or at least it had been for Jet. He was no scientist, and the abundance of jargon made the whole thing feel like trying to chew dry weetabix. Perhaps Oliver was having better luck with it, he mused as he turned the page. Or perhaps he was just skimming through the details until he got to the conclusion.

On the last page was a graph, helpfully summarising the entire study in bold lines of blue and red. Oliver caught sight of the graph and peered at it studiously, brows furrowed in concentration.

Jet knew the exact moment the truth hit home. Oliver's hands tightened on the page, wrinkling the pristine white paper. The harsh intake of breath made Jet wince, a far more controlled reaction than the volley of curses he'd unleashed himself. And then Oliver went deathly still, the colour draining out of his face in a rush. "Average life expectancy post-diagnosis," he read woodenly. "Two-point-nine years." Currently they were two-and-a-quarter years into Oliver's post-diagnosis life. But that wasn't the worst part. "As Caloren's omegas approach seven years post diagnosis, mortality rate…" *approaches one hundred per cent.* Jet didn't need Oliver to read it out to know the dreadful statistic. He'd read that line himself, over and over, until it was seared into his brain. Below the chart, there was a neat, clinical table. *Cause of death: Unrelated causes: 1%. Medical complications from poor management of heats: 30%. Suicide: 69%.*

Sixty-nine out of every one hundred Caloren's omegas took their own lives because living with not only a painful medical condition, but some truly barbaric legal and financial restrictions meant they would simply rather be dead. Statistically, Oliver had just under five years to live – unconventional management techniques aside. But as they'd already seen, even their best efforts had been a bit hit and miss, with Oliver's temperature spiking, one or both of them not managing to make their appointment on time, or Oliver's body playing up now and then in ways they'd had to correct with urgent and chaotic improvisations. Sooner or later, they were going to screw something up, and when they did, there was a very good chance that Oliver was going to join that thirty per cent statistic.

The silence stretched on, and Jet suddenly wished they weren't doing this at nine o'clock in the morning. He felt an urgent need for a stiff drink.

Finally, Oliver moved, taking a deep, shuddering breath. He set the papers back on the coffee table, smoothing the creased lines deliberately.

"I think it's about time we gave this doctor friend of yours a call," he said, in a voice Jet didn't quite recognise. "He's just found his first candidate for a treatment trial."

CHAPTER TWENTY-ONE

CYCLE FIFTEEN
JET

"Okay, so you've got suppositories, pheromone drops, aural thermometer, blood pressure cuff, painkillers… and a giant dildo," Jet recited, checking the items lying on Oliver's bed on by one. "Why did he give you painkillers? I thought the whole idea of this method was that you weren't supposed to be in pain."

"Jet, please relax," Oliver said, sounding far calmer than Jet was feeling. "I'm going to be fine. Dr Kennedy's been through the process with me in detail. The painkillers are just in case. He's still adjusting the dose administered by the suppositories, so he said if it was a bit low for my particular physiology, then I might get a slight headache or mild cramps."

For the past half a dozen heats, Oliver had been helping Sullivan with his trials. They'd been taking detailed measurements of his body temperature and blood pressure. They'd written down exactly how many times Oliver had administered a treatment and how he'd felt after each one. They'd kept charts of any other symptoms he'd experienced and how long they'd lasted.

Since Oliver had signed up, three more omegas had also joined the trial, and Sullivan had compiled the information from each of them, coming up with a treatment plan that he believed would provide sufficient support to get each of them through a heat without needing an alpha's intervention.

The crowning achievement of the research had been the development of suppositories, to be inserted into the omega's reproductive tract, which would provide a slow release of alpha proteins over a twelve-hour period. The packet Sullivan had given Oliver contained five of them, more than adequate for what should be no more than a forty-eight-hour heat.

He'd also developed a liquid form of alpha pheromones, supplied in a tiny vial, and Oliver was supposed to smear one drop on his upper lip every eight hours.

"All three of the other omegas have already been through a heat using the suppositories, and all of them said it worked like a dream." The hopeful smile on Oliver's face was adorable, a far cry from his usual apprehensive self at the beginning of a heat.

"Everything you've ever hoped for," Jet said, attempting to sound enthusiastic. He should be happy Sullivan's research had been such a success. No more ducking out of work to rush home to Oliver. No more Sunday surfing sessions cancelled on short notice. Those small, white pellets signified freedom, not just for Oliver, but for Jet as well. And more importantly, freedom for every other Caloren's omega out there struggling to retain any semblance of control over their own lives.

They sat there, on the edge of Oliver's bed, until the silence suddenly became awkward. "I'd better get going then," Jet announced, standing up suddenly. "Leave you to your... things." It shouldn't be this difficult. Why couldn't he just say 'See you later' and walk out the door? "Well, best of luck," he said, trying to sound cheerful. "If you need anything, I'm just a phone call away. And make sure you tell me how this goes afterwards. If it works, we should get started on that emancipation claim you've been sitting on for the past two years."

Unexpectedly, Oliver laughed. "I'm not going to just kick you out of my life, you know. Even if this works, Dr Kennedy's still working on titrating the right dose. We've got a mountain of paperwork to get through, and the suppositories will have to be signed off by the Pharmaceutical Drugs Authority. That's going to take at least a year. And at the end of all that... who knows, maybe I'll even take you to the pub for a beer." Jet felt himself blush, realising he was being silly. "You've been a good friend," Oliver told him. "More than I could have ever hoped for. And I hope we'll stay friends, once this is all over."

"Absolutely," Jet agreed. "Like I said, if you need anything, even if it's just someone to bring you chocolate and a can of whisky, you're always welcome to give me a call."

It was dark by the time Jet got home, and he let himself into his apartment, feeling oddly let down. He'd known this was coming, had known for the better part of a year, once Sullivan had come up with the idea for suppositories and started trying to work out the correct dose to make them effective. So why was he feeling so damn restless?

He'd cancelled his plans for the weekend, wanting to be on hand just in case something went wrong, but as Oliver had pointed out, the tests with the other omegas had gone off without a hitch.

There was nothing to worry about, he told himself. Nothing at all.

Not yet tired enough to sleep and too restless to do anything productive, Jet poured himself a beer, ripped open a packet of popcorn and settled himself on the sofa. There was a new action movie on Netflix and this was the perfect sort of evening to sit back and take some time out.

Jet jerked awake, tumbling off the sofa as he rolled over, then cursing as he hit the floor. The television was still on, the sound muted, though his movie had finished hours ago. Damn it, he must have fallen asleep on the couch.

The phone rang again – the thing that had woken him up so rudely. He checked the caller, then quickly answered the call.

"Hey, Oliver, what's up, my man?" The clock on the wall said it was ten minutes past two. There was no reply on the other end of the phone. "Oliver? Are you butt-dialling me or what, man?"

Still no reply. "Damn it," he muttered, hanging up. Why was he so excited to be hearing from the guy anyway? With a wide yawn, he stood up, stretching stiff muscles, then headed for the bathroom. Time to brush his teeth then fall into a real bed. Given the time of night, it shouldn't take long for him to get back to -

His phone rang again, and he checked the caller. Oliver. He answered it, wondering if they'd just got cut off before. "Oliver? What's happening, buddy?"

There was no reply. "Oliver? If your phone's in your bed, stop rolling over and elbow-dialling people." Still no reply, though Jet thought perhaps he could hear faint breathing. If it had been one of his work buddies, he'd have assumed this was some sort of weird prank, but Oliver would never do something like that. "Oliver? You're not in bed watching porn on your phone, are you?"

Still nothing, so Jet hung up. That was weird. Maybe he should go over to Oliver's house and see if he was…

No, he was fine, he told himself. He was probably just sleeping and he'd rolled onto his phone. No big deal.

He turned on the bathroom light and picked up his toothbrush.

His phone rang again. "Oliver? Okay, man, now you're scaring me. What's the go, buddy? You need help or what?" Silence. "Oliver?" Shit. Okay, enough of this. "All right, I'm going to come over to your place. And I'm really sorry if I just wake you up in the middle of the night for nothing, but this is weird. So… give me, like, two minutes, and I'll be on the way."

He hung up. A quick visit to the toilet, a swing by his closet to put on socks and shoes, and he was out the door. On impulse, he picked up the duffle bag that was still packed and ready to go by the door. It never hurt to be prepared.

He was just letting himself out the front door when his phone rang again. It was Oliver. "I'm on my way over, buddy. Can you talk to me? Come on man, say something." The line went dead, then immediately rang again. He slammed the door shut, just barely taking the time to lock it, then ran for his car. He jammed the phone into the cradle just in time for it to stop ringing, but it started again a moment later. He started the engine, then answered the call. "Oliver, I'm on my way to your place. I'm going to be there in under ten minutes. You just sit tight, and I'll -"

The line cut out again. Heart thumping in his chest, Jet put his foot to the floor, wincing as he most likely woke up half the neighbourhood as his wheels spun, screeching loudly in the quietness of the night. The phone rang again, but he didn't bother answering it, just focusing on getting there as fast as possible.

The endless sound of ringing was grating on his nerves as he drove, and he was grateful there weren't any cops about at this time of night, otherwise he'd have been booked for speeding at least six times before he got to Oliver's house. But if he'd thought the phone's incessant cry for attention was bad, his night suddenly got a whole lot worse. After cutting out again, he waited for the thing to start up again... and his heart just about stopped when it didn't.

"No, no, no, Oliver, don't you fucking die on me!"

CHAPTER TWENTY-TWO

JET

The roads were deserted, which was just as well, as Jet ran a red light then took a turn too fast. He knew the route to Oliver's house like the back of his hand, and in just over seven minutes, he was pulling up outside.

He grabbed the duffle bag and raced for the front door, knocking loudly. "Oliver? You in there, man? Come on, open the door." His car was in the driveway. The house was dark and quiet, and Jet wondered how he was going to get in. "Oliver?" He thumped on the door again.

Screw this. He ran around to the back of the house, praying that Oliver had left a window open. No luck.

Was he just overreacting, a hopeful part of his mind enquired? In the middle of a heat, there was absolutely no way Oliver would be anywhere but inside his house. Maybe he was in the bathroom, or taking a shower…?

Jet pulled out his phone and rang Oliver. No answer, but somewhere deep inside the house, he heard Oliver's phone ringing.

Palms sweating, heart pounding, he looked around for something to break the window with. A rock? A stray shovel? Damn Oliver for keeping his yard so bloody tidy! A garden chair was the only option, and he picked one up, lining up a shot. Impulsively, he promised himself he'd pay for the window to be repaired, then swung it, flinching as the glass shattered with a crash. A part of him was still desperately hoping he was wrong, and that Oliver was going to spend the next three months laughing at him for overreacting.

It took longer than he would have liked to clear the glass away. If he cut himself to ribbons, he'd be no good to Oliver. Then he climbed through, trying to avoid touching the edges.

The instant he was inside the house, the smell of Oliver hit him… but it was a far cry from his usual enticing scent. This time, the smell was sour, like the tang of meat going off.

He made a dash for Oliver's bedroom, skidding around the corner, then he flung the door open… and his heart all but stopped in his chest.

Oliver lay on the bed, motionless in the dark, his phone near his right hand. "Oliver? Oliver, wake up!" He smacked the light switch and grabbed Oliver, giving him a shake, then swore as he felt the searing temperature of his skin. He was soaked, sweat pouring off him and seeping into the mattress below. He was barely breathing, though Jet caught the tail end of a faint exhale as he leaned his ear down to Oliver's mouth.

His heart racing, he flung the man over onto his side. Why the hell hadn't he used the suppository? Sullivan had reported huge success in his other subjects, and even if it hadn't worked one hundred per cent, it should have had at least a partial impact on Ollie's temperature. Abandoning the slightest pretence of modesty, Jet parted Oliver's butt cheeks and peered in between. A string of curses left his lips. His entrance was bright red, swollen and angry, and a second look revealed a slight trickle of blood leaking down Oliver's thigh. A small string was hanging out the opening, and Jet pulled it out as gently as he could. It was the suppository, though apparently it had been worse than useless.

Hand shaking, sweat beading on his forehead, Jet pulled out his phone and dialled the only person who might be able to help him right at the moment.

"Jet?" Sullivan answered the phone. "It two o'clock in the morning, what are you -?"

"Oliver's dying," he barked out, not caring for an instant what bloody time it was. "The suppository didn't work. He's burning up here. What the fuck do I do?"

Thankfully, Sullivan was a quick study and he didn't waste any time expressing his surprise or muttering about failed experiments. "What's his temperature?" he demanded.

Jet grabbed the aural thermometer off the nightstand and stuck it in Oliver's ear, waiting impatiently for it to beep. "Forty-two-point-five. Shit, that's high!"

"Is he breathing?"

"Just about."

"Keep him on his side. You know the recovery position?"

"Yeah. Got it. Now what?"

"You need to cool him down. Get some ice packs, put them against his armpits and his groin. Remove any clothing. Turn on a ceiling fan, or an air conditioner, if he's got one. Have you taken the suppository out?"

"Yes. As soon as I found it."

"Good man." He heard the sound of a door slamming on the other end of the phone, then an engine starting.

"Should I stick my jizz in his ass?" Oliver would have been horrified at such language, he thought darkly, humour a refuge as fear made his gut roll. He wasn't entirely sure he'd even be able to get it up at the moment, dread and guilt gnawing at him. He should have never left Oliver alone!

"Not yet," Sullivan said. "I'm on my way over. I don't know what went wrong, and I don't want to make things worse. Just try to keep him cool and make sure he keeps breathing. You know CPR?"

"Yeah."

"Good. I'll be there in ten minutes."

He hung up and Jet sprang into action. He ran to Oliver's fridge, praying there were some ice packs in there. There were – thank God Oliver was such a damn boy scout – and he grabbed a couple of tea towels on his way out of the kitchen to wrap them in.

Ice packs in place, he turned on the ceiling fan, then checked Oliver's breathing again. Shallow, but regular. He had his usual t-shirts in his bag, and figuring it couldn't do any harm, he grabbed one of them and stuck it under Oliver's head so he'd get a good whiff of pheromones. What else, what else? The bathroom was the next stop and he got a wash cloth, running it under cold water. Back in the bedroom, he put it on Oliver's forehead. Damn, he was burning up! He opened the window, letting the cool night air in, and at the same time, letting some of the sour stench out. It might not help Oliver, but it would at least make Jet feel better.

Five minutes to go.

Figuring he had nothing to lose, Jet grabbed a plastic cup from the supply in the spare bedroom and returned to Oliver's room. Sullivan might not want to use the samples he could provide, but it wouldn't do any harm to have a couple ready to go in case they were needed. He unzipped his pants and started working his limp member, trying to block out the sickly smell emanating from his partner. The usual scent of his heats was as familiar as the smell of a ripe orange, and he closed his eyes, trying to bring it to mind. Think of all those times you wanted to bury yourself inside him, he coached himself grimly. Think of that time he opened the door in his underwear. Think of that sultry little smile he did when he'd just got out of the shower, hair wet, heat not quite over.

Thankfully, the trip down memory lane was working, and he spent himself into the cup just as he heard a car pulling up outside. He couldn't really have called the experience pleasure, but at least there was a sample in the cup.

He set it on the nightstand, then, checking that Oliver hadn't got any worse, he dashed for the front door. "In here, through this way," he ordered Sullivan, not even bothering to say hello. "He looks like shit. What the fuck is wrong with him?"

Sullivan was all business, pulling out a thermometer, a stethoscope and a pair of rubber gloves. His examination was quick but thorough, and Jet heard him mutter a few curses to himself as he checked Oliver's back end. Cautiously, he inserted a finger into Oliver's passage. "Damn it... What the hell is going on with you, Oliver?"

That's what Jet wanted to know. "Do I call an ambulance? I'm not losing him, man! How the fuck do we save his life?"

"Let me think, let me think..." Sullivan stood back, stripping off the gloves and tapping his foot against the floor. He spun around and checked the bag of suppositories on the nightstand. Just one was missing. A sudden frown creased his forehead, and he grabbed a light from his bag, then tilted Oliver's head back, shining the light on his upper lip. "The skin here is red," he reported, though Jet had no idea why that was important. "In all the time you two have been together, has anything like this happened before?"

"Never," Jet replied immediately. "The only time he's looked even remotely like this is when we've been late getting him a dose of... proteins." Was he supposed to use some sort of medical jargon with a doctor? Did it even matter?

There was a moment of silence, then Sullivan nodded. "Right. Then let's do that... Ah! Way ahead of me." Jet was already holding out the cup and dropper; Sullivan was familiar with the way they'd been dealing with the problem. "Good lad. Go get a couple more doses, and I'll sort this one out."

Shutting himself in the bedroom, Jet unzipped his pants and took a new cup out of the draw. *Okay, Wilder,* he coached himself. *Time to get hot and horny.*

Five minutes later, he was at his wit's end. He wasn't the slightest bit turned on, and the pressure of knowing that Oliver could die if he couldn't perform was doing nothing to help him relax. Without the intoxicating scent of an omega's heat, he was paddling up stream in a leaky canoe, with a paddle made of cotton candy.

Thinking back to Oliver's previous heats, he tried to bring to mind an image that would provide some inspiration. Oliver with his shirt unbuttoned. The decadent desire to strip his pants off him and see those long legs underneath, the bulge of his erection pressing up from his briefs...

Shit, it was no good. All he could see when he closed his eyes was Oliver lying on that bed, his skin an unnatural pink, his face creased in pain, even in his unconscious state.

Damn it, he had to find a way to do this! In desperation, he stripped off his clothes and lay down on the bed, stroking his limp member slowly. His eyes slid shut, and he imagined what it would feel like to have Oliver's hands on his skin, instead of his own. He'd be kneeling between Jet's legs, a sultry smile on his lips, fingertips tracing a heated path up his inner thigh. He'd brush over Jet's balls, bypassing his erection for the moment, and trail a line of kisses up his abdomen. His chest would brush against the head of Jet's cock as he leaned down over him, then he'd whisper seductive words in his ear. *I want you inside me. You feel so damn good, Jet...*

Jet turned his face to the side, amazed that it actually seemed to be working. He was hard now, a trickle of pleasure slowly spreading out from his groin. He pressed his face further into the pillow, revelling in the warm, comforting scent...

Suddenly, he lifted his head, the faint scent breaking through the fog in his brain. What the hell was...?

He leaned down and sniffed the pillow. It smelled of Oliver. The scent was faint, but distinct, the clean, faintly smoky scent of his omega meandering through the first gentle hours of his heat, as his body's pheromones shifted into the intoxicating scent that sent alphas out of their minds. He curled around and scented the sheets, astonished to find more of Oliver's smell there.

Why the hell had Oliver been rolling around on the bed that Jet normally slept in?

The question was dismissed a moment later, as Jet buried his face in the pillow, the horrors and worries of the night put to rest for a few liberating moments as an image flashed through his mind of exactly what Oliver had looked like, writhing on this bed, naked as the day he was born. He spent himself into the cup a moment later, then hung onto the image as he quickly worked himself into a second release.

In a normal heat, Oliver needed at least three doses at the start to get his temperature under control, and given the state he was in, it was a sure bet he'd need at least double that now. Jet ripped the sheet off the bed and wrapped it around his waist. He rushed down the hall, delivering the cup to Sullivan, then rushed back to the bedroom before he could get too caught up in fear and anxiety again, seeing Oliver still lying helplessly on his bed.

Fifteen minutes and three doses later, he stumbled back into Oliver's bedroom, his legs feeling as shaky as a new born deer. "How's he doing?" he asked, thrusting the cup into Sullivan's hand.

Sullivan wasted no time in donning another pair of gloves and administering the fluid. "Blood pressure's come up a little. His temperature's down to forty-two, but I'm not sure if that's because of the treatment, or the ice packs. Still, he's not any worse, so that's a small step in the right direction."

Knowing there wasn't much else he could do for the moment, Jet took a seat on the end of the bed, while Sullivan continued to monitor Oliver's vitals. His breathing was a touch more regular now, the pinched look of pain less pronounced.

It was nearly fifteen minutes later when Jet noticed the first real change. The scent in the room wasn't nearly as unpleasant as it had been when he'd arrived, the open window letting a constant flow of fresh air in, but as the breeze paused for a moment and the air in the room swirled beneath the ceiling fan, Jet caught a whiff of... sandalwood and smoke.

He leapt up, dashing up to the head of the bed.

"What is it?" Sullivan asked, gazing at the thermometer as he took Oliver's temperature for the fifth time.

Jet leaned down, putting his nose right in against Oliver's neck, just next to the discreet little scent gland beside his collar bone. He inhaled slowly, eyes closed...

"His scent's changed," he reported, partly because he could smell it, and partly because his erection was suddenly punching out the front of his sheet like the thing was on fire.

"His temperature's dropped half a degree," Sullivan reported. "But that's not really enough to determine whether it's working." He glanced up at Jet... and froze. "Oh. I see."

Jet was still leaning over Oliver, but his gaze was fixed firmly on Sullivan, a dark, predatory glare on his face. Slowly, he bared his teeth, a low growl rumbling from his throat. "Mine," he snarled, climbing up onto the bed, right over the top of Oliver to put himself between him and Sullivan.

"Jet, we both know that I'm here to help Oliver," Sullivan told him calmly. He didn't move, either towards Oliver, or away from him. "I am a doctor, and Oliver is very ill."

"Get the fuck away from him," Jet growled, climbing off the bed to stand nose to nose with Sullivan. A dim, distant part of his mind was completely baffled by his own behaviour, but he wasn't able to pay it much attention. His inner alpha was demanding that he protect Oliver at all costs, and having another male in the room was absolutely out of the question.

"I am a beta," Sullivan said, still not backing down, even as he kept his voice calm and his body relaxed. "I am of absolutely no threat to you."

Battling for sanity, half of Jet's mind was busy reflecting that Sullivan must have done this before. If he'd moved closer to Oliver, Jet would have gleefully beaten him to a pulp, but even if he'd moved away, Jet would have seen it as a victory, and quite possibly gone after him anyway.

In a move that was straight out of one of those awful, scripted alpha/omega porn videos, Jet took hold of Sullivan's collar and hauled him closer. He bent down, scenting his neck. He smelled a trace of sweat, the lingering scent of cologne from earlier in the day, and a whiff of laundry powder. Damn, his reaction to Oliver had sent his sense of smell into overdrive, as he was even able to detect the faint trace of a domestic cat, and he vaguely remembered that Sullivan had a little tortoiseshell kitten he'd adopted a month or two ago. But the scent of a challenging alpha was completely absent, and Jet reluctantly let him go, the omission just barely adequate reassurance that the man wasn't trying to take his omega from him.

"Oliver needs your help," Sullivan told him. Moving very slowly, he picked up a plastic cup from the nightstand and handed it to Jet. "I'm going to go and wait in the hall. You will *not* lock the door, and when you're finished, you will let me back into the room. Do you understand?"

On a different day, Jet would have told the man he was a total fuckwit for talking to him like he was a three-year-old child. Today, though, he simply nodded. He had to protect his omega, that inner voice was telling him again. Oliver needed a doctor. Sullivan was a doctor...

With Oliver's scent back in full swing, it took him mere moments to have two samples in the cup, and he opened the door, forcing himself not to block the way as Sullivan came back into the room. "Would you like to administer this dose?" Sullivan asked, and Jet nodded. Once it was done, Sullivan did another quick check of Oliver's vitals – with a tense and angsty Jet watching on – and then he breathed a sigh of relief. "His temperature's dropped another few points, and his blood pressure's back to normal. I'd say he's through the worst of it."

The rational man, as well as the caring friend in Jet, wanted to ask what the hell had gone wrong, why Oliver had ended up on death's door from a treatment that had been supposed to *save* his life, not try to end it. But the rioting possessiveness of his alpha was too busy trying to convince Jet to toss away the sheet that was still wrapped around his waist and mount his omega, hard and fast, and it was all Jet could do to keep the warring halves of himself in check.

"What do we do now?" he asked, and that single question was about as coherent as he was likely to get.

Sullivan gave him a long, weighty stare. "I would suggest you lie down next to him. It'll probably do him good to be able to smell your scent... and I have a feeling it might keep you a little calmer, as well."

CHAPTER TWENTY-THREE

OLIVER

Clawing his way up through a thick fog, Oliver came to slowly, feeling like he'd just been run over by a bus. There was a warm, musky scent near his nose, entirely delicious and oddly familiar, though he couldn't quite place where he'd smelled it before. He snuggled closer, enticed by the promise of something wonderful, though it felt like a colossal effort to move even that inch or two.

What had he been doing, he wondered? He couldn't even remember what day of the week it was right now, though he also had the odd feeling that he'd been in the middle of something important.

Something warm touched his shoulder, a gentle, rhythmic stroke running up and down his arm, and he moaned a little at the sensation. That felt nice, so much better than the rough, burning sensation further down his body.

"Hey, buddy," a gentle, soothing voice addressed him. "You coming back to us now?"

Oliver hummed a little, taking a deep breath and letting it out on a sigh. He felt a hand brush his hair back from his face, which made him smile a fraction.

"Come on, Oliver," the voice prodded at him. "Wake up. Let me see those gorgeous green eyes."

Impulsively, Oliver refused, snuggling his face deeper into the pillow and tossing an arm over whoever it was that was lying beside him. *Jet*, his foggy memory supplied. *Your alpha*. His skin was smooth and warm beneath Oliver's arm, both of them naked, and…

Naked?

Oliver woke in a rush, jerking away from the body beside him. Holy fuck, he was naked, and there was another man in the room, sitting on a chair by the bed, watching him and Jet, and he tried to scramble away in absolute terror, convinced he was about to be gang-mated by a group of randy alphas -

"Hey, easy, *easy!*" Jet grabbed onto him, forcefully holding him still, and Oliver was dismayed to realise he felt as weak as a newborn kitten. "No one's hurting you," Jet murmured in his ear. "You're totally fine. This is Sullivan Kennedy. You remember Doctor Kennedy?"

What? He groped around for his glasses, grateful when Jet pressed them into his hand, and then the room came into focus. "Doctor Kennedy," he managed to say, finally recognising the man. "I'm sorry, I didn't realise. I'm…" Naked? Aching? Too confused to even try to figure out what was going on?

Thankfully, Jet seemed to catch onto his embarrassment and tossed the corner of a sheet over his lower half. "The suppository didn't work," he said, by way of an explanation for Oliver's current state. "You were seriously overheated. We've just spent the past five hours trying to save your life."

There was an ice pack tucked up against his side, he realised, now warm and liquidy. "What happened?"

"I'm not entirely sure at the moment," Sullivan answered the question. "My initial guess is that you had some sort of allergic reaction to the suppository. Thank God Jet thought to come and check on you."

A sudden memory flashed into Oliver's mind. "I tried to phone you," he told Jet, twisting around to look at him.

"Yeah. About eleven times," Jet confirmed. "And bloody well done, by the way. You managed to save your own life with that one."

"How are you feeling now?" Sullivan asked. "Your temperature's down to thirty-nine. What about other symptoms? Headache? Cramps?"

"I feel rather sore all over, to be perfectly honest," Oliver said. "And dreadfully tired." His ass felt like someone had shoved a hot poker up there, but he hardly thought it appropriate to mention that particular detail. "Am I still in heat?"

Sullivan nodded. "You've only been going for about twelve hours so far. Jet will have to stay with you for the rest of it. Suffice to say we won't be using the suppositories again. Or at least not until I can get a firm answer on what went wrong. I'm so sorry, Oliver. I had no idea this sort of reaction was a possibility… I feel dreadful for letting you suffer like this. I wouldn't blame you if you decided you wanted to drop out of the trial."

Oliver shook his head, feeling dazed. "I don't know. Right now I don't really want to make any decisions on anything. I just want to go back to sleep."

"That's perfectly understandable. Let me get my things together and I'll leave you in peace. If you start feeling worse, though, don't hesitate to give me a call."

Sullivan left a few minutes later, the front door closing with a gentle thud, leaving Oliver alone with Jet. With a very *naked* Jet.

Oliver looked around the room, as if searching for something that would explain their current predicament, as well as avoiding looking at the very toned and tanned chest sitting opposite him. His brain wasn't functioning particularly efficiently, and it took a moment to find the words to express himself. "Why are we naked?" he asked finally, finding no rational explanation by staring at the carpet or peering at the curtains. "Well, okay, I know why *I'm* naked. But why are you?"

"It's kind of a long story." Jet moved to the edge of the bed, looking for something to cover himself with. There was a spare sheet, tossed to the floor in Oliver's earlier thrashing about, so he picked it up and wrapped it around his waist, leaving Oliver with the other. "The short version is that you were seriously overheated but your scent was off, so I had to try and come up with the goods..." He made a crude hand gesture by way of explanation. "...and that ended up with nakedness and swearing and me threatening to punch Sullivan's lights out."

"Goodness! Why on earth would you do that?"

"Something about your scent hijacked my brain and turned me into a Neanderthal?" Jet hazarded a guess. "Seriously, I just kind of lose the plot when I'm around you."

"I'm sorry."

"Not your fault," Jet reminded him. "None of this is your fault."

Oliver shuffled backwards on the bed, propping a couple of pillows against the headboard so he could lean against them. They smelled of Jet, he noted in passing, and the scent was comforting.

There were still lingering questions, though, and one in particular needed answering, though Oliver wasn't sure how to ask it. "Did we, um... I'm sorry, I don't think there's a delicate way to ask this. Did we... have sex?" It was the natural conclusion to reach, he supposed, given that he was in heat and they were both naked.

But the shocked look on Jet's face made him suddenly wish he hadn't asked. "What? What the fuck, man? No! You seriously think I'd fuck you while you were unconscious?"

"I think – I hope – that you would do whatever was necessary in order to save my life."

"We have a perfectly serviceable method already," Jet snapped at him. "And for fuck's sake, Sullivan was here pretty much the whole time. You think I want to do it in front of an audience?"

"In my defence," Oliver said, "I was unconscious. I have very little idea of what happened while I was out."

Jet calmed down immediately, instantly contrite. "Yeah. Sorry, man. It's just… it's been a hectic couple of hours, you know?" He let out a long sigh, scrubbing a hand through hair that was already unkempt.

"Thank you for coming," Oliver murmured, staring at the sheet. "If you hadn't I…"

"I don't want to think about what would have happened if I hadn't," Jet interrupted him. "But speaking of things necessary to save your life, I kind of… broke one of your back windows. Your doors were locked and there was no other way in. I'll board it up today then I'll pay for it to be repaired."

"Nonsense," Oliver objected. "I'll pay for it. You were saving my life, after all."

"No, seriously, I'll pay for it."

Oliver sighed, too exhausted to bother with a full-blown argument. "I'll split it with you then," he said, an easy compromise that wouldn't weigh on his conscience too much.

"Fine," Jet agreed.

They sat in silence for a while, until Oliver felt a new flush of warmth. He was experiencing none of the usual arousal that came with a heat, his body too sore and worn out to care, but the biochemical reactions still needed to be managed.

"Sorry, Jet," he said, getting the other man's attention. "Would I be able to trouble you for…?"

"For?"

Oliver waved his hand vaguely at the cup on the nightstand. "For another dose?"

"Oh! Yeah. Sure." Jet stood up, grabbing the cup. He took two steps towards the door… then stopped.

"Is there a problem?" Oliver asked. Jet had said his scent was off. Perhaps that was the issue? "Do you need to smell my neck?" he offered, too tired to bother worrying about how crude the invitation was. There was a strange look on Jet's face, and Oliver was vaguely reminded of the time they'd run into that strange alpha in the parking lot.

"No," Jet said, not sounding terribly certain about it. "No, I'm good." A quick peek at his waist region confirmed that he was indeed 'good', the sheet tenting in front of him. Jet turned to leave again, then huffed out a frustrated breath. "Fuck. No, I…" He leaned on the doorframe, facing away from Oliver. "Shit…"

"What is it?" Oliver asked. "Whatever it is, you can tell me. We've come far enough that I think we can deal with a few indelicacies." Maybe it was the tiredness talking. Maybe it was his brush with death making him reckless, though at some level he was aware that he hadn't yet processed the fact that he'd nearly died. Maybe it was just the culmination of four years of intimacy, and the odd friendship that had grown out of it.

"I said before that being near you tends to make me a little crazy," Jet said, turning around. "What happened today was the scariest thing that's ever happened to me. I seriously thought I was going to lose you. So here's the thing…" He looked around, his face flushing pink. "I don't think I'm actually capable of leaving the room right now. I've just got this mad, crazy need to look after you, and some part of me is convinced that if I leave the room, you're going to suddenly drop dead."

His concern was touching, if a little misguided. "I assure you, I'm fine," Oliver said. "You don't have to go far. Just close the door and stay in the hall if you wish." With a good dose of omega pheromones, it never took Jet long to come back with a sample.

Jet glanced out the door, took half a step towards it, then shook his head. As he waited, Oliver felt his temperature rise another notch. It was becoming uncomfortably warm to stay wrapped up even beneath only a single sheet. "I can't," Jet said. "It's like when I wanted to deck Sullivan. Rationally, I know he's a doctor, and he was here to save your life, but instinctively, I just had to get him away from you." He glanced at the door again. "I know it makes no sense, but I physically cannot leave the room right now."

His own mind wasn't working terribly well at the moment either, Oliver acknowledged to himself. What he really wanted to do was curl up next to Jet in bed, both of them naked, and sleep with his head on Jet's chest, listening to the deep thud of his heartbeat. But Jet would think him entirely ridiculous if he dared suggest such a thing. There was nothing soft or romantic about Jet. He was all about action, and bluntness, and reckless abandon.

Maybe, though, that very recklessness would do them both a favour here.

"Come here," Oliver suggested, throwing caution to the wind as he held out his hand. He needed that dose one way or another, and he was beyond caring how he got it. Jet came without protest. "Up here," Oliver said, patting the bed beside him.

"Why?" Jet asked, kneeling on the bed, then shuffling closer at Oliver's encouragement. "What do you… Oh shit, what are you doing?" he yelped, as Oliver began to unwind the sheet around his waist.

"Do you want me to stop?" Oliver asked, his hands instantly stilling. Consent was important, after all, and Jet had always been extremely diligent in sticking to exactly what Oliver had agreed to, and not a fraction more.

"Hell, no," Jet said, his voice suddenly husky. His hips swung forward as if asking for attention. "I just don't want you doing anything you don't want to do. And if you're counting on me stopping you, I really think I'm beyond that this time." His eyes seemed a touch unfocused, hands gripping the sheet spasmodically.

"Kneel down," Oliver said, guiding him to sit back on his own feet. "I promise, you're not taking any liberties with my virtue." Was he going to regret this in the morning, he wondered? It was far more daring than anything he'd done to date. How would it change their relationship? Would Jet expect him to do this again, next time?

And if he did, would Oliver actually object?

Unwinding the sheet, he ran a hand up Jet's back, encouraging him to lean forward, resting his head on Oliver's shoulder. In that position, he would be getting a potent dose of omega pheromones, which should hopefully make this whole process a little less awkward. Though Oliver had no desire to manipulate him, this would be easier if Jet was too distracted to argue. Jet moaned, his arm coming up to drape itself over Oliver's shoulder, his fingers toying with Oliver's hair.

Oliver took the cup from Jet's limp fingers, then reached forward, finding his erection by feel. As he wrapped his hand around it, his eyes opened wide, though he made sure he didn't react physically, not wanting to disturb Jet. Holy hell, he was big! Oliver had known that, of course, having seen the bulge in his pants often enough, but he could barely wrap his fingers around it. In fact, he thought distractedly, he was almost as big as that damned phallus Jet had bought for him all those years ago. Despite a lingering curiosity, he'd never worked up the courage to use the thing, intimidated by its size, and he'd never been quite brave enough to go and buy a smaller one to test things out.

Jet moaned against his skin, and to Oliver's surprise, it took only two quick strokes to have him climaxing into the cup, his hips bucking against Oliver's hand. Seriously? He'd known the pheromones were potent – they'd have to be to have Jet going at it twenty times in two days – but he'd never realised just how effective they really were.

Mission accomplished, he let go of Jet and went to move back, but Jet's arm tightened around his shoulder, and he felt him nuzzle his neck. "No, please... please, Oliver, do that again. I can't..." He moaned again, his breath panting against Oliver's neck in heated puffs.

"Are you sure?" Oliver didn't want to cross any lines – if he hadn't already done so.

"Yes! You smell so fucking good..." Jet reached down and took Oliver's hand, pressing it back against his erection. The thing hadn't decreased in size the slightest bit, Jet's recovery time apparently non-existent. "Stroke me. Please..."

It took less than thirty seconds for Jet to climax again, and afterwards, he was still rock hard. Was this what it was like for him during every heat?

Oliver's sex drive was heightened during his cycle, but he, at least, got an hour or two of relief in between climaxes. By contrast, Jet seemed to be in a permanent state of arousal, and Oliver suddenly felt like a total ass. How had he not even noticed Jet's discomfort? And more importantly, how had Jet managed to cope with a raging hard-on, for two full days every time?

Without really thinking about it, Oliver kept up the steady rhythm of his hand. He thought about putting a bit more effort into it, maybe stroking a thumb over the head, or rubbing his balls – any of the things he did to himself that he enjoyed – but Jet didn't seem to need the slightest encouragement. He rocked his hips into Oliver's hand, making contented little noises… and then Oliver froze suddenly, as he felt Jet give a tentative lick to his scent gland.

At Oliver's sudden immobility, Jet tensed. He pulled back quickly. "Sorry," he muttered, pulling away. "I shouldn't have done that." Oliver was too stunned to answer, that single, cautious swipe of his tongue seeming far more intimate than wrapping his hand around another man's penis. "I'm sorry," Jet said again, when Oliver didn't respond. "Fuck, I'm really sorry…"

"It was a perfectly reasonable thing to do," Oliver said, his voice sounding robotic even to himself. "My neck was right there, and I'm the one who got you to put your head there."

Jet had scrambled off the bed, and he was still standing there completely naked. In a rush, he seemed to realise that fact, and he grabbed the sheet off the floor. His face looked a touch pale, and he seemed unable to look Oliver in the eye. His erection was still there, as hard and eager as ever, and Oliver had been fairly sure he'd been on the verge of climaxing before he'd so foolishly interrupted them both.

Jet spotted the cup, still dangling from Oliver's fingers. "Um… do you need a hand with that? Or do you want to… I could turn around, if you like. I dunno how I'm going to go with the whole leaving the room thing…"

"Actually, I might… If you don't mind, I could probably use your help," Oliver admitted. "Everything's rather sore at the moment, and… but only if you don't mind."

"I'm game," Jet said, his hands shaking just slightly as he took the cup from Oliver. Maybe when this part was done, Oliver could find the courage to help him out a couple more times? Maybe.

Oliver rolled over onto his front, lying passively as Jet administered the two doses in the cup. He winced slightly as the dropper went in, his ass still sore and throbbing, but Jet was as gentle as possible, and a moment later it was done. Oliver rolled over again, tugging the sheet up over his lower half.

"How are you feeling?" Jet asked, sitting down on the edge of the bed.

"Tired. I might just have a nap, if that's okay."

Jet shrugged. "Hey, whatever you like. Do you need anything? Food? Water? Painkillers?"

"No, I'm fine. Just sleep." He settled down in the bed, tugging the sheet up... then he immediately pushed it off, too hot and sticky. He wanted a shower, but didn't have the energy to get out of bed. He turned over onto his right side, forcing himself to lie still. He heard Jet sit down on a chair, and something about that annoyed him. Not because Jet was disturbing him in any way, but because there was just something *wrong* about it.

He turned over onto his left side. The room was too light, though the curtains were still closed. The sun would have been up by now, light seeping in around the edges. His eyes were too sensitive, watering slightly even in the dim light. The ceiling fan was making a faint click-click sound as it spun around, yet another annoyance, though he didn't want to turn it off, knowing he'd be too hot in a few minutes.

"You okay?" Jet asked, and Oliver nodded.

"Fine. Just a little sore." He closed his eyes, deliberately evening out his breathing.

The memory of Jet moaning against his neck echoed in his mind, making him tense. His cock made a half-hearted effort at joining the party, then swelled further as he wondered what it would have been like if he'd had the courage to ask Jet to return the favour...

He opened his eyes, seeing the man sitting there, half-naked in just a sheet, arms folded across his chest as he watched Oliver. He was absolutely exhausted, but sleep seemed an elusive goal.

Maybe... Maybe it wouldn't be unreasonable to... Jet had already said his pheromones were playing havoc with his mind. Perhaps Oliver could claim the same thing, if Jet turned him down. Just say his hormones were playing up, and think no more of it. Maybe, with his head all in the clouds, Jet might actually *want* to...

"Lie next to me?" Oliver asked, before he could think better of it. "I just... want to be near you..."

For a second or two – two seconds that seemed to last an eternity – Jet didn't move. Then he stood up, stiffly, moving like an eighty-year old man. He sank down onto the bed, easing back onto one elbow, the other hand rising to stroke a slow, tender trail across Oliver's cheek. He didn't move, not brave enough to ask for more, terrified that he'd scare Jet away.

But then Jet lay down properly and nudged Oliver to sit up a fraction. He slid his arm beneath Oliver's shoulder, pulling him over so his cheek rested against Jet's chest. The rhythmic thud-thud of his heart echoed just beneath Oliver's ear. He made himself relax, not wanting to ruin the moment by getting all tense and chasing Jet off again.

Two minutes later, he was sound asleep.

CHAPTER TWENTY-FOUR

JET

Three days later, Jet was once more seated in Oliver's living room. Oliver was beside him on the sofa, looking decidedly cosy in sweatpants and a worn t-shirt, while Sullivan had taken the armchair. Oliver had been on strict bed rest since his reaction a few days ago, and today was the first time he'd managed to get out of bed to shower and dress.

"Okay, level with me," Jet said, opening the conversation. Sullivan had arrived ten minutes ago, and at Oliver's request, Jet had prepared the requisite offering of coffee. "What the hell went wrong?" The rest of the heat had passed without incident – if you didn't count the pair of them snuggling on the bed like a pair of kittens an *incident*.

"Firstly," Sullivan began, "let me offer you my sincerest apologies. I had absolutely no idea that Oliver was likely to have that sort of reaction to the suppository. In hindsight, I should have been monitoring him far more closely. I suppose I just got overexcited about the progress we'd made. Very unprofessional of me."

But Oliver shook his head. "Omega physiology is extremely poorly understood, and you've made a wonderful effort in trying to improve that situation. There are bound to be a few hiccups along the way, and I don't hold that against you for a moment. But I am curious to know what caused it. And if it can be prevented in the future."

"I've spoken to a number of my colleagues," Sullivan said, "and we've put together a theory on why your body reacted the way it did. And in support of that theory, I would like to ask you, Jet, to perform a small experiment for me. Nothing dangerous. Just open the lid," he instructed, handing Jet a small vial with a few drops of liquid in the bottom. "Smell this and tell me what it smells like."

Jet raised an eyebrow at the odd request, but nonetheless he took the vial and took a cautious sniff…

"Holy hell, that's disgusting! What the hell is that?"

"What does it smell like?" Sullivan asked first.

Jet wrinkled his nose. "It's like… mould. Something damp, like rotting wood, maybe?"

"Hmm." Sullivan took the vial back and put it away. "That, my friend, is two drops of sweat from an omega in heat."

Jet's first reaction was to glance at Oliver. The man looked as confused as he felt. "An omega in heat? No way. That thing smelled like swamp water!"

"Which very much confirms my theory. How long have the two of you been partnered up for Oliver's heats?"

"Getting on for four years, I guess?"

"And neither of you have had any other partners in that time?"

"No. At least, I haven't."

"Neither have I," Oliver confirmed.

"What has apparently happened," Sullivan explained, "is that your respective physiologies have somehow attuned themselves to each other. Neither of you is now capable of responding to an alpha or an omega who is not your bonded partner. The suppository contained proteins from a foreign alpha, and Oliver's body therefore rejected them. That triggered a serious allergic reaction, resulting in the symptoms we saw – elevated temperature, inflammation at the site of contact, all the usual effects in a Caloren's omega of low blood pressure, migraine, cramping of the internal organs. Once again, I'm deeply sorry for the oversight, Oliver. Bonding between a mated pair – I'm sorry, I know you don't like the term, but it's the most accurate one, medically speaking – had been theorised in the literature, but no one has actually witnessed such a reaction in any medical context in at least the last fifty years. As unpleasant as it was for you to experience this personally, this discovery has actually thrust our research ahead in leaps and bounds."

"So, what does this actually mean for Oliver?" Jet interrupted, before Sullivan could wander off on some medical tangent. "What happens the next time he has a heat?"

"What it means is that Oliver cannot be exposed to the bodily fluids of any alpha other than yourself. The suppositories are no longer an option. The best you can do from here on is continue the methods you've developed amongst yourselves."

A heavy silence filled the room.

"So… there are no other options for…" Jet wasn't quite able to finish the thought. "I mean, the whole point of this was to find a way for Oliver to be independent. We were going to apply for emancipation."

"I sincerely apologise, to both of you. I know it's not an easy thing to hear, but based on my current research, there's really nothing more I can do."

After performing another physical on Oliver, just to make sure he was recovering adequately, and then apologising another five or six times, Sullivan bade them farewell.

Oliver was silent, swirling the remains of his coffee in the bottom of the cup. Jet sat motionless on the sofa, his mind in turmoil.

So... they were stuck with each other. Telling Oliver to go find another alpha would have been heartless before, but if Oliver had wanted out, he could have chosen to leave. Now, that option would literally kill him.

Jet didn't know what to say. The only thing that would be even remotely useful would be to reiterate his previous promise to keep helping Oliver for as long as he needed it, but he was worried that that would only shove the unpleasant truth in his face again. No matter what he did from here on, he would always be tied to an alpha. It was the worst possible outcome he could have imagined, and Jet was at a loss for anything to say that would be even remotely welcome.

Perhaps he should offer to leave? But Oliver was still recovering, and though he seemed a lot better today, Sullivan had said he should keep watching him for another twenty-four hours, just to be sure.

"Do you want a drink?" Jet said finally, and Oliver looked up in surprise.

"Shit, yes."

Jet fetched them two glasses of whisky, with two large cubes of ice in each. He handed one to Oliver, then took a seat again, the only sounds in the room the soft rustle of clothing as one of them shifted position, or the faint clink of ice against glass.

Finally, the silence became too much. "You know, everything I said before still stands," Jet told Oliver. "I'll keep giving you as much freedom as I possibly can. I'm still going to be -" He trailed off as Oliver held up his hand to stop him.

"I'm sorry," he said, avoiding Jet's gaze. "But I... I don't want to talk about it."

CHAPTER TWENTY-FIVE

CYCLE SIXTEEN
JET

Eleven weeks after Sullivan's disastrous news, Jet's phone beeped as he was scrubbing his shower. He squeezed out of the stall and wiped his hands on a towel, then checked the message.

It was from Oliver. Odd. His heat wasn't due for another two weeks. Had it come early? He pulled up the message. *Wondering if you're free for dinner tonight? Got something to discuss. Don't worry, I don't need any babysitting services right now.*

Aside from that one skydiving trip, neither of them had ever suggested meeting up outside of their three-monthly appointment in the whole four years they'd been together – Jet, because he hadn't wanted to impose on Oliver's time, and Oliver, he assumed, because he simply hadn't been interested. So why now?

I'm free, he texted back. *Where? Out or at your place?*

My place, the reply came back quickly. *Best not to discuss in public. I'll cook something nice. Come at 7.*

So presumably, given the need for privacy, it was something to do with his heats. But why couldn't he just wait until the next one started, and say whatever it was then?

But... hang on... Oliver was going to cook for him? The idea seemed oddly intimate. In the past, they'd each either grabbed whatever was at hand, or on the odd occasion that he'd had the energy, Jet had cooked something simple; an omelette or some fried eggs, just to tide them over until the next wave of the heat hit.

It was only 10:30 in the morning, and for once, Jet resented Oliver's tendency to plan everything in advance. Now he'd have the entire damn day to wonder what the man was going to say.

At two minutes past seven, Jet pulled up at Oliver's house, feeling decidedly odd. Despite the lack of pheromones, the simple act of arriving here triggered what was by now an ingrained response. His heart rate had sped up a notch, while his cock was taking an unwelcome interest in things, and Jet had to keep picturing his grandmother doing a strip tease to get the thing to sit down and shut up.

He knocked on the door, then opened it when he heard a faint 'come in' from the depths of the house.

"Wow, that smells good," he said, arriving in the kitchen. Oliver was standing at the kitchen counter, stirring a dish of something creamy, with the scent of garlic and chives lingering in the kitchen.

But instead of saying hello, Oliver burst out laughing. "Nice to know some things never change." Jet didn't quite get the joke, and he said so. "That's pretty much the same thing you say every time you come to my house," Oliver pointed out, and Jet let out a snort, seeing the funny side. After the news they'd received last time, they hadn't really discussed the long-term implications of their arrangement, and it was nice to know that Oliver had reached a point where he could joke about it.

"How's work been going?" Jet asked. They hadn't seen each other in weeks, and didn't tend to cross paths at the ISA base very often. He peered over Oliver's shoulder, seeing chopped mushrooms, onion and bacon frying in a pan. Sneaky fingers attempted to steal a sliver of bacon, only to be slapped away by Oliver.

"Same old, same old," Oliver said, tossing a handful of cheese into the sauce. "The rocket launch is in three weeks, and they found an issue with the bacterial incubation chamber, so the head of engineering has been throwing tantrums all week. It's not going to be a problem," he added negligently, and Jet figured he would have to be pretty confident to be so unconcerned about an engineering flaw. "They just need to reinforce the rubber seal to maintain the air pressure, but Phillip's having kittens over it and refusing to listen to good sense. We're giving him the weekend to calm down, then the rest of us will gang up on him on Monday."

"So that's how you engineers roll, huh? Find the weakest member of the group and pounce?"

Oliver shrugged, shooting a sly grin over his shoulder. "Whatever works."

He seemed to be in an awfully good mood, given what had happened the last time they'd seen each other, and in an oddly macabre moment, Jet wondered if he'd decided to just throw in the towel and commit suicide. He'd read somewhere, many years before, that people under extreme stress could actually seem to improve shortly before killing themselves. Something to do with the relief of having made a decision.

But if that was the case, he reassured himself hastily, then surely Oliver wouldn't have dragged him over here to tell him about it?

Helping himself to a beer out of the fridge – Oliver had told him repeatedly in the past to make himself at home – Jet leaned against the counter and waited while Oliver put the finishing touches on the meal. He drained steaming pasta into a sieve, then mixed in the bacon and mushrooms from the frying pan. Finally, he poured the sauce he'd prepared over the top and followed it up with some hasty stirring.

"Fettucine carbonara," Oliver announced, setting two bowls on the dining table, along with a dish of parmesan cheese and two side plates of salad. "One of my favourite dishes."

"Wow. This is amazing," Jet said, taking a seat. "You know, you always said you could cook, but I've never actually seen you do it before."

"I've got to keep some secrets," Oliver replied with a quirk of one elegant eyebrow. "After all, you've seen my naked ass. There must be some limits to the things you get to know about me."

It was flirting, and it wasn't. In some ways, they'd both become too comfortable with each other, even with their forced intimacy. They both knew where the boundaries were and rarely, if ever, stepped over the line. But that very level of comfort also made it all the more shocking when one of them did decided to push the limits. Jet had still not quite recovered from having Oliver casually offer to jerk him off during his last heat. Nor from the pleasure of it actually happening…

Grandma in high heels. Grandma in a thong. Grandma swinging around a pole… Come on Wilder, get your head together.

"So, as I mentioned in my text message, there's something I wanted to talk about," Oliver said, making a point of twirling his fettucine around his fork.

"Hit me," Jet said. He shoved a forkful of pasta into his mouth and had to close his eyes, moaning in bliss as the flavour hit his tongue. "God, Oliver, this is sinful."

"Just an old family recipe," Oliver said modestly.

"Sorry, you were saying?" Jet said, kicking himself for interrupting. He was desperate to know what the hell had been important enough to drag him all the way over here.

"I've been doing some thinking," Oliver explained. "After what Sullivan said last time, I realised I needed to… readjust my expectations." Uh oh. That sounded ominous. "Not of you, necessarily – you've been an absolute godsend. But of my life in general. Future goals, relationships, family. Any major decisions have to include you now. I can't just wake up one day and decide I want to move across the country. Or, on the other side of that equation, if you come to me and say *you* want to move across the country, I have to be willing to seriously consider it."

It all sounded like sane, reasonable, logical things to say. So why did Jet have a gut feeling this was about to take a dive off a very high cliff?

"Relationships are a part of that whole equation," Oliver went on. "We have quite an unusual arrangement. It takes me a long time to build this level of trust with someone, and I can't see myself starting a relationship with anyone else for as long as we're involved." *Involved* was a good word for it. They weren't *together*, as such, they certainly weren't *dating*. But their lives were inextricably linked. "But the same doesn't necessarily apply to you. Given that we're not sleeping together, it's not unreasonable for you to want to date someone else. So that's my first question for you: do you see that happening, and if so, how would you approach the situation?"

Jet was sitting as still as a statue. He forced himself to chew his mouthful, then swallow, his mind racing the whole time. He took a swallow of beer, then chose his words carefully. "It goes without saying that I'll always put you first, regardless of any other relationship. When your heat hits, I'm here, no questions asked. But aside from that…" He paused, trying to figure out what he really wanted to say. The memory sprang up again, of Oliver's hand wrapped around his cock, Oliver's scent in his nose…

"The honest answer is that I haven't thought about it. Other relationships, I mean. But we've been together for four years, and in that whole time, I've never seriously considered starting something with anyone else. So that says to me that I'm probably not going to." Damn it, he wanted to feel Oliver's skin against his again. That afternoon they'd spent lying in each other's arms, just resting and murmuring reassurances to each other, had been everything he'd ever dreamed of. How was any other relationship supposed to match that?

But the burning question was would Oliver be willing to do that again? The stress of the day, his near-death experience, Jet's own fears and concerns, had made them both vulnerable. Was it foolish to think they could recreate that when they were just dealing with a run-of-the-mill heat?

Oliver nodded at his hesitant explanation, focusing on his pasta for a moment. Jet toyed with his salad, forcing a forkful into his mouth, just to avoid having to think of anything to say.

"I appreciate your honestly," Oliver said finally. "And in that case, I was wondering… the next time my heat starts, perhaps you'd like to deal with it the old fashioned way?"

With so many thoughts swirling in his mind, Jet couldn't quite figure out what Oliver was trying to say. "The old fashioned way being what, exactly?"

Oliver blinked, looking suddenly awkward. His gaze shot to his glass, his plate, out the window – anywhere except at Jet. "I meant, um… we could… We could… have sex."

Jet stared at him blankly, not quite able to believe what he'd just heard. "I'm sorry, we could what?"

CHAPTER TWENTY-SIX

JET

Oliver sighed. "I was wondering if you might be interested in having sex during my heat."

'Yeah, I thought that's what you said." Jet was suddenly finding it difficult to swallow. "How on earth did you decide that was a good idea?"

Oliver rolled his eyes at him – actually rolled his eyes! "This might be news to you, but I hadn't actually planned on being a virgin for the rest of my life. I'm assuming you're astute enough to have figured out by now that I'm a virgin?" he added sharply.

Helplessly, Jet nodded. "I'd… kind of assumed…"

"Yes. Good. Well, then. I hadn't planned on being one forever. I just hadn't met the right man yet. And now it seems that fate has chosen one for me, so I thought…" The sentence went unfinished.

"If that's the case, then why hasn't this come up before? You've always said -"

"What I said, I said four years ago, when I was being forced to have sex with a man I'd never met before and when I was terrified of losing my entire identity. I'd like to think we've made at least a little progress since then." He was sliding towards sarcasm, which he tended to do when he was upset.

But if Oliver was so damn keen on losing his virginity, why would he be upset about it? "It hasn't escaped my attention," Jet said, managing to sound far calmer than he felt, "that I am literally the last man in the world you can sleep with. Which is not a very flattering position to be in." His body helpfully supplied a vivid memory of what it had felt like to have Oliver's hand wrapped around his dick. "Actually, you know what?" he said, a different idea suddenly striking him. "Maybe you're still able to sleep with a beta. I don't know if they have the whole issue with proteins and allergic reactions... but no, I guess given how you reacted last time, you wouldn't be keen on trying that one out."

"Jet, I don't think -"

"But we could always ask Sullivan. Even if he doesn't know the answer, he can probably find out."

"Jet..."

"Or, wait, here's an idea. You could just use condoms..."

"Jet?"

"...and then the whole bodily fluids thing wouldn't be an issue..."

"Jet!"

"I'm sorry," Jet cut himself off sharply. "I'll shut up now."

The sly smile on Oliver's face did nothing for his equilibrium. "You know, you're really quite charming when you ramble."

"I'll take that as a compliment," Jet said, falling back on sardonic humour, when his entire world seemed to have tilted sideways.

There was a pause, while Oliver took a sip of his wine and Jet simply stared at his fork. "I am *not* trying to talk you into anything you don't want to do," Oliver said. "I'm not trying to manipulate you, I am certainly not dismissing your desires or opinions. But the last time we were together, you seemed enthusiastic about me touching you, so I was simply trying to open up a couple of new options. It doesn't have to be full sex, if you're not into that. We could... I don't know. Some kissing, maybe? Some touching each other? I have to admit, I'm curious."

It was all so calm and rational that Jet was having a hard time remembering why it was a bad idea. At a gut level, it was just so *not Oliver*. He'd spent four years being as skittish as a newborn colt, running away the instant Jet moved towards him, changing the subject the moment they crossed onto a sexual topic, and blushing in embarrassment every time Jet handed him one of those god-forsaken cups.

But as he thought about it more, Oliver's strategy in inviting him here was obvious. After having spent four years getting to know the guy, Jet wondered if Oliver knew he was so predictable. He'd left it long enough since his last heat that Jet was supposed to believe he'd thought the matter over thoroughly, but it was far enough from his next heat that there would be no question of him making impulsive decisions based on hormones. Clever, he thought darkly. A clever manipulation that was designed to be subtle enough that Jet wouldn't see it coming.

"I don't think this is a good idea," he said, resenting having to be the voice of reason yet again. Every time things got out of control, it seemed to be up to him to put the brakes on. "It's not because I don't want to sleep with you. Last time was..." No, he probably shouldn't finish that sentence. "But I don't really believe that's what *you* want. This whole plan is impulsive and irrational. You're upset, and I understand why, but jumping into bed together is -"

"No, impulsive and irrational would be asking you to move in with me," Oliver interrupted him sharply. "And I'm not going to do that. This is simply..." He floundered for words for a moment. "...taking the opportunity to experience something that I otherwise couldn't."

"Then why are you suddenly coming up with this idea after we've been told we've apparently *bonded* with each other? If it was pure curiosity, we could have done it a year ago. Two years ago, even! How long do you need to know someone before you decide whether you're attracted to them or not?"

"Well, I'm certain that for me, it would be longer than it is for you," Oliver snapped.

"Ooh, burn!" Jet mocked him. "Yeah, you know what, I've fucked people before. And been fucked by them. But you can't make me regret that, because I went into every one of those relationships with my eyes wide open, whereas I feel like all you're doing here is trying to pull the wool over my eyes. Whether it's a long-term or a short-term thing, I like honesty in my partners. So until you give me that, the answer is no."

The look on Oliver's face was one Jet had never seen before. There was no shame at having been called out, no embarrassment at the crude way Jet had spoken. Instead there was a dark shadow, like a foreign being had taken up residence behind Oliver's eyes.

"You want honesty?" he said darkly, and Jet suddenly regretted his impulsive words. "Then here's some honesty for you. My life was taken away from me the instant I had that first pin-prick gender test as a minute-old baby. I have worked my ass off, not to become someone special or elite, but just to be considered a *human being* by the rest of the planet. And then just when I think I've actually made something of my life, some screwed up quirk of biology and a bunch of archaic laws means that I get to lose it all again, unless some random stud takes pity on me because he likes the way my ass looks wrapped in tight denim. And now I know that there is absolutely *nothing* I can do to change any of that." Jet was shocked, almost as much by Oliver's anger as he was by the bitterness in his words. Aside from a few brief instances when he'd been addled on hormones, he'd never seen Oliver lose his temper before.

"So here's where I'm at. I want to know what it's like to have sex. And I want to do it with someone that I trust at least enough to know they're not going to steal my wallet and run off in the middle of the night while I'm sleeping. And given the absolute dog's breakfast of a hand I was served by life, or fate, or whatever the hell you want to call it, that means that you, Mr Wilder, are my one and only option."

As he'd already told Oliver, the assessment of the situation was not a flattering one. But it was tempting. So very, very tempting…

"I, for one," Oliver went on, his rant gathering steam now, "am tired of pleasuring myself in my bedroom and pretending I'm not picturing how big your penis is or how it would feel to have your mouth sucking on me. Is that honest enough for you? Have I shocked you yet? Would you believe me if I told you that yes, I do actually feel aroused when my hormonal cycle sends my body into a biochemical horror-show that could kill me if I miscalculate what day I'm due?

"So my offer stands, Jet. The next time you walk through that door and get punched in the face with a wave of pheromones so powerful they could knock out an elephant, do you want to keep hiding in the spare room jerking off to a mental image of my ass, or do you want to come into my bedroom and find out what the reality's like? You've got just under two weeks to make a decision. Think hard."

That, right there, was the last part of the plan, a trap set so well that Jet had never had a chance of escaping it. Oliver had given him enough time before his heat to have a good, long think about his request, to remember just what it felt like to spend forty-eight hours with a raging hard-on, to envisage every wayward fantasy he'd ever had about Oliver, and to talk himself into, and out of, and back into the idea that it wouldn't be such a bad thing to dip his toes into the well of desire that was Oliver Levy.

Well played, my friend, Jet thought, knowing his defeat was all but secured. *Well played.*

CHAPTER TWENTY-SEVEN

JET

Two weeks later, Jet stood awkwardly in Oliver's living room, watching Oliver fumble and blush his way through an apology. He'd arrived here just moments ago, and Oliver hadn't even waited until he'd put his bag down to launch into what sounded like a rehearsed speech.

"You were right," Oliver was saying, while Jet slung the strap of his bag off his shoulder and let it thump down onto the floor. "I was upset. I still am, in some ways, but there was no reason for me to take that out on you. So I apologise unreservedly for snapping at you and for making you uncomfortable. It was never my intention, and I hope you can forgive me."

"Yeah, man. Look, it's cool," Jet said dismissively. "You've got a lot going on, and I'm not the type to hold a grudge. So let's just move on, okay?"

In all honesty, Jet didn't quite know what to make of all this. Oliver had apologised for losing his temper... but not for suggesting they have sex in the first place. Was he just too embarrassed to even mention it? Or was he actually retracting his offer? Jet had worked himself into a bundle of nerves before coming here, entirely uncertain about what to expect. It was equally likely for Oliver to be determined to follow through with his intention to sleep with Jet as it was for him to have changed his mind and want him to forget all about it.

But there was a set of plastic cups sitting on the coffee table, and Jet decided to take that as his cue. He gestured to them vaguely. "Do you want me to...?"

Oliver nodded. "Yes. If you wouldn't mind."

Right. Well, that answered that question, at least. Jet took one and disappeared into the spare bedroom. He wasn't sure if he should be feeling relieved or disappointed about Oliver's apparent change of heart, but either way, the scent in the room was still working its magic, so he unzipped his pants and got to work on providing the first couple of doses. His erection was hard and ready, and he sat on the edge of the bed, stroking himself lazily, closing his eyes as pleasure pooled in his groin.

What was Oliver doing right now? Was he just standing there in the living room waiting? Or had he scampered off to the kitchen to make the customary offering of coffee?

Or perhaps he was picturing what Jet was doing. In his tempestuous rant, he'd admitted to imagining what Jet looked like naked while he took care of relieving his own arousal. Was he standing outside the door, listening to Jet's breathing, waiting for the moan that signalled his climax?

The image of Oliver naked had haunted him for the past two weeks. Oliver had said he'd fantasised about Jet's mouth on his cock, and Jet couldn't help wonder what other erotic gems were floating around in his mind. Had he pictured them both in bed together? Their hands on each other as they jerked each other off? Had he imagined how it would feel if they actually had sex? Which position would he prefer? Given that Oliver was a virgin, Jet wasn't expecting it to be anything too adventurous, but he'd had plenty of fantasies himself, the image burned into his mind of Oliver on his knees on the bed, hands gripping the headboard as Jet entered him from behind.

He climaxed a moment later, a harsh gasp escaping him as his essence hit the bottom of the cup.

What about if Jet was sitting in the armchair in the living room, Oliver climbing up on top of him, knees resting on the cushions as he settled himself down over Jet's cock? Jet let himself fall back onto the bed, his hips bucking into his own hand at the mental image. Oliver would rock his hips against him, and Jet could all but feel the slick heat of his passage, sliding back and forth. Oliver's eyes would be closed in pleasure, his hands gripping the back of the seat to keep himself steady.

Or what about in the bathroom, both of them dripping wet after a shower? The shower stall itself wasn't really big enough for too much vigorous activity, but he could picture Oliver bent over the sink, their eyes meeting in the mirror as Jet fucked him from behind, slow and deep...

He cursed as he came again, frustration building as the second climax did absolutely nothing to take the edge off his raging arousal. Why had nature designed them this way, he wondered as he shifted around, making himself more comfortable against the pillow. While Oliver had admitted to being aroused, he seemed to suffer a far less potent version of it than Jet was subject to. Based on long observation – and a bit of guesswork, given the few telling comments he'd made – Oliver seemed ready to go at it once every two hours or so, while Jet could have happily climaxed every five minutes, given half a chance.

He flipped over onto his front, then rose to his knees. He rested his forehead on the headboard, one hand still stroking himself while the other held the cup ready. But in his mind, instead of thrusting into his own hand, he was buried in Oliver's body, his slick walls spasming around him while Jet's arm was around Oliver's waist, their bodies pressed together from shoulder to hip.

This time when he climaxed, he cursed not only his own body, but fate itself, and Anderson, for introducing them, and his father, for causing him to develop these unrealistic ideals of an alpha's behaviours, and his own damning lack of foresight, right back when he'd first met Oliver all those years ago. Why the hell had he been thrown into this accursed arrangement, temptation dangling just beyond his reach while his body betrayed him at every turn?

It was only the knowledge that Oliver was waiting for him urgently outside the door that forced him not to keep going, instead clambering off the bed and fastening his pants.

He was breathing hard as he re-entered the living room, finding Oliver sitting rigidly on the sofa. "Here," he said, holding out the cup. "That'll do for a start."

"Thank you," Oliver said, standing up. There was a split-second's hesitation before he took the cup, then he headed off into his own bedroom, and Jet wasn't even going to pretend anymore. He made a beeline for the bathroom, pants around his ankles a moment after the door was shut, climax number four spilling into the toilet bowl. Oliver was at this very moment inside his bedroom, stripping his pants off, revealing that firm, toned ass. Did he get himself off before, or after he administered the doses? Did he take his shirt off? Was he picturing Jet's body at this very moment?

CHAPTER TWENTY-EIGHT

OLIVER

Inside his bedroom, Oliver leaned against the door, letting his head fall back with a thunk. Damn it all. Why hadn't he had the courage to say what he really wanted? The simple answer was that he was too much of a damn coward, taking the easy way out when Jet suggested they use the cups again.

So now, here he was, alone in his bedroom once more while Jet was no doubt jerking off in the bathroom. *You're an idiot*, he cursed himself. A virgin idiot who was likely to remain that way for the rest of his life.

Stepping away from the door, he moved towards the bed, unbuckling his belt as he went. He discarded his pants on the floor, then grabbed the dropper and quickly administered the doses Jet had left in the cup.

Job done, he lay down on his back, staring at the ceiling as he stroked himself. The image sprang to mind of what Jet had looked like, that one time he'd actually dared to touch him. Tanned muscles had shuddered against him as he'd pleasured his alpha, and he replayed the feel of that warm tongue stroking his scent gland. It had felt sublime, sensation trickling down his back and settling in his groin, feather light, but no less compelling for all its ethereal quality. He'd frozen out of pure surprise, not from any kind of shock or disgust, though Jet had understandably taken the action in a negative light. But what might have happened if he hadn't frozen, if he'd instead encouraged the move?

Perhaps he could have tilted his head back, giving Jet better access to his neck? What if he'd kept stroking him, letting him climax a third, or a fourth time? He closed his eyes, imagining how it would have felt if he'd had the courage to take Jet's hand and guide it to his own groin. Jet would have pulled back in surprise, startled eyes seeking confirmation that his touch was welcome... but then he'd have willingly followed through, stroking slowly but firmly, a sultry smile playing over his lips, always making sure to gauge Oliver's reactions. Did he like it faster? Slower? Perhaps a fraction harder?

Yes, to all of the above, Oliver through frantically, his hips bucking into his own hand. Yes to everything, if Jet was the one doing it.

Would they have kissed? Oliver liked to think they would have, then Jet would press him backwards to lie down on the bed, trailing kisses down his chest, until his mouth reached Oliver's groin…

Oliver came on a gasp, feeling hot fluid spurt between his fingers, and he let his legs flop down on the mattress with a sigh. The fantasy was no match for the reality, and he cursed himself again. It had taken him weeks to work up the courage to ask Jet to sleep with him, and then he'd gone and blown it, his fears and anxiety getting the better of him when Jet hadn't responded the way he'd expected.

Gradually, his breath slowed and his heartrate returned to normal. Feeling oddly let down, he got up and went to the bathroom to clean himself up, then reluctantly put his pants back on. But when he went to open the door, he stopped, dreading the idea of having to face Jet again. If only he hadn't made such a damn fuss last time, it might have been easier to brush off the idea to have sex as a whim, or a mere suggestion. But as it was, Jet was almost certainly going to ask him about it at some point. What was he supposed to say? Could he say he still wanted to do it? But if so, then why hadn't he just said so when Jet first arrived today? Maybe he should apologise, not just for yelling at Jet, but for raising his expectations in such an unrealistic manner.

It doesn't have to be unrealistic, a small voice pointed out. He could just walk through that door, tell Jet the option was still open, and see what he had to say.

A strangled sort of laugh bubbled out of his throat, and Oliver sank down onto the bed, letting his head fall into his hands. It was a fantasy, nothing more. And that was what it would ever remain, because he was a damn coward who would never work up the courage to ask for what he really wanted.

Three hours later, Oliver's courage had not returned. His temperature had risen, but he kept putting off the inevitable request for Jet's assistance, caught in an endless inner debate about whether to ask Jet to accompany him into the bedroom, or just accept that damned cup again.

It got to the point that Jet started shooting him worried glances every thirty seconds, no doubt aware of how long it had been since his last dose, and in the end, he decided to just bite the bullet. A light cramp had started up in his abdomen, and if it went on much longer, he'd be suffering from his own indecision in a far more physical way.

"Excuse me, Jet," he said, falling back on manners in the absence of the words to say what he really meant. "Might I trouble you for…" He waved his hand at some vague midpoint between Jet and the cup sitting on the coffee table.

Normally, Jet was quick to respond, and Oliver now knew that it was not so much out of a desire to be helpful as it was a keen urge to go and relieve the ache in his groin. But this time there was a pause, just long enough to make him look twice. Then Jet stood up and picked up the cup. "Yeah. Sure. Be right back."

He was back less than a minute later, and Oliver felt his face flush as he took the cup and excused himself into his bedroom.

It was no better this time than it had been the last. He took care of the necessities quickly, then once more found himself lying half-naked on his bed, contemplating how Jet would react if he stood up, opened the door and asked him to join him in the bedroom.

What had that pause meant? Was it possible that he wanted Oliver to repeat his invitation? Had that been disappointment that had flashed so briefly across his face?

Or perhaps it wasn't disappointment, but rather resentment? He still didn't really know what Jet thought of the news that they'd bonded with each other, never quite having had the courage to ask. When Anderson had first proposed Jet as an assistant, Oliver wasn't really sure how long he'd expected the arrangement to go on. A year? Two? Ten? He'd been eager to find a cure at the time, indulging the fantasy that one day medical science would produce the required miracle and set him free from the indignity of forced intimacy with a dreaded alpha.

What had Jet thought of the arrangement? Had he expected it to go on this long? Or had he thought he'd put in a year or two of service and then go on his merry way, leaving Oliver with a new partner, no longer his concern? They were both meandering through their early thirties now, the age at which most people were contemplating serious, long-term relationships and planning families of their own.

Unbidden, the image came back again of Jet, kneeling on the bed, muscles tightening as he neared his climax. He regretted not paying more attention at the time, not having known that it would end up being a one-time-only event. He longed to go back to that morning, to put his hand on Jet's leg and feel the coarse hair along his thigh, to stroke the back of his neck in encouragement and murmur seductively in his ear…

He came into his own hand a moment later, feeling no satisfaction in the rough, pulsing release. He'd royally screwed this up, chasing dreams that were not meant to be, and using Jet as a scapegoat for his own disappointment. Perhaps, if he'd suggested a change in their arrangement earlier, Jet would have taken him up on the offer, instead of misconstruing it as an idea born of despair and desperation.

Disheartened, he got up and headed for the bathroom. Perhaps a cold shower would go some way towards relieving the persistent ache in his nether-regions.

Afternoon faded to evening, a hasty dinner of scrambled eggs on toast punctuating what was otherwise a slow and agonising trudge though a minefield of potential missteps and unintended insults.

Jet still hadn't mentioned his reckless request to move their arrangement onto a more physical level, and Oliver was finding the oversight disconcerting. Jet was usually far more predictable in calling Oliver out over his shy reticence and embarrassed assumptions.

After his shower, he'd changed into a worn t-shirt and a pair of cotton sleeping shorts, too tired to bother with real clothes. With his temperature still hovering just above thirty-eight degrees, his current attire was far more comfortable than his usual jeans. Now, it was getting on for 9 p.m. and he knew he'd need another dose before he attempted to get some sleep. It was early to be heading to bed, but the night was going to be disturbed with sleepless fantasies, erotic dreams, and waking every three hours to administer another dose, so it was a good bet that he'd be tired in the morning, regardless of what time he went to bed.

Curled up in his armchair, Oliver drained the last of the hot chocolate from his cup. He stood up and went to the kitchen, his heart pounding as he contemplated what he wanted to do next. He'd spent the last fifteen minutes rehearsing the conversation in his head, trying to anticipate how Jet would respond, bracing himself for a harsh answer and another argument. Should he even try? Would it be better to forget the whole idea? It would be far easier to just ask for another dose to be deposited into a cup, regardless of what Jet thought of the idea. That way, the whole thing would be over in a few awkward minutes, without risking a prolonged debate that would doubtlessly just re-open tender wounds and prod at injured pride.

But the lingering idea refused to let him be, floating around in his head like a leaf caught in an eddy in a river.

He washed his cup and set it upside down on the draining board, changing his mind once every three seconds. He should let it go. He should just accept that Jet wasn't interested. And yet…

He went back to the living room, the decision still swirling back and forth. Trying to look natural, he headed for his bedroom, wondering if he should just keep walking, go and have a cold shower and pretend all was right with the world. Right at the door to the hallway, he stopped, hating the awful rush of anticipation and dread swirling in his gut. Feeling like he was watching himself from outside his own body, he turned to face Jet, sitting sprawled out on the couch as usual, flicking through a magazine. "You once told me," he said, "that you spent a lot of time during my heats wondering how to convince me that I should let you come into my bedroom so I could see what an alpha was really capable of." Time seemed to stop for a moment, then the words flowed out of him, like they'd been spoken by someone else. "How'd you like to come in and show me?"

Jet's eyes met his. The seconds ticked by, Oliver's world taking on a dream-like quality as they simply stared at each other. A muscle beside Jet's eye twitched, and Oliver felt his own fingers curling into a fist, his whole body fraught with tension.

Then, finally, Jet moved. He stood up, a cautious look on his face, like he was approaching a wild deer that was likely to bolt at any moment. His magazine hit the couch with a light thump. Oliver was half-expecting Jet to tell him to go fuck himself and stop asking inane questions. Jet took another step closer, and Oliver wondered if he was going to ask him if he was sure, if he really wanted him this time? He honestly didn't know what the answer would be. Was he sure? Would he regret this tomorrow? Or, if he chickened out, would he forever regret not taking the risk?

But Jet said nothing. He walked slowly across the room, and Oliver was struck by the memory of jumping out of that plane. One moment he was agonising over the small movement of extending his leg to step onto the railing outside the plane's door, and the next he was falling, the decision entirely out of his hands.

He reached out and took Jet's hand, stepping backwards along the hall and through his own bedroom doorway, and then he was freefalling, with no way out, and no real desire to find one.

CHAPTER TWENTY-NINE

OLIVER

Oliver's legs were shaking as he led Jet towards the bed. He stopped as the back of his knees hit the mattress, not knowing what he should do next. Should he kiss Jet? Take his shirt off? Climb onto the bed?

Jet solved the problem for him by leaning forward, a slow movement that, for all its cautious progress, was not lacking in confidence. He brushed his lips gently against Oliver's.

When Oliver didn't pull away, he did it again, then again, more firmly this time. "I thought you'd changed your mind," he said, a note of wonder in his voice.

Oliver shook his head. "No. Just... taking my time."

"That's a good way to do things," Jet agreed. This time the kiss was accompanied by a hand curling around Oliver's waist. He forced himself not to move – once more, he had no objection to the touch, but the sensation was something of a surprise. He leaned into it, his own hands rising to rest on Jet's waist, then he parted his lips at Jet's urging. The kiss deepened, and Oliver felt his head spin. Were they actually going to do this?

"How about you lie down and make yourself comfortable?" Jet suggested. Oliver climbed up onto the bed, feeling terribly self-conscious. Would Jet like his body? Was he attracted to him? Or was this all just driven by hormones? For Oliver's part, he was throbbing in his pants, eager to see all those firm muscles revealed to his gaze, even as his nervousness made him doubt his own role in this. Jet had far more experience than he did. Would he be disappointed?

Jet bent down to remove his shoes, then joined Oliver on the bed, stretching out beside him. "How do you like things?" he asked, running one hand slowly up Oliver's thigh. "Slow? Fast? Gentle or more vigorous?"

"Um… I don't…"

"Slow, then," Jet decided. "Tell me if I do anything you don't like." He would like it all, Oliver knew, having spent far too long anticipating how this would feel, but he nodded anyway, appreciating the concern. A warm hand stole up inside his shirt, and his abdominal muscles contracted.

A smirk appeared on Jet's lips. "Are you ticklish?"

"No!" Oliver denied, even as he squirmed beneath the touch.

"Don't worry. I'm going to make you feel good."

He was already feeling good, his body temperature rising another notch. His passage felt slick and ready, though they'd only just begun, anticipation riding him hard. Jet wriggled an inch or two closer, then pressed his knee between Oliver's legs. He rocked his hips forward, pressing their erections together, and Oliver gasped at the sensation. It was shockingly intimate, despite the two layers of clothing still separating them.

How the hell was Jet staying so calm, he wondered, feeling a touch resentful at his seemingly unshakable patience. He already knew that alphas were more susceptible to heat pheromones than omegas were, but here Oliver was, desperate to just rip his clothes off, while Jet was…

But no, actually, he wasn't, Oliver realised. He saw the tell-tale twitch of muscles as Jet clenched his jaw, and when his hand rose to stroke Oliver's hair out of his eyes, it was shaking just a fraction. "Are you okay?" he asked, aware that he sounded a touch breathless.

Jet let out a laugh, then a soft curse as he ran a hand through his own hair. "Holy fuck, Oliver, you… You would tempt the virtue of a saint. And God knows, I'm not one of those." His eyes were roving all over, down to his waist, up over his chest, then back down again, to the prominent bulge in his shorts. "May I…?" Jet asked, his hand sliding downwards, stopping just shy of touching it.

Oliver nodded, then his eyes slid closed as he felt the heat of Jet's hand through the thin cotton. Jet squeezed him gently, then more firmly. Impulsively, Oliver reached out to return the favour, but Jet suddenly took his hand in his own and moved it away. "No, sorry… If you do that, I'm just going to come in my pants."

'So take your pants off' was the obvious answer, but Oliver wasn't quite brave enough to say it. "Do you want to…?" He leaned over to kiss Jet again, sliding a hand beneath his t-shirt in the process. He tugged the hem up a fraction, hoping Jet would take the hint.

He did, stripping the t-shirt over his head and tossing it off the side of the bed. But then he seemed to freeze for a moment, and Oliver frowned, trying to work out what the problem was. Jet rolled away from him suddenly, lying on his back with his hand over his eyes, breathing fast. Oliver heard him swallow hard.

"Fucking hell," Jet muttered. "I'm sorry, I'm just…"

"Do you want to stop?" Oliver asked dreading the answer. Was he having second thoughts already?

But Jet shook his head, turning to look at Oliver with a faint desperation. "No, that is definitely not the problem here." He swallowed again, then his hand slid down his own chest, stopping just shy of his belt. Oliver's eyes followed it… and then got a look at the prominent ridge of Jet's erection, pinned to his thigh inside his jeans in a way that looked almost painful.

Actually, it probably was painful, and Oliver realised without being told what the problem was.

"Maybe I could…" Could he actually say it? "… help you with that? I mean, you're going to come more than once, aren't you?"

There was a moment of stunned silence. "Yes," Jet confirmed, an odd note in his voice. "Definitely more than once."

"So I could…" He placed his hand carefully on Jet's stomach, tentative fingers toying with his belt.

Jet flung one arm above his head, his fingers gripping a fistful of the pillow and hanging on like his life depended on it. His other hand flexed just above his groin. "Whatever you like." He sounded like he meant it. Oliver reached out to undo his belt… but then stopped, another idea occurring to him. He sat up, stripping his own t-shirt over his head in a quick movement, before he had a chance to talk himself out of it.

Jet simply gawked up at him, his eyes fixed on Oliver's chest… then he was suddenly undoing his belt as fast as humanly possible, snapping the button open, ripping down his fly…

Spurts of white fluid spilled across Jet's stomach a split second after he'd managed to get his dick out of his pants. "I'm sorry," he apologised immediately, reaching over to grab a handful of tissues from the nightstand. "Shit, I'm so sorry…"

Oliver bit his lip, watching Jet clean up, not entirely sure how he should feel about it. The blatant display of desire was deeply flattering, but at the same time, it was daunting to see once again how fierce Jet's sexual needs were. What would happen when he was inside Oliver? Would he be able to control himself? Climaxing too early wasn't the concern – Oliver had seen first-hand how quickly he could be ready to go again. But would he be rough? Forceful? What if Oliver wanted him to stop at some point? Would he be able to?

"I'm sorry," Jet said again, and Oliver realised he must be looking rather shocked about the display. Jet tossed the tissues into the bin and went to cover himself, attempting to fit himself back inside his pants.

In a quick movement, Oliver stopped him. Keeping his eyes on Jet's, he pushed his hand away. Feeling bold, and brave, and terrified beyond words, he slid his hand down, wrapping it firmly around Jet's erection. Last time he'd done this, he'd been exhausted, his mind fuzzy, rational thought a distant memory as he'd just tried to get through the day without falling apart. Today, though, the entire experience was crystal clear, every sound crisp, every sensation vivid and captivating.

He stroked his hand up and down, slowly but firmly. He ran his thumb over the head and heard a hitch in Jet's breathing. His hips bucked upwards, a surprised little moan escaping from his throat. Oliver glanced down, expecting him to be about to come again, but Jet let out a chuckle. "Not yet, buddy. I'm not far off, though. But maybe you want me to…?" He put a hand on Oliver's thigh, then slid his fingers a fraction higher.

But Oliver shook his head, surprised to find that he was perfectly content just watching Jet enjoy himself. Later, certainly, he'd like to get in on the fun, but for now…

"Um… yeah, so… this is going to make a mess," Jet gasped out, his hips rocking in time with Oliver's hand now. This time, it was Oliver's turn to laugh.

"I think I'm familiar with the result of this sort of thing," he said, quirking an eyebrow at where his hand was still working Jet's flesh. He quickened his pace and was rewarded a moment later when Jet groaned, arm flung over his face as he climaxed again. He mumbled what sounded like a curse, then took his arm away.

"Hey, I was supposed to be the one showing *you* a good time," he griped. "That's two I owe you now."

Oliver smiled. "Omega's aren't capable of orgasming anything like as often as an alpha can," he pointed out. It was a scientific fact, one he'd looked up in a medical textbook after he'd seen how quickly Jet had been back in action during his last heat. He didn't let go, continuing to move his hand in slow, even strokes, and Jet made no move to stop him.

"What were you thinking about the last time you did this?" Jet asked, peering at him from beneath hooded eyelids. "You seem to be enjoying yourself, which makes me wonder."

Oliver shrugged, plans forming in his mind as to how to spice things up a bit. Though Jet was making no complaint about the rhythmic stroking, Oliver was sure he could make things a little more exciting. "Half of me was stunned by how fast you recovered, and the other half was…"

"Was what?"

He felt a shy, bashful smile settle on his face. "Was wondering what it would feel like if I could convince you to return the favour."

Jet's expression turned suddenly serious. "I would have done, you know," he said, even as the words caught in his throat, punctuated by a moan. "All you had to do was ask." His hips curled upwards, and Oliver's eyes met his again. Deliberately, he leaned down, shuffling his knees backwards and, he hoped, giving Jet a clear indication of what he was about to do before he did it. Not entirely sure how to proceed, Oliver ran his tongue in a long, wet stroke from the base of Jet's cock to the tip. Jet cursed again, sitting half-way up in shock.

Then he laughed, flopping back onto the bed as Oliver took a second swipe at him. "You know, this is a whole lot more fun than doing it alone."

Oliver wasn't going to disagree. He was paying attention this time, each moan, each ridge and curve of Jet's body eagerly catalogued in his mind – just in case they didn't get the chance to do this again. That would be a shame, he thought, in a distracted sort of way. But most of his attention was focused on making sure his first ever blow job was up to scratch. Jet's cock was far too big to get much of it in his mouth, but he sucked on the tip, then ran his tongue around the head, a stray part of his mind contemplating how odd it was that all his nerves seemed to have vanished now that they were actually doing this. He tilted his head... and then paused, catching a unique scent. It was familiar, yet at the same time he was sure it had never smelled quite like this before.

He pulled back, brows furrowed as he wondered why it was different from usual? He would recognise Jet's scent anywhere, having spent a good portion of the last few years breathing in his pheromone-laden shirts. But as he peered down at Jet's groin, his cock still throbbing in Oliver's hand, the answer was suddenly obvious. Alphas didn't just have scent glands in their necks. They also had them in their groin. And obviously, Oliver had never scented him from quite this angle before.

"You okay?" Jet asked, sounding worried, so Oliver shot him a quick smile.

"Fine. Do you like this?" The apprehension was back, but only as a faint concern that he wasn't pleasing his alpha well enough.

"Bloody fantastic," Jet muttered, rocking his hips upwards again. "I hadn't really expected you'd go for... Oh, fucking hell, do that again!" Oliver did, engulfing as much of Jet's cock in his mouth as he could, then pulling back slowly, and after the second time, Jet quickly guided his head away, climaxing again across his own stomach.

He fell back onto the bed, eyes closed, lips parted, his hand still stroking himself slowly. "For fuck's sake, can't I get a break for a minute?" he muttered, asking no one in particular. His hand quickened, fast, impatient strokes while he seemed almost angry over his body's reaction. Multiple orgasms had always seemed like an enticing idea, but Oliver supposed the incessant arousal could also be intensely frustrating, if there was no way to get away from it.

"Here, let me," he offered, taking over from Jet. He didn't bother with any theatrics this time, just pumped him hard and fast until he was arching his back again and groaning out another release.

This time, though, when Oliver went to keep going, Jet put his hand on Oliver's, stopping him. "Ollie, we could just keep doing this for the next six or seven hours, and it wouldn't make a difference." Was he serious? "Really, it wouldn't," he added, at Oliver's stunned expression. "But sooner or later, you're going to need some of these helpful little proteins." He dipped a finger into the mess on his stomach to make the point. Oliver must have looked apprehensive about that, because Jet shook his head, reaching for more tissues to clean up. "We don't have to go all the way right now. If you like, we can just do it the usual way and work up to something more later. That's assuming you still want something more?" he added, raised eyebrows and an upward lilt to his voice indicating that it would be perfectly fine if Oliver said no.

"I do," he said firmly. Part of his brain was already rushing ahead, urging him to take his pants off and mount Jet right then and there. But a more rational part of him reminded him that this was his first time, and Jet wasn't going anywhere, so there was no reason to rush. He thought about having Jet up inside him and…

No, that was a little too much, too fast, particularly with the pressure of his own biology demanding that it should happen *right now*, before the tension in his abdomen turned into a real cramp.

"Let's just go with the dropper for now, then we can pick up where we left off."

"Sure." The cup Oliver had used earlier was still on the nightstand, so Jet picked it up, rising to his knees as he began to work himself. He paused a moment later and shot a tentative glance Oliver's way.

"Do you want a hand?" Oliver asked. Somehow it was more awkward now, back to just being a biological function, and he wasn't sure what he was supposed to do; sit back and wait, or keep up the seduction routine?

"No, but could I…?" This time, it was Jet who couldn't seem to find the words he was looking for.

"Could you what?"

"Sorry if this is a bit stereotypical alpha and all that, but could I…?" His gaze flickered down to Oliver's neck.

Oliver's eyebrows rose. He'd had plenty of fantasies about Jet licking his neck, tasting his scent glands, but the reality seemed far more intimate, and he suddenly realised why he'd baulked when Jet had dared to lick him, all those weeks ago. Sex was one thing, but this was something only a *mate* would dare to do. Or be *allowed* to do.

His heart gave an odd little lurch as he shuffled closer. Not trusting his voice, he nodded instead. He rested one hand on Jet's shoulder for balance, then tilted his head back. He felt Jet's nose graze his skin, the warmth of his breath, then the rasp as his inhaled. Jet pressed his lips to that sensitive little patch of skin, then Oliver felt his tongue sneak out, caressing the gland in a smooth, wet glide.

Jet groaned a moment later, and he pulled back suddenly. Oliver felt a moment of panic, worried he'd done something wrong again, until he realised that Jet had just climaxed into the cup, and he'd pulled away to avoid spilling it.

Jet seemed a little dazed this time, different from how he'd been after his previous climaxes. He handed the cup to Oliver. "Do you want to do it, or should I?" Was it Oliver's imagination, or were his words slightly slurred?

"Could you?" he asked, reaching for the dropper on the nightstand. It wasn't because he specifically wanted Jet to do it; rather it was because trying to do it himself invariably meant he ended up in a rather undignified position, twisted around with his ass sticking up in the air, and he'd rather Jet not see that when he was supposed to be seducing him.

Jet, though, didn't seem to mind either way. He took the dropper, sucked up the liquid, and looked at Oliver expectantly. "I think you're going to have to take your pants off for this part," he pointed out, when Oliver didn't move.

"Right. Of course." He stood up, put his hands on his waistband… and froze.

Just push your pants down, he ordered himself, when the pause stretched on. His body refused to obey him, a wave of sudden fears assailing him. What would Jet think? Was he too skinny? Too pale? What if his penis was too small? It was certainly smaller than Jet's, but then again, even the smallest alphas tended to be well above average in the downstairs department. What was average for an omega? Oliver had no idea.

"Hey," Jet said suddenly, his voice calm and even. He slid off the bed, setting the cup and dropper on the nightstand. He came to stand in front of Oliver, tilting his chin up so he could look him in the eye. "We can stop any time you like," he said gently.

"I don't want to stop," Oliver replied firmly. "I'm just…"

"Taking your time?" Jet suggested, a hint of amusement in his voice.

"Yes. Exactly."

Jet glanced down, raising an eyebrow at the prominent bulge in the front of Oliver's shorts. "Maybe you'd like a hand with that?"

It was so easy to let Jet take over. Oliver lifted his arms to rest on Jet's shoulders. His hips rocked forward as Jet's hands took him by the hips. Nimble fingers took hold of his waistband and tugged the fabric down, caressing Oliver's bare buttocks as his clothing dropped to the floor. "Shit, you're really hot," Jet muttered. Oliver began to smile at the compliment… but then the context of the statement hit home. His body temperature was climbing again, rapidly heading for a point that wouldn't be considered healthy. "We should get you dosed up, then come back to this," Jet told him, and Oliver was inclined to agree.

"Okay, sure. Just let me..." He knelt on the bed, facing away from Jet, and leaned forward, his hands spread out on the blanket. He heard Jet pick up the dropper, felt him put his hand on Oliver's back... and then he realised his own mistake a moment too late. He was hopelessly aroused, having had no relief since they'd come into the bedroom, and in his naivety, he'd somehow expected this to feel the same as it usually did, his own hand administering the treatment in a purely perfunctory manner.

But Jet's hands were deliberately tender, impossibly warm against his skin. He felt careful fingers part his buttocks, then felt the dropper slide in, and he almost gasped at the tantalising sensation, even from so light a pressure. It was over a moment later, the dropper landing on the nightstand with a light tap, and Oliver went to move, to turn around, to say thank you, perhaps. That was the intention, at least. What he actually did was arch his back, thrust his hips backwards and let out a mewl that was one hundred per cent omega, a pleading invitation to his alpha to *please* hurry up and fuck him already.

CHAPTER THIRTY

OLIVER

Oliver clamped his jaw shut a moment later, utterly mortified by the sound he'd just made. He spun around, his eyes wide, his face bright red.

Jet seemed just as surprised. He was standing by the nightstand, mouth open in shock, one hand floating uncertainly in the air after he'd let go of the dropper. "Holy shit, Ollie, you just…"

"Uh… please ignore that," Oliver said, staring at the blankets. "I didn't mean to… um…"

Jet took a step closer. Instinctively, Oliver backed up a foot, crawling backwards onto the bed.

"You liked that, didn't you?" Jet asked, his eyes roving over Oliver's naked form.

Oliver grabbed the blanket and pulled it up to cover himself. He retreated until his back hit the headboard. Jet lifted one knee onto the edge of the bed, leaning forward to rest his weight on one hand, the other reaching out to touch Oliver's ankle, peeking out from beneath the blanket.

"Jet, please, I… I didn't mean to do that." Such a blatant invitation, from an omega in heat to an alpha high on pheromones… There was no possible way this was going to end well.

Jet ran his fingers higher, up Oliver's calf, while he squirmed back another inch or two. There was nowhere else to go, the edge of the bed to his left, the wall behind him, and Jet positioned firmly between himself and the door.

"Jet, stop," Oliver said sharply. "This isn't what I want." Were they going to end up in a fight? Oliver was fairly sure he'd lose to Jet even on a normal day, never mind when he'd triggered every alpha instinct the man possessed.

143

"I'm not going to hurt you," Jet said dismissively. He plucked at the edge of the blanket. "You're going to get hot, all covered up like that."

Was Jet even aware of what he was saying? He'd admitted in the past that he'd tried to punch Sullivan when the doctor had unknowingly triggered a possessive instinct in him. Was that what was happening here? Would Jet be able to control himself? Or had Oliver finally pushed him too far?

"You need me," Jet said, tugging lightly on the blanket. "This is gonna feel good. I promise." He took hold of his own cock, still sticking out the front of his pants, and stroked himself lazily. "Come on, Ollie. Let me see you."

"You need to stop this," he repeated, praying that some part of Jet's mind was still functioning. "You're not in control of yourself, and you're scaring me."

A look of cool anger settled on Jet's face. He sat back on his knees, withdrawing the hand that was fiddling with the edge of the blanket. "You said you wanted me." It was hard to tell whether the statement was warning, or a threat.

"I did," Oliver admitted. "And I still do. But you're…"

"What do you want?" Jet asked, in that same, not-quite-threatening tone.

"I want to do this *slowly*."

"I can do slow," Jet purred, a predatory smirk on his lips.

"And I want to know that you're in control of yourself!"

The heat in Jet's stare got a fraction warmer. "Always," he promised, looking Oliver in the eye. He trailed one finger across Oliver's foot again. "I'm not going to hurt you."

For all his eager assurances, Oliver was far from convinced that Jet was in his right mind. If he was, he'd have been backing away, apologising for letting things get too intense, and offering to take a break, maybe come back to this later.

What was he supposed to do now? He thought about demanding that Jet put his clothes back on and get out his room, but he couldn't quite bear the inevitable look of stark disappointment on Jet's face. He could just go along with the sex – he had invited it, after all – but he'd also promised himself that he would never, ever submit to an alpha just because it was the easy way out. He felt like he was at a dead end, unwilling to say no, unable to say yes…

But as he contemplated the odd situation, Jet still stroking his foot with a morose expression, one glaring truth suddenly stood out to him. He'd asked Jet to stop… *and he had*. Okay, so he was still trying to talk Oliver into continuing, but he had actually stopped. He'd tried to coax the blanket from around Oliver's hips, but he hadn't removed it by force. He was currently stroking gentle lines up and down his foot, but he wasn't going any higher than that.

Oliver had no idea what to do with that knowledge. No, he still didn't believe Jet was processing reality properly, but on the other hand, he knew perfectly well that even if he had been, he would still be willing and eager to have sex.

Needing to test the theory, to know that Jet really wasn't going to push things too far, Oliver slowly and deliberately lifted the blanket and pushed it aside, revealing his naked body to Jet's gaze. Jet was immediately transfixed. One hand reached towards Oliver's groin… then pulled back, his eyes flicking back and forth uncertainly.

"Slowly, yeah?" Jet asked, staring at Oliver's erection.

"Slowly," Oliver confirmed.

"Okay." He edged closer and ran a gentle hand up Oliver's thigh. It bypassed his groin, rising higher to stroke his waist, his pecs, then over his shoulder and down his arm. Jet leaned closer, pressing small, nibbling kisses to Oliver's lips.

Oliver was trying to reciprocate the attention, letting his hands wander over Jet's shoulders, down his back, but his progress was suddenly halted by the waistband of Jet's pants. He dipped lower, feeling firm buttocks encased in faded denim.

He was about to ask Jet to remove them when he suddenly felt a hand on his thigh again, tentative fingers migrating gradually higher. "Is this okay?" Jet asked.

Oliver nodded, swallowing hard. He felt his erection throb. "Yeah…"

That hand slid higher, pausing to caress Oliver's balls, then wrapped firmly around his cock. "I want you to feel good," Jet told him, peppering kisses along his jaw and down his neck. Oliver lifted his chin to give him better access. The hand at his groin stroked him slowly, with a sure, confident grip that drew a moan from his throat.

"Lie down on the bed," Jet suggested, moving back to give him room. Oliver obeyed, but tensed when Jet's hand slid lower, past his balls, around to his entrance. He felt one cautious digit probing for access, and he tried to squirm away.

Jet immediately removed his hand. "I think you'll like it," he said, stroking the back of his knuckles along Oliver's thigh. "If you let me keep going?" It was reassuringly phrased as a question, and Oliver could feel his passage throbbing with need.

"Just… go slowly," he said, trying to make himself relax. He let Jet part his legs, then closed his eyes, working on keeping his breathing slow and even as he felt one finger tease his entrance. The tip slid inside, and Oliver's hips bucked in surprise.

"Sorry. Did that hurt?"

"No, it's fine." The sensation was deliciously erotic, but also unfamiliar.

The finger slid deeper, making Oliver moan and squirm again. "Here, let me do this," Jet muttered, wriggling around to get more comfortable. Then Oliver felt a wet heat against his cock. His eyes flew open, and he looked down to see his length slowly disappearing into Jet's mouth. Perhaps feeling himself being watched, Jet looked up, eyes meeting Oliver's even as he kept his mouth where it was. He swiped one long, wet stroke up to the head, at the same time as pressing his finger deeper inside Oliver. He gasped at the sensation, feeling his cock throb.

"You like that?" Jet asked. Oliver tried to say he did, but couldn't quite get his brain to figure out the words. Instead he nodded, bucking his hips up into Jet's hands. He felt that one finger slide out again, and he frowned in disappointment, but a moment later, it was back, this time joined by a second. Jet's mouth was back on his cock as well, moving in rhythm with his hand. Oliver gave himself up to the sensations, hips tilting upwards in invitation. In all his fantasies, he'd never quite managed to capture the odd combination of apprehension and longing currently pulsing through his veins.

He felt a climax building, but didn't want this to end so soon, so instead, he wriggled away, batting Jet's hands out of the way.

"Want you," he stammered, at Jet's look of disappointment. "Inside me." The frown disappeared instantly, replaced with a sultry smile. Without being asked, Jet quickly shimmed out of his pants, dropping them over the side of the bed. But instead of climbing in between Oliver's parted legs, he lay down on his back beside him.

"Come on. Up on top," he said, trying to guide him via a hand on his hip.

That was not what Oliver had expected. "Why?"

"It'll be more comfortable for your first time. You can decide how fast you want to go."

That might be true, but it also meant that Oliver would be entirely in control of the experience. For all his earlier reticence, it was far easier to let Jet take control, as it had been jumping out of the plane. Jet should be deciding when they jumped, when he pulled the chute, where they landed once it was over.

But the look on Jet's face was determined, and it seemed he'd regained some of his usual awareness over the last few minutes, no longer quite so driven by pheromones and instinct. And because of that, Oliver knew there would be no abdicating of responsibility this time. He was either all in, one hundred per cent committed, or this wasn't going to happen at all. Mustering what little courage he could, he rose to his knees and slid a leg over Jet's thighs.

"That's it. It's just like riding a horse. Go as slow as you like."

Feeling terribly self-conscious, he reached back, guiding the head of Jet's erection to his slick entrance. The position wasn't the most stable, and he wobbled to the side, before reaching out to grip the headboard for balance. Breathing fast, he pressed backwards, teeth gritted as he felt the thick head stretch him open.

He paused a moment, running a quick mental check of himself. Did he really want this? Was he finally ready to lose his virginity?

Jet stroked his thighs, his hands shaking, but the look on his face was one of composed patience, and Oliver suddenly knew that if he pulled the plug now, if he climbed off and said he wanted to stop, then Jet would absolutely respect that. He'd let him go, spend himself into a cup and then tell Oliver that everything was totally fine.

That made up his mind. He pressed back again, feeling his body resist for a moment, then suddenly give. Jet slid inside him, maybe only an inch or two, but that short length was enough to send a shockwave of pleasure through Oliver's groin. He let out a moan, not caring this time that he sounded wanton and needy.

He heard an answering moan from Jet, and a wave of satisfaction hit him. He was pleasing his alpha! He was causing pleasure, where for so long there had been frustration and endless delays.

Oliver felt stretched wide, his hand tightening on the wood of the bedframe as his cock throbbed in front of him. He pressed back again, another moan escaping him as he felt Jet slid in another inch or so. Flaming heck, how big was he? Oliver felt full already, his thighs shaking from the effort of holding him up, but his hand was still around the base of Jet's cock, and it was telling him there were plenty more inches left to go.

"Go slow, Oliver," Jet said, his voice sounding tight. "You don't have to
—"

"Want you!" Oliver insisted, pressing back again, another thick inch sliding in. He rose up a fraction, then gasped as the move created a delicious friction against his inner walls. He sat back again without even thinking about it, rocking up and back in an instinctive rhythm.

"Fuck, I'm going to come," Jet muttered from beneath him, and Oliver nodded, humming a vague reply. Jet grabbed his hips a moment later, holding him still, and Oliver felt a spurt of wetness inside himself. As soon as Jet let him go, he was moving again, pressing back, gasping out a moan as Jet filled him even more.

He was teetering right on the edge of an orgasm now, though he resisted the urge to stroke himself, wanting to draw out the sensation. He rose up again and pressed back, and he was almost surprised when he felt his thighs hit Jet's, unable to go any further. He opened his eyes, not having realised he'd closed them.

"Oh God, keep going. Please…" Jet muttered, his head thrown back, mouth open as he panted for breath. Oliver did, the world feeling suddenly surreal. He felt an odd, lurching sensation in his chest, like he'd just taken a corner too fast in a powerful car.

In a rush, his orgasm swept over him. Unable to help himself, he wrapped his fist around his cock, thrusting into his own hand as hot fluid spilled across Jet's stomach. He felt Jet grab his hips and urge him to move faster, harder, then he came as well, faint curses muttered on the tail end of a husky cry of pleasure.

CHAPTER THIRTY-ONE

JET

Jet lay limply on the bed, completely dazed. He felt like his brain had just short-circuited. Oliver's hands were braced against his chest, his upper body slumped over like a rag doll while Jet's cock was still buried deep inside him, and he felt a moment of pride that he had been the one to put him in that state. He'd pleased his omega. There was no better feeling in the entire world.

Panting for breath, Oliver suddenly leaned down and kissed him, hard and wet, with open mouth and probing tongue. Jet accepted the kiss willingly, but he was surprised at the force of it. He tried to pull away at one point, but Oliver wouldn't have it, demanding more.

When he finally pulled back, Jet let his head flop back onto the pillow. Oliver knelt up, Jet's dick sliding out of him in a tantalising caress, then lay down beside him. "Sorry," he said, though Jet wasn't quite sure what he was apologising for. "I just... I got this crazy urge to kiss you. Sorry. That was odd."

"It's fine," Jet told him. "I wasn't complaining. How are you feeling?"

A sly smile appeared on Oliver's face. "Good. Tired. What about you?"

Strangely, Jet was feeling rather wiped out himself. Normally during a heat, he was revved up and raring to go the entire time, constantly restless and only able to nap for an hour or so at a time, even in the middle of the night. Now, though, he felt oddly sleepy. And even more odd was the fact that his erection was softening quickly, the urgent arousal fading out in a way that was unfamiliar, but not unwelcome. He sniffed the air, surprised to find that Oliver's scent was far less intense than usual. Was that one of the side effects of a real mating with an alpha? Or maybe it was the physical stimulation? Oliver had admitted in the past that he'd never used the dildo, but maybe Sullivan had been right after all; maybe they'd managed to stimulate some nerves that they hadn't before, and this was the result?

Like a cat in front of a fire, Oliver curled into his side, resting his head on his chest, and Jet put an arm around his shoulder. "Take a nap," he advised him, more than happy to have a little time to just cuddle. "Wake me up if you need me."

Jet lurched awake on a moan, a demanding pressure in his groin and a fiery heat pressed against his side. A hesitant hand crept across his chest, that light touch sending shafts of sensation straight to his cock.

Jet turned his head, getting hit with a blast of pheromones when he accidentally stuck his nose right against Oliver's neck. "Need you," Oliver murmured.

Thank God for that, Jet thought dazedly, because he was about ready to come just on that husky request. Oliver tugged him over on top of him, and Jet went without protest, not really thinking about what they were doing. He was still half asleep, and even the wakeful part of his mind was addled with lust, so there were no guarantees it would be able to make any sensible decisions anyway.

"God, you're burning up," he muttered as he reached down between them. Oliver was already hard as a rock, parting his legs without being asked. Jet kissed him hard, his hand moulding his erection, then he moved further down, around to his entrance. Two fingers slid inside, and Oliver arched his back. "This okay?" he remembered to ask, mind still foggy from sleep.

"Yes," Oliver gasped out. "Hot."

Jet wondered just how long they'd slept for. They should have learned by now that they needed to set an alarm! His fingers pressed deeper, but Oliver was squirming away almost immediately.

"No… want your cock."

"I don't want to rush you," Jet replied. This was only the second time they had done this, and -

"I ready! I need you!"

With the heat pouring off him, that was probably true, and the desperation in Oliver's voice was enough to assuage his guilt about not taking longer to prepare him. He replaced his fingers with his erection and pressed just the head inside. He gritted his teeth as he felt how tight he was. "You okay?"

Oliver was trying to push himself further onto his cock. "Yeah." He tried to tug Jet closer. "More."

The omegan body was an amazing thing, Jet thought dimly, as he pushed in further. Oliver opened to him readily, his passage slick and welcoming, needing no more stimulation to be able to accept something that by all rights should have been too big to fit into that tight passage.

Jet groaned, climaxing almost immediately. But that small dose of fluid was far from enough to counteract the burning need in Oliver's body, and for once, he was grateful for his ability to pump out three or four ejaculations in a row. He pushed in again, then pulled out, thrusting gently as he felt Oliver's natural lubricant seep over his groin.

"Feels good?"

"Yes! Keep going…" He felt Oliver reach down, his hands cupping Jet's buttocks as he tried to persuade him to move faster. Jet obliged, feeling his second climax rising swiftly. He didn't try to hold back, spilling himself inside Oliver with a rough moan. He slid his hand down Oliver's thigh and tugged it up over his hip, resuming his pace after the briefest of pauses. The bed squeaked beneath them, and Jet gave in to the desire to bury his nose in Oliver's neck. He mouthed his scent gland, stroking it with his tongue. The taste was indescribable, sweet and smoky, and from the way Oliver's body bucked beneath him, it was a fairly sure bet that Oliver was enjoying it as much as he was. He slid a hand down to stroke Oliver's erection, rewarded when he thrust up into his hand.

"Come for me, babe," he murmured into Oliver's ear. "I want you to feel so good…"

Oliver froze, fingers digging into Jet's shoulders, and he felt a spurt of wetness between them. Oliver's passage clenched around his cock like a vice, and he came a moment later, finally feeling a little relief from the urgent desire in his groin.

Oliver lay limply beneath him, both of them slick with sweat and messy with other fluids. As his breath began to slow, Jet moved to pull away. But before he could, Oliver reached up, grabbing the back of his neck and pulling him down to kiss him, hard. Jet didn't try to pull away, opening his mouth as Oliver's tongue pushed inside. But as the kiss wore on, Jet once more felt that odd sensation in his groin, his erection fading, moisture seeping between them as he softened inside Oliver's body.

Finally, Oliver let him go, and he pulled out, flopping down on the bed beside him.

"Let me guess – you just had this crazy urge to kiss me?"

"Sorry," Oliver said, but Jet brushed the apology aside.

"I think there's a reason for that," he said, an idea forming in his mind. "I think maybe that's some kind of ingrained reaction to mating." Lazily, he reached over for some tissues to clean them both up, doing a cursory job of it before tossing them in the bin.

Oliver arched one eyebrow at him. "You think it's a what?"

Tentatively, Jet sniffed the air, and wasn't surprised when he found he could barely detect Oliver's scent. "I think you kissing me does something to my hormones. No, hear me out," he went on, when Oliver tried to interrupt him. "We have sex, you get a dose of proteins, and then you get this urge to kiss me. And that seems to hit some kind of off-switch for me." To show Oliver what he meant, he took his hand and pressed it down over his dick, which was now lying limply between his legs. Oliver gave a few experimental strokes, surprised when there was no response.

"But you're usually... You said before that you could keep going for hours."

"Normally, I can. Seriously, I've never felt like this before." He wrapped his hand around himself, feeling a faint twinge of excitement, but it faded again quickly. "I feel like I could still give you a work out, if you really wanted me to, but that manic, driving need is gone. I can hardly even smell you anymore."

"You're saying there's a pheromone blocker in my saliva?"

Jet shrugged. "Maybe." If that was the case, it came as an enormous relief. "That would actually make a lot of sense," he said. "Think about it; why would an alpha need to have sex continuously for as long as a heat lasts, but an omega only needs it every couple of hours? That just means the alpha ends up wasting a whole lot of energy, and from an evolutionary perspective, that makes no sense. But if your body can tell mine when to take a break, that means you still get what you need, but I don't wear myself out giving it to you. Sullivan actually suggested something like that the first time I spoke to him about this. His theory was that your body needed some kind of chemical signal from my saliva, but what if the opposite it true? That I'm actually picking up on a signal that *you're* giving *me*?"

There was a pause as Oliver thought about that. "That is simultaneously absolutely fascinating, and really, *really* annoying. Why the hell don't we know that already? I mean, why doesn't *science* know that? Alphas and omegas kept the human race going for millennia, but now we've just forgotten everything we knew about our own physiology!"

Jet lay back on the bed, huffing out a deep sigh. "I don't know what to say, man. It sucks, I agree, but humanity's real good at only remembering the bits of history that we want to. There have been huge chunks of it effectively deleted because it didn't match up with someone's religion, or some king's power trip, or whatever. Fifteen hundred years ago, betas started being able to reproduce, and our genders just became superfluous."

Oliver sighed, his eyes fixed on the ceiling. Then he shook his head. "I feel like I should be apologising. Not knowing this means you've had to go through a huge amount of unnecessary frustration for the last couple of years."

"How many times do I have to tell you this is not your fault? I didn't know any more about the way our bodies work than you did. Makes me wonder, though, how much more there is that we haven't figured out yet."

They lay in silence for a while, Jet listening to the sound of Oliver's breathing. After a time, his breaths slowed and deepened. But just as Jet thought he'd fallen asleep, Oliver suddenly rolled over. He slid an arm across Jet's chest and tucked his face in against his shoulder. He made a contented murmur, and Jet felt his heart do an unhappy little stutter in his chest. Once this heat was over, he was going to have to walk away, to pretend everything was back to normal, unable to see Oliver again for three months. No touches, no kisses, no peaceful cuddling beneath the blankets. The idea was just about enough to break his heart.

CHAPTER THIRTY-TWO

OLIVER

Not quite thirty hours later, Oliver was lying face down on his bed, his legs spread, his hands gripping the pillow as he felt Jet's cock slide up inside him, slick, hot, and impressively large. It was eight o'clock in the morning. Oliver had woken about half an hour ago, tired after two nights of broken sleep, but his body had ignored his exhaustion, demanding more attention from a willing and eager alpha.

Behind him, he felt Jet pause to reposition himself slightly, then he started up again, a languorous, rocking rhythm that was fast enough to keep Oliver on edge, but slow enough that he knew Jet was trying to draw things out. Deliberately, he clenched his passage around Jet's cock and chuckled when the man swore.

"Damn it, Oliver, you… Ughh, fuck…" He climaxed a moment later, as Oliver had known he would. Jet paused to catch his breath, hot puffs against Oliver's neck, then pressed a kiss to his naked shoulder. "That's five times in a row," he griped, though the complaint lacked conviction. "Aren't you supposed to be getting near the *end* of your heat?"

Oliver shrugged, then wriggled his ass against Jet's hips. "Feels good," he said, knowing the weak excuse would be more than enough to convince Jet to keep going. He felt Jet caress him from shoulder to hip, and he could well imagine the look of admiration, of lust colouring the man's face. Then he began to move again, long, satisfying strokes right up to the hilt, then out again, once more stoking the fire in Oliver's groin.

But as Oliver felt his own climax approaching, he was grateful for a moment that Jet couldn't see his expression. He buried his face in the pillow, a grimace of despair driving away any thoughts of ecstasy, while a sob of anguish rose up to choke him. He turned the latter into a moan, only half a lie, as his climax was building quickly, and kept his face hidden to stop Jet from noticing the former.

Jet paused a moment later, pressing kisses all over Oliver's back. "Come on, up on your knees," he urged him. Oliver complied, lifting his ass while resting his weight on his elbows, and predictably, Jet reached around to stroke him while he continued pumping in and out of him. Oliver felt his breathing speed up, then he came into Jet's hand, feeling one final spurt of fluid fill his passage as his alpha spent himself as well.

Gathering control of his facial features, Oliver turned around as he felt Jet pull out. He leaned over to kiss him, allowing the embrace to linger, long enough to be sure that he'd transferred enough of whatever chemical signal was in his saliva. Jet pulled back with a smile and a contented sigh, and Oliver watched out of the corner of his eye as his erection softened, feeling a poignant sense of loss. That was it, the last time they would make love until his next heat arrived. In another hour or two, his hormonal cycle would switch gears again, and there would be no more excuse to keep Jet here.

He wasn't entirely sure when it had changed in his own mind from 'having sex' to 'making love'. He hadn't said anything to Jet that might betray his change of heart, and Jet himself had neither said nor done anything to indicate this was anything other than an enjoyable physical experience.

"I'm going to take a shower," Oliver said, knowing by now that whatever was in his saliva tended to make Jet sleepy, and it was a good bet that he'd spend the next half an hour taking a nap. Sure enough, Jet nodded disinterestedly, rolled over in bed and let his body relax.

Satisfied that he wasn't going anywhere, Oliver got up and went into the bathroom, closing the door gently behind himself. He started the shower and waited until the water warmed up, then got in, adjusting the tap when it was a fraction too hot.

And then he leaned his face in under the spray, finally letting the tears he'd been holding back come rushing out, immediately washed away in the cascade of water. The hiss of the shower would disguise the faint sobs that escaped his throat, as he once more cursed himself as a coward. Telling Jet he wanted to sleep with him had been agonising, a decision full of self-doubt, and fear of rejection, and the shame of giving in to carnal desire. Telling him he was in love with him was a far higher hill to climb, and Oliver knew he'd never have the courage to jump off that particular cliff, with no assurance whatsoever that there would be a parachute to slow his fall.

He was a fool, he knew, as the water washed away the evidence of both sorrow and lust alike. A coward, and a fool, and he had no one to blame for the ache in his chest but himself.

CHAPTER THIRTY-THREE

CYCLE SEVENTEEN
JET

Two days after the decadent and sensual rollercoaster than had been Oliver's latest heat, Jet's phone rang. Sitting sprawled on his couch, he glanced at the thing vibrating happily on the coffee table, and swore at it, not at all inclined to pick it up. It wouldn't be Oliver, he reminded himself irritably. No, Oliver was not going to call him and invite him over for dinner, or ask him to meet him at the pub after work, or any one of a dozen other bland social events that the pair of them had *never* engaged in, in the entire four years of their arrangement.

Okay, so they'd had sex. And maybe they would again, next time Oliver's heat hit. But that was it – a simple, physical solution to a purely biological need. Jet had no right to be expecting anything more – and possibly no right to even expect that much again. Oliver had said nothing on the subject as Jet had left his house, and given the way Oliver's mind worked, it was entirely possible that now that his curiosity was assuaged, he'd have no desire to repeat the experience.

Jet finally bothered to pick up his phone, still merrily chirping away, and he was surprised to see the call was from Sullivan. "Hey, man. Wasn't expecting to hear from you again for a while. What's happening?"

"I'm not surprised you don't want to speak to me," Sullivan said. "I made a serious error of judgement last time, and I'm deeply sorry for the pain it caused Oliver."

Jet snorted. "You've apologised about nineteen times now. It's water under the bridge. Shit happens and all that. Seriously, you didn't just phone me to say sorry again, did you?"

"No, I didn't. I'd like you and Oliver to come over to my office, if you wouldn't mind. I have some news that I think the pair of you would find rather interesting. I've already phoned Oliver, and he said he's free at three o'clock this afternoon. Does that work for you?"

Sullivan's office was typical of most doctor's surgeries, two stiff, plastic chairs facing his desk, an array of anatomy charts lining the walls and shelves that were filled with medical paraphernalia. Oliver was already there when Jet arrived, and Jet felt his heart skip a beat as he turned around to greet him. Did he look tired, Jet wondered, feeling a sudden protective urge. Had he been sleeping properly? He forced a casual smile onto his face, shook Sullivan's hand, and took a seat next to Oliver.

"Let's get right down to business," Sullivan said. He shuffled a few papers, then handed two neatly stapled bundles across the desk, one for each of them. "A new research paper has just been released out of Australia. A colleague of mine has been conducting post-mortem histopathology on the endocrine glands of Caloren's omegas."

"He's what now?" Jet asked, glancing at the first page of the report. As with the other medical reports he'd read, much of the jargon was beyond him.

Sullivan pursed his lips. "He's been analysing the ovaries of omegas who've committed suicide."

"Charming," Oliver muttered.

"It's not a pleasant idea, I agree. But it was with the full agreement of the omegas' families – their natural families, not the alphas who made their lives hell. And his research has had some quite staggering results."

"Don't keep us in suspense, man," Jet prodded him. "None of us are getting any younger."

Thankfully, Sullivan wasn't one to beat around the bush. "What he's discovered is that in each and every case, one of the ovaries had developed a small but highly active tumour, which resulted in the omega producing an overload of hormones during their heats – the cause of Caloren's Syndrome. We're still not sure exactly *why* this tumour develops – as with most cancers, there's likely a genetic component involved. But it's the first time anyone has found an explanation for why some omegas develop Caloren's Syndrome, and others don't."

Oliver looked a little stunned at the news. "You're saying I have a tumour on one of my ovaries?"

"It's not malignant," Sullivan told him hastily. "My colleague has never found any case where the tumour has spread, but in a nutshell, yes, you most likely have a tumour. And what he's also discovered," he rushed on, "is that if the affected ovary is removed then the omega returns to having normal heats. He's discovered a cure for Caloren's Syndrome."

A stunned silence followed.

"Hold on, wait just a damn minute," Jet blurted out. "We've been down this road before. *'Here's a marvellous treatment that's going to make your life so much better, but oops, it nearly just killed you.'* Because I'm guessing what you're going to say next is that Oliver should book himself in to see this magical doctor and start getting parts of his internal organs removed."

"I'm not suggesting you *should* do anything," Sullivan said, turning to Oliver. "I made a significant mistake last time, and I wouldn't blame you at all for a certain level of scepticism. All I want to do here is alert you to the results of the research, and let you make your own decision from there. That's why I've given you a copy of the paper; so you can read it for yourself. I can answer a certain number of questions you might have, and I'm more than willing to put you in contact with the doctor if that's what you want. Or, on the other hand, if you want nothing more to do with this research, then fair enough. That's your call."

Oliver sat in silence, processing the news. Jet had about a thousand questions to ask, but he bit his tongue, sitting quietly while his heart was beating so hard it felt like the thing was about to burst out of his chest. This decision wasn't his to make, he reminded himself. Whatever the risks, it was Oliver's right to choose his own medical treatment.

Oliver cleared his throat. "Surgery is never an easy decision," he said cautiously. "So let's start there. What are the possible complications from that alone, leaving aside any effect it may have on my hormonal cycle?"

"Surgery of any sort comes with its share of risks. You may have a bad reaction to the anaesthetic. There may be excessive bleeding during an operation. You may develop adhesions afterwards – that's when the internal organs stick to the scar tissue and it can cause ongoing pain or blockages to the intestines, for example. The procedure would be done via keyhole surgery, so the risks are minimal and the recovery time is usually short, but it's still a possibility. You'd end up with a couple of small scars on your abdomen and you'd have to spend a night in hospital. Afterwards, the doctor would monitor you through your next heat to make sure your cycle is back to normal, and Jet would need to be on hand, of course, in case it's not successful. And there's the added complication that you'd have to travel to Australia to have the operation done. You'd have the cost of the flights there and back, and the surgery itself would cost a couple of thousand dollars."

"Hold on, why Australia?" Jet interrupted. "Isn't there a surgeon here who could do it?"

Sullivan didn't answer right away, and Jet braced himself for more bad news. "The thing is, in America this operation is currently illegal."

"What? Why?"

"According to our laws, it would interfere with an alpha's rights over his omega. Even surgical sterilisation is illegal in a post-diagnosis Caloren's omega. The only reason Oliver was able to have it done was because he hadn't been diagnosed at the time." Sullivan had been fully briefed on Oliver's medical history before he'd joined the original research trial.

Jet scowled. "That is seriously fucked up."

"I'm not going to disagree with you. But given the declining number of omegas, no one is particularly interested in changing the laws at the moment. I'm not saying I agree with it, but right now, travelling to Australia is by far the easier option."

"You said before that Jet and I have bonded," Oliver said, breaking into the conversation. "What's to say that's not going to cause some unforeseen complication after the surgery?"

Sullivan shrugged helplessly. "That's something you'd need to discuss with Doctor Briggs. He's the man who's been running the research. I'll be perfectly honest; there's very little we know about bonding or its consequences at the moment. Even if your cycles were returned to normal, you'd still be bonded to Jet, and you still wouldn't be able to have sex with any other alpha."

"What about a beta?" Jet asked, forcing himself to do so though the question made him feel sick. "Do omegas have the same reaction to proteins in beta semen?" The thought of Oliver having sex with someone else made him want to punch his fist through a wall. On the heels of that surge of rage, though, Jet suddenly felt another rush of disgust, but this time it was aimed at himself. His father had had the same reaction every time his mother had so much as tried to leave the house. He had absolutely no right to be acting possessive over Oliver. He was his own person, with the right to make his own decisions. But a small, selfish part of him hoped Sullivan was about to say there was no way for Oliver to have sex with anyone else…

"The short answer is we don't know. As I mentioned before, no one's seen a case of bonding in at least fifty years, and medical research has come a long way in that time. Based on what I know of the differences between alpha and beta biochemistry, I'd guess that it shouldn't be a problem, but I can't rule it out entirely. But, if Oliver wanted to have intercourse with a beta, they could always use a condom, and that would bypass any potential complications."

Oliver was being awfully quiet, ruminating over all the new and startling information, and Jet forced himself to shut up and sit quietly. This wasn't his decision, he reminded himself again. The thought of Oliver being put at risk again scared the shit out of him, but if he decided to go ahead, Jet promised himself that he'd authorise it. Even if the laws were different in

Australia, Oliver would still need his permission to travel, and as Sullivan had said, Jet would have to go with him to make sure nothing went wrong during his next heat.

This was everything Oliver had ever wanted, freedom once more dangled enticingly in front of him. So what Oliver said next wasn't a great surprise, even if it felt like he'd just stuck a knife through Jet's chest. "I think you need to put me in contact with this doctor," he said finally. "At the very least, it's worth asking a few pertinent questions."

CHAPTER THIRTY-FOUR

OLIVER

"What am I supposed to do?" Oliver asked, staring mournfully into his coffee. Celeste was curled up on his sofa, having eagerly answered Oliver's request for a figurative shoulder to cry on. Little Hazel was now two and a half years old, and Celeste had left her at home with her father for the afternoon. "Given what happened last time, I'm not very keen on doing anything that could mess things up worse than they already are." With Jet's permission, he'd explained the whole situation to her, the disaster with the suppositories, the new research Sullivan had told them about, and Jet's offer to grant him emancipation if they could find a cure for his condition. The only part he'd left out was the detail that he and Jet had slept together during his last heat.

"Have you spoken to this doctor in Australia?" Celeste asked, a sympathetic frown on her face. "Because that should really be the first step."

"Yes. At length. We had a Skype meeting. I've got an MRI booked for two weeks' time to have a look at my ovaries. I figured there's no harm in making the appointment, at least, while I think about it."

"This is everything you wanted," Celeste pointed out, a complete lack of judgement in her voice. "You've said yourself, the way you and Jet have been handling your heats can be a bit hit and miss. Leaving aside the fact that you have an unusually good situation with your alpha, the rate of medical complications for Caloren's omegas is still high. So what's holding you back?"

"Well, for one thing, it's a lot of money. The trip to Australia for both of us, the surgery's going to cost about seven thousand dollars, and then I'd have to stay there for about two weeks until my heat hits. The doctor said they could schedule the surgery so that I don't have to spend months in Australia just waiting around, but it's got to be a couple of weeks before to give my hormone levels time to adjust. But at this stage, they don't even know if it's going to work. Detecting the tumour in living patients is a lot harder than it is in a post-mortem. Doctor Briggs said he's managed to correctly identify the affected ovary in seventy-five per cent of his patients."

"That's a pretty good statistic," Celeste pointed out. "No medical treatment is ever one hundred per cent effective."

"But he's only treated twelve omegas, so it's hard to get a good feel for the real chances based on a sample size that small. He did surgery on one of his patients, and ended up taking out the wrong ovary. The scan showed some odd results, and he couldn't quite pin down which one was causing the problem."

"Okay, so let's think about it this way," Celeste said, sitting up and taking on a stern, business-like expression. "What's the worst case scenario if you go through with it? I'm not trying to scare you, I just think it's worth knowing where all your cards are."

"If it doesn't work, then I've spent a lot of money for nothing. That's not the real issue, though," he went on, as thoughts continued to swirl through his mind. "No one seems to know how it would affect me, given that Jet and I have bonded. The sudden change in my hormone levels could throw my entire physiology out of balance. Imagine if I ended up going through a heat every month. Or every week, even!"

Celeste winced, and this was why Oliver had decided he needed to talk to another omega about it. As supportive as Jet was, he didn't really have an omega's perspective on things. Not to mention the fact that right now, he wasn't sure he could actually face Jet without breaking down and blurting out how he felt about him.

"But if it does work," Celeste asked, "what's the outcome? Are there any downsides to the surgery?"

"Best case, my heats go back to normal, but I'd hit menopause a few years earlier than I otherwise would. Given what I have to deal with at the moment, I think that's a small price to pay. I get emancipation from Jet and life goes back to normal." The thought of being permanently separated from Jet sent a cold rush of horror through him. He folded his hands in his lap to stop them from shaking.

"What does Jet think about it?"

Oliver shrugged. "He's just said it's my decision, and he'll support me, whichever way I decide to go. I feel like I should do it, though, for his sake. He's already done more for me than I could ever have expected, and I don't think it's fair to keep him locked in this arrangement when there could be a perfectly viable way out."

"Has he ever said he wants out? Or implied that he's not happy with the way things are?"

That, right there, was the real crux of the problem. If he had surgery to cure his Caloren's Syndrome, he would have no further reason to ever see Jet. As things stood at the moment, he could spend two glorious days once every three months making love, using his hormonal cycle as a convenient excuse to throw himself at the man like a puppy whose owner had just arrived home from work. That scant frequency was far from enough, the weeks in between feeling like a long, slow drudgery, but at least it was *something*.

But if he found a cure, even that would be taken away.

But on the other hand, as they'd discovered via brutal experience in the past, if anything happened to Jet, Oliver was as good as dead. It was hard to justify risking his life every time his heat hit just because he was too scared to tell Jet how he felt.

"He hasn't said he wants to leave," Oliver said finally, answering Celeste's question. "But he's an exceptionally decent man. Given that I don't have any other options, I'm not sure he'd say anything even if he did want to end things." He sighed and leaned his head back on the sofa, closing his eyes. "Half the problem is that I'm trying to make a decision based on information I don't have. I don't know if the MRI will show up anything unusual. I don't know if the doctor will agree to do the surgery. I don't know if there could be any unexpected side effects."

"I think you've answered your own question right there," Celeste said gently. "Have the MRI. See what the result is. Talk to Doctor Briggs again, and in the meantime, see if Sullivan comes up with any more information about the effects of bonding. You said he's looking into the literature to see if anyone else has developed any useful theories. So by the time you have to make a decision, you'll have more information, and everything might make more sense."

It was good advice, and really the only sensible way to go about things. Now, if only he could come up with as sensible a course of action to deal with his feelings for Jet...

CHAPTER THIRTY-FIVE

JET

Jet stood in front of the massive glass windows, staring at the planes lined up outside. "So. Australia. They damn well know how to make things happen in a hurry."

Standing at his side, Oliver smiled, though Jet could see how nervous he was. "Well, Doctor Briggs did say he'd called in a few favours at the hospital to fit me in so soon. The Australian government gave him a grant to try and improve omega suicide rates. There's been a big push in the media over there about how it's become a national crisis, so I'd imagine he gets a fair bit of leeway."

It was ten weeks since they'd first been told of Briggs' research, and Jet felt like he'd been on a whirlwind ride ever since. The MRI had come back with a clear positive result. Oliver had been sent for a seemingly never-ending list of tests – something he'd found a challenge to endure, given how many tests he'd had to have prior to his Caloren's diagnosis. And then there had been appointment after appointment with Sullivan, as he'd liaised between them and Briggs to ensure Oliver understood all the relevant information and had completed all the required pre-screening. There'd been a mountain of paperwork to go through as well, Jet having to sign off on each of Oliver's medical visits, approve the sharing of his test results with an overseas doctor and authorise his travel itinerary.

Despite no clear answers on how their bonding was going to affect the outcome, Oliver had finally decided to go ahead with the surgery. "I want to live a normal life," he'd reiterated, one evening over a meal at a pub with Jet. They'd stopped for a bite to eat as a convenient option after a late appointment with Sullivan, though Jet would never have complained about the chance to spend an evening with Oliver. "I don't think I could live with the idea that I'd been too scared to take that risk. And who knows; if this all goes well, maybe I can start lobbying for omega rights in America. Australia seemed to be leaps and bounds ahead of us, so we've got some serious catching up to do."

"Attention passengers on flight MS105 to Australia. Your flight will begin boarding shortly. Please wait for your row to be called, and have your boarding pass and passport ready."

"So this is it then," Jet said, shooting Oliver a hopeful smile. "Freedom and normality, here we come."

"Ladies and Gentlemen, we are beginning our descent into Melbourne. I expect to have us docked at the terminal in a little over thirty minutes. Local time is 9:45 in the morning. Please note that the fasten seatbelts sign has been switched on, and I hope you've enjoyed your flight."

"It's a fairly simple procedure. It should only take about half an hour, but it could be up to two hours before Oliver's transferred out of recovery to a ward. He'll be awake fairly quickly, but it depends on the availability of beds. If you have any concerns in the meantime, phone this number, and the nurses will be able to give you an update."

"Mr Wilder? Oliver's being transferred to the ward now. The operation went very smoothly, and Doctor Briggs will be sending the tissue sample away for pathology. We'll email you the results as soon as they come back from the lab. That usually takes about three days. If you come this way, I'll take you through to see Oliver."

"Your heat is due to begin in about eight hours, is that correct? A nurse will be coming in to monitor you every hour. We're going to take your temperature, blood pressure and heart rate, and monitor you for any other symptoms. Now, I understand there's a strong desire to believe that everything is back to normal, but I can't stress enough how important it is that you let us know if anything feels off. Jet will be in the room right next door, just in case the procedure hasn't been successful, but it's imperative that we keep you apart until then to properly assess the result of your surgery."

"Ladies and Gentlemen, you'll notice that the fasten seatbelt sign has been turned on. We're experiencing a degree of turbulence, which may last for the next ten minutes or so. We're expecting to be landing about half an hour behind schedule, as there's a storm currently making its way up the west coast, and we're going to have to take a small detour around it."

"Holy shit, how many bloody forms are there? I should just get my signature printed on a rubber stamp and stamp the lot of them. What's this one? Release of financial claim to omega's property. Yes, I agree. Next one... Waiving of sexual rights to omega- For fuck's sake! Alphas do not have the fucking *right* to use an omega for their own sexual gratification!"

"Actually, they do. Legally, at least. Morally, it's a whole different story, but no one's arguing that point at the moment."

"How are you so damn calm about this? Some of these forms are downright obscene!"

"Yes, but you're signing them all. So obscene or not, in a very short time, they're no longer going to be my problem."

"Bloody sanguine personality types. How's your scar, by the way?"

"It still itches. I'm seeing Sullivan on Tuesday to get my final check up. Oh, that's another form I'll need you to sign. Where did I put it...? Ah, here we go. Just one more, at the bottom."

"Are we done yet?"

"No, there still the one where you agree to pay all legal fees on my behalf – until the emancipation is final, I'm still your responsibility – and one to authorise the solicitor to act on your behalf to action the necessary claims."

"Okay, hand them over. I swear, I'm going to have repetitive-strain in my wrist by the time we're done here."

CHAPTER THIRTY-SIX

OLIVER

Oliver shuffled through his front door, a bag of groceries in one hand, his work bag in the other, and a large envelope tucked under his arm. It had been stuffed haphazardly into his mailbox, but his hands were too full at the moment to give much consideration to what was in it. He dropped his keys on the table by the entrance and kicked the door shut, wincing as it slammed just a little too hard.

He set his work bag by the coffee table, ready to check over a new report from the international space station. It had come in at five minutes to five, and he'd decided to print it out and read it at home, rather than spending another half an hour at the office and running into the evening rush hour as a result. The envelope was dropped beside it, to be dealt with later.

He took the bag of groceries into the kitchen, putting milk and yoghurt into the fridge before they had a chance to warm up, then the rest of it away in the cupboard.

It was just over five weeks since he'd got back from Australia. He'd seen Jet three times in that period, once at an appointment with Sullivan, once to fill in that abominable pile of forms, and once at work. They'd run into each other in the hallway and had stopped for a quick cup of coffee, chatting about nothing in particular until Jet had had to leave, heading off for a test flight in the simulator, putting a new flight module through its paces.

Feeling peckish, but knowing it was too early for dinner, Oliver fetched a slice of bread from the fridge and smothered it with cream cheese, adding a few pieces of shredded ham to make a quick snack.

The report was niggling at the back of his mind, but from the length of it, he knew it would take him a fair while to read through it all, so he set the bread on the counter and headed for his bedroom to get changed. It would be far more comfortable snuggling up on the sofa in jeans and a t-shirt, rather than his work shirt and trousers.

But as he passed the coffee table, his eye caught the red and white print on the envelope. He'd all but forgotten about it in the few brief minutes since he'd walked in the door. Curious, he picked it up and ripped the tab off the side, two thick bundles of paper spilling out into his hand.

It was a bunch of legal documents, and he recognised the name of his and Jet's solicitor at the top right hand side. Again, it looked like it was going to take him a while to work through all of it, so he went to set it back down on the coffee table, eager to get more comfortable for a long, boring slog through mountains of legal jargon.

But before he put it down, one sentence suddenly caught his eye. Down at the bottom of the page, in bold font, sat a declaration that made his heart thump in his chest and his lungs suddenly feel like all the air had left the room.

Application for emancipation from Jet Wilder: Granted.

The words blurred in front of him, his entire world seeming to spin on its axis as his mind tried to process the news, but it was only when a drop of water landed on the corner of the page that Oliver realised there were tears running down his face. He sank down onto the sofa, relief and regret warring within his mind.

It was over. The risk to his life from his heats, the legal roadblocks, the archaic laws that had tried so hard to rob him of his identity. It was all over.

And so was his arrangement with Jet. No more hasty phone calls in the middle of the night when his heat started unexpectedly. No more quiet chats over a cold beer on the back patio. No more bashful silences as Jet handed him his next dose.

No more making love, sprawled out on Oliver's bed, or tentative morning kisses, or sighs of pleasure as they both finally learned to embrace their biology, instead of fighting against it.

A low, keening cry rose up in his throat, and Oliver buried his head in his hands and wept.

CHAPTER THIRTY-SEVEN

JET

Jet was sprawled on his couch, watching a game of football when a thumping knock sounded at his door. He muted the television and went to answer it, checking through the peephole before he opened the door.

A short, slender woman stood on the other side, looking thoroughly pissed off, though Jet didn't recognise her. Assuming she might have the wrong address, he opened the door, ready to point her in the direction of one of the other apartments once he found out who she was looking for.

But he didn't get the chance. The instant the door was open, she launched into a tirade, fiery eyes and accusing finger making Jet back up a step, despite her small size.

"You are a complete and total asshole! I've listened for the past two and a half years to Oliver harping on about how you're a gentleman, and an honourable man, and the last decent alph- I mean, *person* in the world, " she corrected herself hastily, "and now you just turn around and stab him in the back! You're just like every other self-absorbed, narcissistic *person* I've ever met, control freaks, and liars, and militant little dictators who run around using your ego to hide the fact that you're all insecure little boys who can't deal with someone else running their own life! How dare you do this to Oliver! How dare you just dangle happiness in front of him and then rip it away again! Was it really so damn difficult to give him the *one thing* in the world that he really wanted?"

Jet gaped at the woman in shock. "What the flaming hell are you going on about?" he demanded, the instant he could get a word in edgeways. "He wanted freedom! So I gave him freedom. I went with him to Australia, I authorised his surgery, I signed three hundred bloody forms for him. The emancipation came through, by the way," he added sharply. He ducked back into the living room and grabbed his papers off the coffee table. They'd arrived three days ago, though after the most cursory of glances at their contents, Jet hadn't been able to work up the enthusiasm to read much of the report. "See?" he said, returning to the door and brandishing the bundle at the woman. "Freedom. Exactly like he asked for. So what the fuck is it that I've supposedly done to wreck his life now?"

The woman stared at the papers, a stunned look on her face. "You gave him... You agreed to emancipation?" She took the forms from him, glancing over the details quickly, the anger melting off her face to be replaced with awe. "Wow." She peered up at him, looking genuinely surprised. "I seriously didn't think you were going to do it."

"Shows how much you know," he muttered darkly.

The woman opened her mouth to answer... but then suddenly paused. "Do you even know who I am?" she asked, giving him a sceptical frown.

Jet rolled his eyes, trying to rein in his temper a little. "I would assume you're Celeste. You're the only person other than Anderson and a handful of doctors who knows there was anything going on between me and Oliver."

She looked a little surprised that he'd known the correct answer. "Oh. Well. Okay, then. Um... I'm sorry, I don't really know what to say now. I honestly didn't think you'd signed the forms."

"Look, do you want to come inside?" Jet asked, feeling miffed. He opened the door wider. "I really don't feel like having a shouting match where my neighbours can hear every word."

"Yes. Sorry. My bad." She hurried through the door and into the living room, and he closed it behind her.

"How did you get the idea that I'd gone back on my word?" he asked. Clearly there had been a serious misunderstanding somewhere along the line. "What exactly has Oliver said to you?"

"Nothing," Celeste said flatly. "Absolutely zero. He's not answering his phone, he's not replying to my text messages. I went by his house earlier, but he's not home. I even tried calling him at work yesterday. The receptionist said she'd passed on a message, but he never called me back. The last time I spoke to him, you'd just got back from Australia, and he said he was going to start working on the application for emancipation. And then suddenly he's avoiding me like the plague. The last time he did that was just after he'd been diagnosed with Caloren's Syndrome. That's what he does when he gets upset; he shuts himself off from the world and tries to deal with all his problems on his own. So that brings me back to my original question – What did you do?"

"Why does it have to be something I did?" Jet asked, annoyed at her assumptions. "Like I said, the emancipation papers came through." He waved the pages at her again. "I would have thought he'd be swinging from the chandeliers in celebration, not sulking in his bedroom." Damn it, could he at least put in a little more effort to avoid sounding like a sullen teenager? Jet himself had felt no joy when the paperwork had arrived, knowing it was the final nail in the coffin for their unorthodox arrangement, and the timing couldn't have been worse. They'd only just broken down that last barrier between them, opening the way to more affection, a deeper connection, and lots, lots more sex… But then Sullivan had come along with a miracle cure and ruined everything.

But Oliver should have been over the moon. Actually, now that he thought about it, he was surprised he hadn't heard from Oliver himself. He hadn't expected a call right away on the day his own paperwork had arrived, assuming that maybe Oliver's hadn't got there yet, but three days should have been enough time to solve any minor delays in the postal system.

Impulsively, he pulled out his phone, dialling Oliver's number. The phone rang four times, then went through to voicemail. Jet hung up without leaving a message. "No answer," he reported to Celeste. "That's not like Oliver."

Celeste was peering up at him expectantly, and it took him a moment to work out what she wanted. When he did, he sighed and muttered a curse. "Fine. I'll go over to his place," he said. "But I'm sure he's fine. He's perfectly capable of looking after himself."

But if that was true, then why did he feel a slow, simmering knot of dread in his stomach?

CHAPTER THIRTY-EIGHT

OLIVER

It was dark when Oliver got home. He parked in the driveway and fetched his bag from the passenger seat. He'd gone to the beach after work and sat staring at the water for what seemed like hours. In the end he'd got cold and forced himself to go home, dreading walking into his empty house, but knowing he couldn't very well sit outside all night.

He was so caught up in his thoughts that he didn't notice Jet sitting on the porch steps until he very nearly walked over the top of him. He pulled up sharply, cursing uncharacteristically in his surprise.

"Jet! What are you doing here?"

Jet stood up, brushing off the seat of his jeans. "I tried to call you earlier. When you didn't answer, I thought I'd come see how you were doing."

"Oh. Well, thank you." That was just like Jet, always the gentlemen, always looking out for his friends. "Um… would you like to come in?"

"Sure."

Oliver stepped around him, careful not to accidentally brush against him, and let them into the house.

"The legal papers came through," Jet said, standing awkwardly in the living room. "I wasn't sure if you'd got your set."

"I did," Oliver confirmed. He forced a smile. "Good news all round."

From the look on Jet's face, he knew he wasn't fooling anyone. "I thought you'd be happy about it," Jet said, shoving his hands into his pockets.

"I am," Oliver said automatically. "It's just… it's all a little overwhelming at the moment." There was a pause, and Oliver fumbled for something to fill the silence. "Would you like some coffee?" If nothing else, it would give him something to do with his hands.

"Yeah, that'd be great."

He headed for the kitchen, not surprised to find Jet following right behind him. He went through the automatic motions, grounds spooned in neatly, water in the back, milk in the jug. The machine began gurgling happily, a comforting scent filling the kitchen. Oliver busied himself with heating the milk, trying not to look like he was avoiding looking at Jet.

He heard the faint rustle of clothing as Jet leaned against the counter, and assumed he'd just folded his arms. "Talk to me, Oliver," Jet said, his voice soft and soothing. "I know you well enough to see that something's eating you. So what's going on?"

"Nothing. Everything's fine. I'm really very happy the legalities have been finalised. We'll have to tell Anderson," he added, talking just to fill the silence. "He'll need to know our legal situation has changed again. Really, I'm fine," he repeated inanely, not sure whether he was more interested in convincing Jet, or himself. "It's just a bit of an adjustment."

The milk was done now, so he switched off the frother and poured it into the cups. One sugar for himself, two for Jet. He turned around and nearly jumped out of his skin, finding Jet standing right behind him. He could detect the gentle waft of alpha pheromones, fainter than his usual scent during Oliver's heats, but no less enticing. "I'm fine," he repeated, then cursed himself silently as his voice cracked on the last word. He looked down, unable to bear the open concern on Jet's face.

"Then why didn't you answer my call? Why haven't you been talking to Celeste? She said she's been trying to reach you for more than a week." He felt a light brush of Jet's hand against his own, a tentative touch that nonetheless rocked him to his core. "Seriously, Ollie… What's going on?"

"Its just that I hadn't really considered… I hadn't thought about what would happen when this ended." He wasn't ready for this. He hadn't had time to think about the best way to phrase his feelings, how to add a light-hearted flavour to avoid it all sounding too intense. He hadn't had time to gather his courage and consider all the pros and cons of telling Jet how he felt, or to wonder what would happen if Jet said no.

He wasn't ready for their arrangement to end. He hadn't come up with a list of casual outings he could invite Jet on, just for the excuse to see him again, or thought of how to suggest they did something that Jet enjoyed, like going skydiving again. He could ask Jet to teach him how to surf, he thought desperately. That would give them an excuse to spend time together, without putting too much pressure on either of them.

Or maybe Jet was really just glad this was over, he thought blackly. Maybe he'd only come over here because Oliver was being a big baby and refusing to answer his calls.

"What do you want to happen?" Jet asked. Damn him for sounding so calm! "You could come over to my place for dinner. I still have to prove to you that I can cook something fancier than scrambled eggs. Or we could go out for a drink to celebrate." There was a pause. "Or do you want me to just leave you alone?"

"No!" Oliver blurted out, then cursed himself for not thinking before he spoke. That single word had sounded so abrupt, so desperate, and his gut lurched at the thought that Jet would think him needy and weak. "That is to say, I... I said before that we should stay friends after we found a cure. A drink would be nice. Tomorrow, maybe?" Damn it, he was still being a coward! He'd jumped out of a plane, he'd travelled halfway across the world to have surgery, he'd risked unbalancing his entire hormonal cycle to secure his freedom. Surely he could manage to say two damn sentences to let Jet know how he really felt. "The truth is, I..." *Don't chicken out now, Oliver!* he scolded himself. "I was rather hoping we might..." He looked up, daring to meet Jet's gaze. "The truth is, I've grown rather fond of you. And I thought..." His throat closed up, the words refusing to come out. He looked away, feeling a fool all over again.

"I've become rather fond of you too," Jet murmured, his fingers stroking uneven lines over Oliver's hand. "And if you're interested, I was hoping we might..."

Oliver dared to glance up again. The look on Jet's face was so familiar, the one he got when Oliver had said something daring and he was trying to decide whether to follow through on it, or give him the chance to back out.

Screw backing out, he thought suddenly. He hadn't backed out of that skydive, though he'd been terrified beyond words at the thought of going through with it. Not giving himself a chance to second guess himself, he leaned forward, capturing Jet's mouth in a kiss that was clumsy and chaste, no more than a brief meeting of lips. But it was more than enough to say how he felt, when words seemed woefully inadequate.

He pulled back, heart pounding in his chest. "I was hoping we might..."

"Hell, yes," Jet said, all the tension suddenly leaving him in a rush. He leaned forward, returning the kiss, then upped the intensity, hands cupping Oliver's face as their tongues met in a hot, wet embrace that made Oliver's head spin and sent a rush of sensation to his groin.

A moment later, he was leading them both towards the bedroom, the coffee left abandoned to cool on the counter.

EPILOGUE

OLIVER

Oliver lay on the surfboard, feeling the ocean rocking soothingly beneath him. Lying on his own board just a few feet away, Jet was grinning at him like a cat that just ate a canary. "Okay, ready?" he asked, and Oliver nodded, scared and eager at the same time. "When the next wave comes along, you're going to start paddling when it's still a way back from you. Keep paddling until you feel it pick up the board, then get up on your feet, and ride it in to shore. Don't worry about any fancy moves at this point, just get yourself standing up and stick it out as long as you can."

Oliver nodded, feeling like a gangly teenager again. His arms and legs just seemed to splay everywhere, no matter how hard he tried to keep everything in place.

"Okay, here it comes. Start paddling... paddle, paddle, paddle! Now stand up!"

Oliver did, pushing himself upwards and jamming his feet in underneath himself. The wave thrust the board forward, and he wobbled precariously, trying to keep his balance... and then suddenly he was doing it. Arms out to the sides, knees shaking with the effort to stay upright, he was hurtling towards the shore, feeling a heady thrill of satisfaction as he rode the wave. Behind him, he heard Jet let out a whoop of encouragement.

Nearing the shore, the wave petered out, and Oliver jumped off, landing in waist-deep water. He grabbed the board and turned around, a huge grin on his face as he tried to spot Jet, still out beyond the breakers.

Jet sat up on his board, holding his hands in the air to give an exaggerated round of applause. Then he waved at Oliver vigorously, a gesture that seemed to say *'now get your ass back out here and do it again!'*.

Grinning from ear to ear, Oliver tossed his hair out of his eyes, clambered back onto the board, and began to paddle his way back to Jet's side.

Sign up for Laura Taylor's Newsletter

If you enjoyed this book, you can sign up for my newsletter by going to
https://laurataylorauthor.com/newsletter/

By signing up, you get a FREE romance novel, as well as updates on new releases, discounts, short stories, book recommendations, and lots more. I will never spam you or give your contact details to anyone else. Ever.

REDEMPTION OF A SLAVE
An Omegaverse Romance

As an omega in the 1800's, Dante's life was never going to be an easy one. Kept as a slave and sold from one master to another, Dante has suffered far too much cruelty, and even he would admit that the harshness of life has turned him from a civilised, obedient omega into a broken man bent on violence and revenge.

Antoine Calvet has lived a blessed life. The alpha son of a wealthy farmer, he is an anomaly among his own gender, wanting to use his position to protect those he cares about, rather than flaunting either his money or his power. So when Antoine meets Dante at a slave auction, his heart goes out to the bruised and battered man, unwilling to leave him to endure even more suffering.

But once Antoine gets Dante back to his estate, he has to wonder if he's taken on more than he can handle. Dante's trust in alphas has been completely destroyed, and he veers between cowering fear and outbursts of anger, unsettling the entire estate.

But Antoine is convinced that kindness can win over the hardest of hearts and that with enough time, even Dante can be redeemed. But as his quest to show Dante that he matters delves into uncharted territory, Antoine will be forced to confront the very foundations of the society he lives in, and for the first time in his life, he'll have to question whether an omega can truly be more than just a slave.

WOLF'S BLOOD
Book One of The House of Sirius

Dee Carman considers herself to be quite ordinary, your average, run-of-the-mill office worker. But her quiet life is turned upside down when she's kidnapped by the ruthless Noturatii and converted into a wolf shape shifter.

When a shadowy figure helps her escape from the lab, it seems she's been given a second chance… until she's kidnapped once again, this time by a pack of wolf shifters living in England's north. The pack's leaders try to help Dee adapt to her new abilities, but her animal side is the opposite of Dee in every way; wild, violent and unpredictable, and making peace with the fiery wolf seems an impossible task.

But as she struggles to come to terms with her new life, Dee finds herself caught up in an ancient war between the shifters and the Noturatii, a six-hundred-year-old conflict that threatens not just Dee's newfound family, but the survival of their entire species.

HURRICANE
Book One of The Elements

Lieutenant Azure Lynwood has worked hard to earn his place in the Space Corps, overcoming centuries of bias and discrimination against omegas. Travelling across the solar system and exploring new worlds comes with its share of complications, but Azure has proven himself a worthy member of his team, and he's ready for anything the solar system can throw at him.

Or, at least, he thinks so, until a supposedly routine mission goes awry. An inspection of a remote outpost on Titan turns into a murder investigation, then a blizzard traps Azure and his crew inside the base, cut off from any contact with civilisation, and finally, without access to his supply of hormonal suppressants, Azure realises he has only a couple of hours until he goes into heat.

But just when Azure thinks his situation can't get any worse, he finds out one last, staggering piece of news. Major Tor Savan, his commanding officer and one of the most respected men in the Space Corps, is an alpha.

Refusing to be mated means enduring twelve hours of the worst pain imaginable. But allowing Tor to mate him is unthinkable. Alphas in rut are notoriously violent and aggressive, and if anyone ever found out about the illicit encounter, Azure's career would be over. Can he really trust Tor's assurances that he has both the skills and the discretion to see Azure through his heat unharmed?

UNTIL DAWN

The end of the world is no place for the faint-hearted…

After five long years evading bands of slave traders in a post-apocalyptic wilderness, Dusk of the Two Swords has honed her survival skills and her prowess in battle. In a world where women are commodities and the roaming tribes are ruled by the most ruthless of men, Dusk has maintained her freedom by trusting no one and by being willing to slit the throats of those who stood in her way.

But it seems that Dusk has finally met her match. Captured and en route to a slave camp, she is desperate for a way to escape. But when hope seems nearly lost, a miracle occurs – she is freed by the rivals of the slavers; a band of fierce warriors led by a towering mountain of a man; Aidan the Ferocious.

Aidan offers Dusk a deal; become his wife and he will defend her from the lecherous advances of all other men. But even when the alternative is starving to death in the wilderness, only a fool would trust a man who promises safety and security while the blood from his latest victims has not even dried on his blade.

ABOUT THE AUTHOR

Laura Taylor is a pseudonym for Gabriel Danes. Gabriel is a bisexual, transgender writer of fantasy and romance novels. He likes watching ice hockey, reading about vampires and werewolves, cooking, and has fantasies of one day becoming a firefighter.

Gabriel lives on the Far South Coast of New South Wales, Australia.

Email: laura@laurataylorauthor.com

Website: http://laurataylorauthor.com

Facebook: https://www.facebook.com/LauraTaylorBooks

Amazon: https://www.amazon.com/Laura-Taylor/e/B06XC3TZZH

Goodreads:
https://www.goodreads.com/author/show/7336592.Laura_Taylor